PROBLEM

E. Charle

First published by Ward, Lock and Co. (London, 1939)

This edition first published electronically by Black Heath Editions, 2020

This paperback edition published by Black Heath Editions, 2022

CHAPTER I

The Victims

THE ticket-collector on duty at Crandon station when the 2.45 A.M. train arrived and left, on the morning of the last Thursday in March, was able to testify when his turn came for questioning that ten third-class and two first-class passengers had given up their tickets to him, and that he recognised the two firsts as Mr. and Mrs. Houghton of Castel Garde, while he could also place three of the ten thirds, but not the other seven. Quite a number of people in the district went to London on Wednesdays because of this train, which, beginning its journey at 11.40 on Wednesday night—it ran only that one day in the week—admitted of winding up a day in the metropolis at a theatre. Since there was no restaurant car attached, passengers solved the problem of supper as best they could, or dispensed with that luxury and dozed the journey out.

The guard of the train, Robert Potter, flagged it out from Crandon on time and swung himself aboard the forward brake van, and the big engine with its seven heavy corridor coaches gathered way in the cutting which begins some quarter-mile on the Westingborough side of Crandon station, plunged with a roar into the tunnel which pierces the long ridge of which Condor Hill is the highest point, and emerged to cross the Idleburn bridge and then curve to follow the course of the river to Westingborough. Less than a quarter-mile beyond the bridge, everyone in the train was jarred wide awake by the sudden application of the brakes, and Robert Potter said a bad word as he hurried along to ascertain who had pulled the communication cord—for the first time in his experience as a railway official.

He had not far to go. The coach next the forward van was composite, with third-class compartments at each end and two firsts in the middle, and from the second third-class compartment in the coach a youngish, bronzed-face man looked out. He had opened the sliding door just far enough to admit of sticking his head through the opening; the three blinds of the compartment had been pulled down, and that head was all of him that was visible as the guard halted at sight of him.

"Did you pull that cord?" he snapped out harshly.

"Come in here," the passenger answered.

He slid the door open, and revealed himself as stark naked, a leanly built, well-muscled individual. Potter started at him with dropped jaw until he reached out, got a grip on the uniform sleeve, and pulled. Then Potter entered the compartment, and the naked man slid the door closed.

"Whereabouts are we?" he asked calmly.

"Wu-whereabouts?" Potter echoed, almost stupidly. Then, with sudden fierceness—"'Ere! Whatcher reckon you're doin' of?"

"Do you think I run about like this for fun?" the passenger demanded acidly. "You can see for yourself—whoever did it hasn't left me a stitch. Suit-case gone, everything gone! I woke up and pulled the cord. Whereabouts are we, I asked you?"

"Just out of Crandon. Strike me pink!"

"That's—we haven't passed Westingborough yet, then?"

"Next stop. But——" Potter broke off. The situation was beyond him. He took out his watch and looked at it, but gained no inspiration thereby. A voice called from the corridor—

"Oh, Bob! You anywhere about?"

"That's Starkey, my driver," Potter said, and did not answer the call. "We're ten minutes behind time already, too."

"Yes, but where are my clothes and suit-case?" the naked man asked.

"How would I know?" Potter snapped, in sudden exasperation.

"No." It was an acid rejoinder. "You wouldn't know—much."

Again the voice called from the corridor —"Bob?" and footsteps sounded as coming along from the forward end of the coach. The guard slid the door open and put his head out.

"All right—let her go," he said. "Bloke here lost a few things, that's all. We'll lose a bit more time at Westingborough, I reckon, over it, so we better not waste any more here. Better get on."

"Righto." The footsteps receded, and Potter closed the door again.

"Now what happened?" he asked the naked man. "To you, I mean?"

"Happened?" There was satiric resentment in the word. "I landed in London to-day, and got aboard this train to-night—last night, I suppose it was, now. Went to sleep. Wakened up—like this."

"Booked to where?" Potter asked. "I clipped you for Westingborough, though, didn't I?"

"I'd booked to Westingborough—yes. That was why I pulled the communication cord—in case we'd already passed Westingborough."

"Next stop." Potter spoke morosely.

Then—"Crikey!" An exclamation partly of incredulity, partly of disgust.

"Well, what are you going to do about it?" the other demanded impatiently. "What about my clothes—and suit-case, too?"

"What in Pete's name can I do?" Potter asked in irritated reply. "Here, though—wait a bit. Every time I've come through since I clipped your ticket, these blinds. Did you pull 'em down?"

"No. They were down when I woke up just now."

"And been down since a half-hour after we started, too. And the first next but one to you along here—he's got his blinds down too. Hold on, and I'll go and have a look in there."

"Damn it, man, what he does is nothing to do with me! I want some clothes—something to cover me. They've left me nothing."

"Who've left you nothing?" Potter asked, with sudden suspicion, and as he spoke the train began moving again.

"How the hell do I know?" the naked man fired back angrily. "Do you think I helped whoever it was undressed me and left me like this?"

Sniffing, Potter detected a faint, sweetish odour in the compartment. In his surprise at the sight of a stark naked passenger, he had not remarked it before. He shook his head gravely.

"You was drugged, that's what it was," he said. "But I'm going to see why that bloke in the first's got his blinds down too."

He went out, closing the door on the naked man, and, passing one empty third-class compartment and one empty first, reached the other first-class compartment of the coach, of which the three blinds were drawn down. He slid the door back and looked in, to stand frozen to horror-struck fixity for a period of which he could not estimate the length.

"Oh, Gord!" he whispered at last. "What is this? The eleven-forty, or a blinkin' travellin' madhouse?"

He entered the compartment, emerged from it again after one fearful look at the figure lying face upward on the floor between the seats, and went along the corridor to look into the remaining third-class compartments, all empty, now. The lavatory at the end of the coach, too, was unoccupied, as he discovered by looking in. Then he returned to the compartment in which the naked man waited, and looked in.

"Stop there," he bade. "We'll pull into Westingborough in another five minutes. Don't come out of there when we stop."

"Am I likely to, like this? But what's wrong with you, man? You look as if you've seen— what's wrong?"

"What's wrong?" Potter echoed grimly. "Bloody murder—that's what's wrong. You stop where you are, mind."

A change in the rhythm of the wheels on the rail joints announced that the train was slowing as it approached Westingborough.

* * *

Pyjama-clad and barefooted as he held his telephone receiver to his ear, Superintendent Wadden shifted his weight uneasily from one bare foot to the other, and back again, for the uncarpeted tiling of the hallway was uncomfortably cold. After one incredulous interruption, he listened to all that Samuels, the Westingborough stationmaster, had to tell him.

"I get it," he said, when the report was complete. "Disconnect the coach and run it into a siding, and keep that guard, Potter."

"But we can't keep the guard," Samuels protested. "And the train is over half an hour late already——"

"I don't care a hoot in a coal-yard," Wadden interrupted testily. "Not if it's half a year late. If you choose to deliver us cases by rail when we haven't got any in the district of our own, you've got to take the consequences, and if you let that guard go on with the train I'll run you in as accessory after the murder—if it is a murder. Replace him with anyone you like, and I'll answer for it if the company raises hell—which they won't. I'll be along with Inspector Head as soon as we can get some clothes on, and I want the coach and the guard for examination—both of 'em—when we get there——"

"But, superintendent——"

"No buts," Wadden interrupted in turn. "I'm not going to freeze on this cold floor any longer."

And he slammed on his receiver.

Within a quarter of an hour the big police saloon drew up in the railway station yard, and Wadden, uniformed to the last button and wearing his winter overcoat, since the early hours of this March morning were decidedly chilly, descended, to be followed in turn by Inspector Head, a tall, kindly-looking man in civilian clothes, and by Sergeant Wells, whose night on duty at the police station it happened to be, and who carried the finger-printing outfit which, as a rule, he manipulated when need arose. Jeffries, driving the saloon, remained at the wheel in compliance with Wadden's order, and the other three passed through the booking hall to the platform, where Samuels, the tubby little stationmaster, awaited them in a camel-hair dressing gown which revealed no more than that he had put on trousers before coming to investigate the trouble. With him were Potter, the guard of the train, and Tom Adams ticket-collector. The train, of course, had gone on, and such passengers as had left it here had all gone their ways.

"Morning, Samuels." Towering over the stationmaster, Wadden greeted him. "Doctor Bennett not arrived yet—no. Well, what have you?"

"It's pretty ghastly, superintendent," Samuels answered. "There." He pointed to the siding platform reserved as a rule for branch line trains to Carden and beyond.

Now, against its buffers, stood the composite coach detached from the train, still lighted from its accumulators. The corridor side of the coach was toward them, and both Wadden and Head noted that the blinds of two compartments were drawn down. In addition to the end exits, there were two doors in the side of the coach, one directly opposite the drawn-down middle blind of the first-class compartment, and the other abreast the third-class compartment of which the blinds were lowered. The station was eerily, even ominously still, and Tom Adams, abruptly coughing, raised a volley of echoes.

Wadden rocked his eighteen stone on his toes, and blew gently—it was a habit of his, an expression of annoyance, and the fact that he blew gently showed that his irritation was slight, so far.

"Is that all?" he demanded crisply.

"All?" Samuels looked puzzled as he echoed the word.

"What do you know, man?" Wadden amplified.

"I—well, the guard here asked Tom to call me, and told me he'd got one corpse and one naked man in that coach. So I rang you. I ordered the coach taken off the train, and held the guard, as you asked. In addition, I told Tom to wait, in case you wanted to ask him about the passengers who got off here. The guard can tell you the rest, I think."

"Your name, guard?" Wadden inquired, turning to him.

"Robert Potter, sir," he answered.

"Well, what have you to tell? Tell it all, from the start of your run—eleven-forty out from London. Begin with that, and carry on."

"Well, sir, we left on time, of course. A pretty full train, first stop Watford. There were people in every compartment of that coach to there, and quite half of 'em got out there. It was after Watford I noticed the two sets of blinds were down, but I didn't pay much attention to it, because passengers often pull down their blinds on this train and turn down the lights for a snooze—or they may be spooners, sometimes. I'd checked tickets, and nobody got on at Watford —nobody got on anywhere on the run, as far as that goes. We left Crandon on time, and this side the river bridge the cord was pulled— communication cord, I mean. I went along from the forward van, and found a man stark naked in that third with the blinds down. After a bit of an argument with him I told the driver to run on, as we couldn't do anything there——"

"Have you any idea whether anyone left the train while it was at a standstill this side the river bridge?" Head interposed.

"None at all, sir," Potter answered. "I was— well, a bit stupefied over finding a passenger without a stitch on him. Then I thought of the first with the blinds down, and went to look in. The dead one is in there—the sight of him nearly made me sick, too. And they were the only two in the coach. I disconnected it and coupled up the rest to the forward brake van, and then waited as Mr. Samuels ordered."

"Did anyone leave that coach at Crandon?" Head asked again.

"No, sir. As nearly as I know, all the other compartments emptied at Watford. But whether there was more than one man in either of the two compartments with the blinds down—well, I dunno."

"You mean you didn't look in either of them after Watford?"

"Well, sir, why should I? I'd done their tickets, and knew nobody else got aboard. It's not my job to worry passengers."

Head nodded agreement: he had no intention of irritating this man in any way by the form of his questions.

"Do you remember what were the bookings of those two men?" he asked.

"Yes, sir. Westingborough—both of 'em."

Head turned to the stationmaster. "Do you know either of them?" he inquired. "That is, I suppose you've seen both?"

"Seen 'em, but don't know 'em," Samuels answered.

"I don't think anyone's going to recognise that corpse in a hurry, unless by the suit of clothes he's got on. I lent the live one a blanket."

"Then I don't think we shall need you any more for the present. You, Potter, and you, Tom, had better wait in case we have more questions to ask you. Ah! There's Bennett." For the doctor who acted at need as police surgeon appeared from the booking-office doorway. "Now we can go and see what there is in the coach. Chief, if you'll go with Doctor Bennett and see what you make of the body, I'll have a word with this nudist. That is, unless you wish me to see the body first?"

"Oh, no!" Wadden answered. "You'll have all the spade work—make your own arrangements. Morning, doctor. They've started to ship us cases by rail, because we haven't enough of our own. In that coach over there, the stationmaster tells me. Will you come and see what there is?"

With a mere nod of assent, and an equally silent greeting to Head, Bennett accompanied him. They entered the coach by the door opposite the first-class compartment, while Head went to that opposite the third with its blinds down, and Sergeant Wells, in the absence of any order, waited to find out where he would be needed. Wadden pulled open the sliding door of the first-class compartment, and for a second or two, hardened though he was to casualties of most kinds, stood aghast. Then he backed out, and beckoned through the corridor window to Wells.

"Carry on, doctor," he bade. "Garrotted and

disfigured, I make it!"

Entering the compartment, Bennett looked down at the body, and at the face. The protruding tongue, swollen and discoloured features, and staring eyes, all symptoms of strangulation, rendered identification difficult, but, in addition to this, both cheeks had been slashed open by vertical, deep cuts reaching from the level of the eyes to the line of the chin, and a similar but horizontal cut had been slashed to bone depth across the forehead. Opened out as they were, and added to the disfigurement caused by garrotting, these cuts made it difficult to determine the age of the victim, and obviously altered him almost beyond recognition, even by one who knew him well. He was dressed in a suit of grey tweed, with black shoes of which the soles declared that they had been worn only once or twice, black socks, a soft-collared blue shirt and a dark blue tie. A black soft felt hat, a fawn rainproof coat, and a very new suit-case were up on the rack in one corner of the compartment. Ash on the carpet, and two stamped-out cigarette ends, were almost directly in front of the things in the rack, indicating to some extent that as passenger the dead man had occupied that corner—farthest from the corridor and, Wadden calculated, facing the engine.

Bennett beckoned him in and pointed at the cord round the neck of the corpse, a thin, greyish line sunken in the flesh.

"Want that in situ, or do I take it off?" he asked.

"Leave it, for Head," Wadden answered. "The way it's knotted may tell him things, for all I know. Can you hand me down that raincoat and case? We may get his identity from one or other of them."

Bennett reached up and handed him both articles, and began unfastening the dead man's vest as the superintendent went out to the corridor to make his examination. The suitcase proved to be locked. The raincoat, perfectly new by the look of it, yielded an ordinary shilling packet of cigarettes of which five were missing, a carton of "book" matches from which ten had been torn for use, and, from a tiny, inconspicuous pocket located inside the right-hand outer pocket of the coat, a single London-Westingborough ticket, dated for the preceding day, and third-class. With that, Wadden stepped out to the platform, went to where Potter and Tom Adams still waited, and held the ticket for the guard to see.

"I thought you said you'd inspected tickets," he said.

"And his was a first," the man answered unhesitatingly. "That's not his, I know. I don't make mistakes of that sort."

"Unless he moved into that compartment after you saw this."

"No. There was one third—that stark naked

bloke—and two firsts left in that coach after Watford, I'm dead certain. And nobody got in."

"Came along from another coach," Wadden suggested.

Potter considered it. "Just possible," he admitted. "The blinds being down. But—would he barge in with the blinds down?"

"You've got brains," Wadden remarked after a moment's pause. "Wait on a bit longer—you too, Tom. We'll let you both go as soon as we can manage it, and I'll have a word with Samuels about giving you time off to make up for waiting about, Tom."

"That's all right, sir," and the ticket-collector nodded good-humouredly. "I'll wait as long as you're likely to want me."

Wadden went back and faced Bennett in the compartment entrance.

"Well?" he asked.

"Age, thirty to thirty-five," Bennett reported concisely. "Height about five feet eleven, weight I should estimate at between eleven and twelve stone. Strangled by the cord not less than three hours ago, and the disfiguring slashes were made by a razor or very sharp knife after his heart had ceased to beat—practically no blood exuded. No disarrangement of clothing, no bruises, no sign of struggle."

"You went through the pockets?" Wadden asked.

The doctor nodded. "No papers of any kind,

except for seven one-pound notes in the left-hand breast pocket of the coat. Silver and coppers—I haven't counted them—in the right-hand trouser pocket. Nothing else whatever. His clothes appear to be quite new, and I can find no laundry marks on the shirt or collar—and the handkerchief is new too. Everything new, by the look of them."

"A key for the suit-case?" Wadden suggested.

Bennett shook his head. "I didn't find one," he said.

"We'll have to break it open, then. Finger-prints, though—I'll leave it to Head. Take charge of it, Wells. And that hat, too. Head's a long while operating on his man—shut in with him, too. No sign of struggle of any sort, you say?"

"None. A post-mortem might show heart trouble—or anything. He may have been doped—the far-side window is half down, which would have got rid of the smell in three hours."

"Would it, though?" Wadden reflected.

"If what wind there is were on that side of the train," Bennett half-insisted. "I'd get it on the lungs, probably—but not in there. After you've let me move him to where I can get at him."

"Post-mortem—yes," Wadden assented. "Well, it's Head's pidgin, and I don't envy him, this time."

"If an earthquake shot you into the middle of the next county, superintendent, would you still keep calm?" Bennett asked abruptly.

"Very calm, I expect—while the undertaker measured me," Wadden answered. "Why, though?"

"Well, a murder thrown at you in the small hours of the morning, a naked man added in, and you seem to take it all as a matter of course."

"Whaddye want me to do—stamp around and make faces? I'm too wild for that, doctor. Every time I think about resigning and starting to grow tomatoes under glass, something happens to stop me. Like this. I've got to hold myself in, bottle it all up. And here's Head, at last."

CHAPTER II

Leo Thane Explains

"WHATEVER it is that you want, please come quite inside and close that door before you ask for it. What little warmth there is in here seems to be evaporating rather quickly."

Without changing the direction of his gaze, Inspector Head moved forward a step into the third-class compartment and, reaching behind himself, slid the door fully closed. The voice that had made the request and comment was that of a well-bred man, and had the faintest tinge—so faint as to be beyond locating—of a foreign accent. As if, Head felt, the speaker were one who, English in origin, were more used to speaking and thinking in some other language than his own. The face and neck and a small V of chest of the man were deeply tanned, as were the hand and arm to the elbow that the brown blanket in which he had wrapped himself left exposed: where, normally, a short-sleeved singlet would cover him, his skin was ivory white, rippled with fine muscling on such of his chest as showed, and the arm and shoulder appeared to be fined down to little more than bone and sinew. He looked like one trained to the last ounce; the grey eyes in his lean, sunburnt face had a humorous gleam in them, though he sat in the corner of the compartment stark naked except for a borrowed blanket; his tousled hair was a silky brown, his nose too large, his mouth firm almost to hardness. A strong man in every way, Head decided in the second or so that he paused before declaring the object of his entry to the compartment.

"I am a detective-inspector," he said, and my name is Head. Will you tell me who you are, and how you come to be in this state?"

"Who I am—yes," the other man responded calmly. "My name is Thane—Leo Thane. If I knew how I came to be in this state—well, I should not be in it. Head—yes, I've heard of you. Read, rather."

"Indeed," Head observed. "Our local paper, I suppose?"

"No, a paper sent out to me. Murder of a man named Gatton, and there was a reference to another case of yours. I gathered that you were regarded as something more than an ordinary country policeman—it was a London paper. I am honoured to meet you, Inspector Head."

"You know your predicament is not the main cause of that—you know, I mean, that something worse happened on this train to-night?"

"The guard made a remark about bloody murder," Thane assented. "I suppose that is what you mean, isn't it? Why the query, though?"

"You seem rather cool about it all," Head answered sharply.

"Cold, say," Thane amended, quite calmly. "This blanket is thin and old. And why should I be enthusiastic? You've told me you're police, so I don't expect any help from you—expect no more than to be asked to account for myself. And in an altogether different way, this is not the first time I've found myself like this."

"Just explain that, before we go any farther," Head asked.

"Willingly. In the hills behind Duran—I got caught by one of the thunderstorms that happen in that district, and had a peon with me. I remember the flash, and no more. When I waked up, the peon was lying dead about a yard away from me, and every stitch of clothing was burned off the front of me, while I and the back half were untouched. Not a burn to show anywhere—nothing. I went back in the peon's trousers and blanket—what was left of my clothes was quite useless, of course."

"Where did you say this happened?" Head's question expressed no disbelief: incredible as the story sounded, he knew that lightning plays utterly fantastic tricks at times.

"In the hills back of Duran—that's across the estuary from Guayaquil," Thane explained. "It's the terminus of the railway line to Quito —Ecuador, I'm talking about. That's where it happened."

"I see. And your present address, Mr. Thane?"

The other man hesitated. "Here, I think," he said at last.

"Meaning that you have none, or decline to give it?"

Thane smiled, bleakly. "Mr. Head—or Inspector Head, if you like that better—I seem to myself to have been sitting here like this for quite a long time, and I've been thinking. I landed at Folkestone to-day, and decided to come straight on here after fitting out. Whoever played this trick on me not only robbed me of everything material, but of my identity as well. To the best of my knowledge, there is not a soul in this country who could swear to my being Leo Ashford Thane, and my chance of getting even another suit of clothes, except by charity, appears rather small to me. I have no address. I have nothing."

"Here—take this." Head stripped off his fleece-lined overcoat and put it down on the seat. "Put it on, for the present. Then, if you don't mind, Mr. Thane, we'll begin at the beginning of things —for my purpose—and work on to the present moment."

"Your purpose being the bloody murder

the guard remarked upon," Thane suggested. "Well"—dropping the blanket, he donned the coat, which proved a loose fit for him, and then draped the blanket over it—"this is an unexpected kindness. Now tell me what you want to know."

"Landed at Folkestone to-day—from where?" Head seated himself as he asked, and offered his cigarette case. Thane took one, and a light.

"Thank you, inspector. From—well, Lima in the first place. That's in Peru, if you didn't know. If you did, I apologise. From there I got a berth in a coaster to Guayaquil, and from there by P.S. N.C. to Panama. There was a German cargo boat just through the canal, discharging at Panama before she made for Hamburg again by Pacific ports and the Suez and Mediterranean— a round-the-world cruise. I got a berth on her, intending to see something of the Pacific and leave her at Port Said. She loaded copra at half a dozen places and caught fire two days before we reached Aden. The *Weissgartner* was her name. They let me take nothing but the clothes I wore and essential papers when we took to the boats, and the *Strathconal*, Orient liner, picked us up and took us on to Port Said. I crossed to Alexandria, picked up the Messageries boat to Marseilles, and came across France to Boulogne. Arrived at Victoria at four o'clock yesterday, still in my dirty old tropical kit, and went to one of these reach-me-down places where they supply everything. I bought a complete outfit, shed all the old stuff, had a bath, and felt quite new when I dressed myself. Tried London by night, took a dislike to it since I was such an utter stranger, and booked for Westingborough rather than stay there. I suppose you could get in touch with the captain of the *Weissgartner* to prove that I am Leo Ashford Thane. If not, you'll have to apply to Felipe Gutierrez, better known as Felipe the Torero, and to find him you've got to go to the posada of Juan Hurtada in Guayaquil, for I don't know his private address, if he has one."

There was a brief interval of silence, in which the draped man inhaled luxuriously at his cigarette, while Head reflected that Wadden and the doctor were evidently busy over the body in the other compartment, and would get all possible information there, and that the story this man had told, speciously plausible as it sounded, could not be confirmed at any one point nearer than either Guayaquil on the other side of the world, or the present whereabouts of some member of the crew of the burned German vessel on which Thane—if that were his real name—had travelled from Panama. Beyond the sinking of the vessel, if he had actually been on it, he might have assumed any identity he chose. And Head felt certain that he was in some way connected with the body in the other compartment, while his cool acceptance of his predicament told as much against as for him, almost appeared to indicate that he had expected it, and prepared in advance to explain it. On the other hand, if the story were true...

"Why come to Westingborough, and at such an hour?" he asked.

"Why not?" answered the man who called himself Thane, with a smile.

"Yes, but what was your reason for choosing Westingborough?" Head insisted, with a passing reflection on Wadden's assertion that even the railway service shipped trouble to them.

"Oh, I see! Yes, of course. Well, my mother was a cousin of Sir Bernard Ashford, and I understand he lives at Carden Hall."

"Other relatives, capable of identifying you?" Head persisted.

Thane shook his head. "My father was an only son of an only son, and my mother the only representative of her branch of the Ashford family. I don't expect Sir Bernard to recognise me, but it's a link, and—well, I am a lone wolf, and felt like—making acquaintances, say."

"You are—well-to-do? Or looking for more than social openings?"

"Fairly well-to-do, I suppose you'd call it. I uncovered Cinquefuego and managed to hold my own till the flotation."

"Which means nothing to me," Head pointed out.

"Means—no, of course not! I'm sorry, Mr. Head. Cinquefuego is copper, and some silver.

A mine—a valuable one. I discovered it, and managed to get my rightful share in the proceeds when it was turned into a company—it took five years of careful work on my part, because people in that part of the world are not over-scrupulous. I estimate myself at about five thousand a year in English money."

"And travel third-class," Head observed.

"I went to the *guichet*—the window where one buys a ticket—and said 'Westingborough.' The man inside asked whether I wanted single or return, and I said single. When I saw I had a third-class ticket, I was already on the platform, and seeing how good the third-class compartments are decided me not to change it. English railways are well run."

"What baggage had you?" Head asked.

"One suit-case. New—everything I had was new, had been bought to-day—yesterday, it is now, of course."

"You had a passport, I suppose, or some papers proving identity?"

"A passport—yes. Issued by the consulate in Lima. And a draft on Barclay's head office for four thousand pounds English. Both in the left breast pocket of my new coat, when I got on the train."

"That is to say, your signature will be available at Barclay's head office in London?" Head suggested after a pause.

"The draft is to bearer," Thane dissented. "It and the duplicate forwarded to Barclay's independently are both signed by the managing director of Cinquefuego, and countersigned by the consul in Lima."

"Is there any specimen of your handwriting in this country?"

"Not that I know of. You see, I anticipated spending the rest of my life prospecting in the Andes, or wandering elsewhere if I got tired of that. Cinquefuego altered everything, and I decided to come home."

"Does 'home' mean that you were born in England, Mr. Thane?"

"Yes, and lived here till I was ten. Then, since my mother was dead, my father took me with him when he got an appointment in Talcahuano —that is in Chile, as you may or may not know. He left me enough when he died to follow my inclination and go prospecting. Enough, and no more."

"Now let's consider your journey here," Head suggested. "I take it you got into this compartment at the beginning of the journey?"

"It was the only empty one I could find," Thane assented.

"Did it remain empty till the train started?"

"No. A tall, rather effusively pleasant man got in and accused me of having been abroad. We got talking, but he bade me good-night and left the train at its first stop—Watford, I believe."

"Got talking—on what grounds? Did he open the conversation?"

"Yes, by saying—let me see! Yes, that my complexion proved I had been out of England, and would I like a cigarette? I took one, and he told me what the weather had been like when I told him I hadn't seen England since I was ten years old until to-day. Small talk, until we got to Watford, and then he left me and I went to sleep, to waken feeling very sick and with a reek of ether, but with nothing else. No suit-case or clothes, I mean. Then I pulled the communication cord."

"Did you see or speak to anyone else before going to sleep?"

"Nobody. I felt confoundedly sleepy before my pleasant companion left me, and very irritated by a pack of fools in the next compartment who were singing choruses—rather drunk, I reckoned them. But they too left the train at Watford, and I know practically nothing after that."

"What became of your cigarette end?" Head asked.

"I dropped it and put my foot on it—here." He pointed down between his bare feet. "But it isn't here!" he added, in some surprise.

"Naturally," Head commented drily. "That cigarette prevented you from wakening before the ether rendered you completely unconscious. And now, give me as good an idea as you can of this pleasant companion of yours. A tall man, you say. What can you add to that?"

"But I'd never—yes, I see, though. A dark

grey, fleecy overcoat. Loose brown trouser legs showing from under it, and heavy-soled brown shoes. A soft brown felt hat, which he didn't take off. Brown eyes, I remember, and a rather purplish nose and a close-clipped brown moustache. Nice eyes, I thought, and a very nice smile, and good teeth. Rather stringy sort of neck —I should say he was in the late forties and had not spent all his life in this country, comparing his yellowish complexion with the rest I'd seen to-day—yesterday, I mean. But he might have been younger. Well-spoken, and told me nothing about himself. He had very strong-looking hands, I noticed, and as far as the overcoat let me see was strongly-built altogether. I think that's all."

Head glanced at his wrist watch, went to the compartment door, and slid it back to look out. Then he closed it again and faced Thane.

"You tell a story well," he said. "What are you going to do now?"

"What can I do?" Thane asked in reply. "I can't prove I am myself."

"No. I suggest you come with us to the police station, and we can find you blankets and possibly clothes of some sort as well. If you can give me the names on that bearer draft to Barclay's head office, I can get in touch with them and not only stop payment, but make sure that any person presenting it will be held for inquiry, while it will be some evidence that you are Leo

Ashford Thane—their identification of it will, I mean. Now I want you to—what's that, though?"

He knelt on the floor and, reaching far under the seat on which Thane was sitting, retrieved a shining nickel-plated key little more than an inch in length. He held it up, and Thane took and inspected it.

"One of the two keys of my new suit-case, I think," Thane said. "There were two, on a piece of pink tape. I untied it and put one inside the case. If this is the other, it was in my vest pocket."

He held it out. "Take it, if you like," he said. "Since I no longer have the case, the key is no use to me."

Head slipped the key in his pocket. "I want you to stay here a little longer, while I see what the others are doing," he said, and went out to the corridor, closing the door behind him.

"A very distant relative of Sir Bernard Ashford of Carden Hall," he answered the query in Wadden's eyes, out on the platform, "or else a perfectly beautiful liar. I suppose it is murder, in there?" He pointed at the first-class compartment as he spoke the question.

"No doubt of that," Wadden answered. "Moreover, gloves, or wiped down. Wells has done some dusting, and there's not a print anywhere."

"Killed how?" Head asked. Then, before Wadden could reply—"I'll see for myself, though," and he entered the corridor of the coach and pulled back the door of the first-class compartment to look in.

A long look, and then he entered the compartment to bend over the body, unmoved, outwardly, by the ghastliness of what he saw. Out on the platform, Doctor Bennett turned to Wadden.

"What about letting me go?" he asked.

"Yes. Tell Jeffries to come here, will you. I want him to help move that body somewhere else, ready for the ambulance, before this station wakes up again. As soon as Head has finished with it, that is."

Kneeling beside the head end of the body, Head managed to get the small blade of his penknife under the cord round the dead man's neck, and, severing it, examined the knot and then put the cord in his pocket. He put the knife away too, and rejoined Wadden and Wells on the platform just as Jeffries, police clerk and chauffeur at need, appeared.

"What's that?" he asked, raspingly, pointing at the suit-case which Wells kept close beside him as he waited.

"Belonged to the dead man," Wadden answered. "Wells has tried it for prints, and there aren't any. Gloves, or wiped off."

"Have you looked inside it?" Head inquired—thoughtfully, now.

"He'd locked it, and Bennett says there are no keys in his pockets, though I haven't been through them myself," Wadden told him.

Head took out the key he had retrieved from the floor of the compartment in which he had left Thane. "Try that on it, Wells," he suggested, handing the key to the sergeant.

Both locks of the case clicked, easily, and Wells pulled back the catches and lifted the lid. A neatly packed and strung brown-paper parcel appeared. Under it Wells found handkerchiefs, socks, a pair of hair brushes and a comb, a safety razor in its case, a new packet of blades, shaving soap and brush, and a toothbrush still in its cellophane casing. The parcel, opened, revealed five new shirts with their collars and two suits of pyjamas, also quite new. Head looked at the label on one of the shirts, and then rose to his feet, frowning.

"Shut it up, Wells," he said. "And still it proves nothing."

"Meaning what?" Wadden asked.

"Not a scrap of writing in it, don't you see?" Head said. "Wait."

He went back to Thane, thrusting back the sliding door.

"I want you to come and view the body," he said. "I think it's quite unidentifiable, owing to the way in which the face has been mutilated, but there may be some point about it over which you might help us. First, though, you say you fitted out with everything new in London at a reach-me-down place. What place was it, can you tell me?"

"The name was Reed," Thane answered. "Not far from Piccadilly Circus. I got everything there from hat to shoes, and the case too."

"Now come with me and see the body," Head asked.

Thane padded barefooted along the corridor to the entrance of the compartment in which the body lay. He looked in, and gripped the framing of the doorway so hard that his knuckles whitened.

"My God!" he whispered.

"Do you recognise him?" Head asked.

"No—how could I? But—but I'll swear that's the suit of clothes I bought to-day! Yesterday, I mean."

"By the way"—Head spoke quite calmly —"was your suit-case locked when you got on the train?"

"Locked? I—let me think. No, though. I put one key inside, and you have the other. But I didn't lock it. You see, I had my passport and the draft on Barclay's in my pocket."

"What was in the suit-case?"

"Let me see. The other five shirts and two suits of pyjamas—not unpacked. Eleven handkerchiefs, because I was using the other, and five new pairs of socks—I only got half-a-dozen pairs. A new pair of hair brushes and a comb, a shaving kit—oh, and a new toothbrush. I think that's all. Why, have you found the case?"

Head did not answer. The list was complete, but still, he felt, it proved nothing.

"Do you approve of my suggestion that you should come along to my office for what's left of the night?" he asked at last.

"Under arrest?" Thane had turned his back on the corpse he had viewed, and faced Head as he put the question, harshly.

"No." The reply was baldly non-committal.

"At hand in case you decide on arrest, then?"

Head shrugged. "Take it how you like," he said. If you don't accept the offer, what will you do—where will you go?"

For a few seconds Thane hesitated.

Then—

"I accept the offer," he said.

"And you claim that suit is yours?"

"Yes, but—I'd never wear it again. I'd sooner stay as I am than put it on. But it is the one I bought at Reed's."

"Very well. Now we can go." He opened the door leading to the platform. Through the booking office, and you'll see a big saloon car outside. Get in and wait for the rest of us—only a few minutes."

He went to where the two railwaymen waited apart from Wadden and his two men.

"Potter," he said, "I shall call here for you as soon as it's daylight, and drive you out to show me where you stopped when the communication cord was pulled. That's all for the present. Now,

Tom"—he addressed the ticket-collector—"who got off this train here?"

"There was Mr. and Mrs. Enthwaite," Tom Adams answered without hesitation, as if he had expected the question, "and Mr. Ednam and his daughter—the oldest one, Bella—and the two Miss Frosts, and Mr. Parham, and young Tom Cosway with that girl he's goin' to marry, they say—I've forgot her name, for the moment. Snell, it is, though—I remember now. And the barmaid in the saloon at the Black Lion. That was all."

"You're quite sure it was all?"

"'Less somebody got down the other side an' dodged down on to the line," Tom answered. "It was all that come out the reg'lar way."

"Thank you, Tom. I know your memory's good. Sorry to have kept you so long. Good night —or good morning, if you prefer it."

"All clear, Head?" Wadden asked, as Tom Adams retired.

"All ready to go, chief—but far from clear, yet."

"Near enough. Get that body out as I told you, you two. You wait with it till the ambulance comes along, sergeant."

"While you're waiting," Head added, "get at the stationmaster somehow and tell him that coach is not to be touched till I've had a good look over it in daylight. I'll go along to the car and wait for you, chief."

CHAPTER III

Among the Ashes

ALTHOUGH Head had made a thorough daylight inspection of the coach in which the murder had been committed, and had informed Samuels that he had no further need of the vehicle, the sun was but a little way above the horizon when the old two-seater irreverently known to Westingborough police as "the inspector's barrow" drew into the side of the road where a bridge led over the railway just outside Crandon, and Head got out, after removing the ignition key, and, together with Robert Potter, climbed over the railings at the end of the bridge and got down on to the line. They took to the six-foot-way, and followed it toward the bridge by which the double track was carried over the Idleburn.

"Watford, Tring, Crandon, Westingborough," Head observed thoughtfully. "That is, practically a local for the first part of the run, two hours without a stop after that, and then stops at two stations only ten or twelve miles apart. I wonder why that is?"

"People wonder lots o' things about trains," Potter said. "But you see, sir, they got to be fitted in, and the worst jig-saw puzzle ever cut is child's play to fittin' in the trains on a time-table. I don't know myself, but most likely this eleven-forty is hurried over that two-hour part of the run to leave a clear line for some bigger trains. And quite likely it ain't run for the sake of the passengers it'll carry on that particular run, but because the rolling stock is wanted at the other end for the return trip. There's all sorts o' reasons."

"I see that—yes. How many people got aboard at Euston last night, would you say, at a rough estimate?"

"I'd recken 'em at nigh on two hundred, sir. There was a swarm got off at Watford, and as I said, nobody got on, there or anywhere else."

"And I suppose you lost still more at Tring?"

"Pretty near half what was left. I took a walk down the train an' back after we left Tring, an' there wasn't more'n two score left in it altogether, I'd say. Mostly all dozin', too, or else sound asleep."

"Knowing they had two undisturbed hours, and the stopping of the train would waken them. Yes. Were the blinds of both those compartments in the forward coach drawn down, then?"

"As I remember it, sir, the third—where the naked man was—that had the blinds down, but not the first. And there was one man in there!"

"That would be the one you found dead later, I take it?"

"I couldn't say, sir. I didn't take much notice of him. He looked to be asleep, an' had a soft black hat down over his eyes an' his overcoat collar turned up—head dropped down so I couldn't see much of his face. An' you couldn't make anything o' that dead man's face, only a sort of horror. Made me near sick when I spotted him, it did."

"Quite so. Where was this sleeping man sitting?" Head continued.

"Corner next the corridor, faced toward the engine. So, you see, sir, he'd be faced a bit away from me as I went along, like that."

"A soft black hat. What sort of overcoat, could you say?"

"Brownish, as near as I remember, but I'm not sure. Smoothish sort o' stuff—might be grey, but I think it was brownish. Light coat, not a heavy winter one, as near as I remember. I didn't take close notice."

They came to the river bridge, and were in the middle of it when an up-bound express roared by and shook them and the iron fabric.

When it had passed, they plodded along the ballasting for some distance, and the guard stopped and looked back, doubtfully.

"It wouldn't be any further'n this, when we pulled up," he said.

"Would you place this as the position of that coach?" Head asked.

"Half a mo, sir. If you'll stop there for a bit ____"

He walked on for some distance, while Head waited. Then he began returning, and evidently counted his paces as he came. He passed Head by about ten yards, stopped, and faced about.

"This'd be about the position of the third with the naked man in it, sir," he said. "There's fresh ash an' clinker up where I went to, which means the fireman raked his box a bit while we were standin'—engines don't drop stuff in a place like that as a rule, not in heaps. An' I've paced back the length o' the tender, the length o' the brake van, an' as much o' the coach as'd bring me to that compartment—about."

"Good for you, man! Now pace on till you're opposite the first-class compartment with the body in it, mark that point, and then pace to the rear end of the coach and wait there, will you?"

"Right you are, sir."

As he moved on, Head went along to the point at which he had stopped, and there halted to give only a brief glance to either side. From here to within a few yards of the river bridge the line was neither embanked nor cut, but level with the wooded tract through which it ran. A wire fence on iron posts bounded the tracks on either side, and, where the ballasting ceased, a mat of last autumn's dead grass began, extending under the fences to the undergrowth of the woods, which was composed of hazel clumps, hawthorn and blackthorn bushes, the latter already in blossom, silver birch saplings, and all the varied growth of an area in which the botanic life had been allowed to run wild. Head knew the ground from the days of a childhood in which he had played and birds-nested and poached and illicitly fished the river, as boys will, and his scant survey convinced him that nobody had left the train at this point to climb either of the wire fences. He went on to where Potter had scraped the ballasting with his toe to indicate the position of the first-class compartment with the body in it, and dismissed it as affording no evidence after as brief a scrutiny as before. Then he went on to where the guard stood, the estimated end of the coach.

"I expect you're a bit tired and fed-up, aren't you?" he asked.

"Sleepy, sir, but—well, I wouldn't say I'm fed-up. First time I've ever done any police work, an' it's interestin', so far."

"I'm glad you find it so. I think—yes, we'll walk back toward the bridge, now. There's nothing at this point, as nearly as I can see!"

They made twenty paces, or thereabouts, and then Head stopped, at which Potter halted too and looked round at him.

"Somewhere about the back end of the next coach, isn't it?" Head asked. "I take it the ordinary coach runs about sixty feet in length."

"About that, sir, corridor stock of the sort that train carries."

"Yes. Well, this is where he got out. But why he made for the river instead of taking to the woods on the other side——"

He did not end it, but crossed the down line of rails to stand gazing at the dead, tussocky grass for a few seconds. He looked back at the corresponding strip in which the other fence was set.

"You see"—he pointed as he spoke—"someone has made a track in the grass both sides of this fence—got over the fence, lately. And they didn't come over the other fence and cross both pairs of rails—there are no marks on that other grass strip. This has been untrodden and untouched all winter, and"—he put a foot on the grass and lifted it—"any impression shows. I'm following this. You can go back to the car and wait for me, or come too—just as you think best."

"I'll come along, sir. I'm new to this game, an' a Londoner at that, not knowin' anything about the country, but they say two heads are better'n one, an' mine might come in handy some way or other."

"Well, that's very good of you, Potter. Here goes—over the fence, and if we can only find a suit of clothes sunk in the river——"

"You mean—the suit belongin' to that naked chap, sir?" Potter inquired, after he too had climbed over the fence.

"Possibly," Head answered, and led slowly along the trail that had been left for him. "Whoever we're following had an electric torch, I think. And starlight to guide him for direction, probably."

"How d'you make the electric torch, sir?" Potter asked.

"No clear footprints," Head answered. "His feet dropped on heaps of dead leaves or tussocks of grass every time—never on bare earth, you may notice. Without a torch he'd have struck earth, some time."

"Shows how you see things an' don't see 'em," Potter commented.

They came to the osier-fringed bank of the river, and here a trail led plainly over the long grass, between two clumps of the "pussy-willows," to the water's edge. Head pointed across to a corresponding trail on the other side, apparently leading into the woods which, forming part of Squire Hastings' property, extended up from the stream to near the crest of the long ridge of which Condor Hill was the highest point.

"We'll part here," Head said. "I'm going to wade over."

"Mind if I come too, sir?" Potter asked.

"Not a bit, but it's nearly waist deep, in the

middle. If the weather hadn't been so dry this winter, it'd mean swimming."

"Umm-m! Did *he* wade it, d' you reckon—in the dark, too?"

"He did. It begins to appear that he knows his way about, here. Though why he didn't go round by the bridge—wanted to keep away from the road, though, I expect, until—wait a bit before we muddy it."

He paced a dozen yards or more up-stream, gazing at the clear water, and, returning, walked over a score yards in the other direction. Then he came back to where Potter waited.

"If he'd thrown anything in, he'd make sure that it sank," he remarked, "and obviously nothing has sunk near here."

"He might reckon whatever it was'd float far enough to get lost," Potter dissented. "So's nobody'd connect it up, I mean, sir."

"I can try that out later, if necessary," Head said. "For the present, I'm going over, but I'll keep my socks and shoes and trousers dry."

He took them off and, estimating the depth of the water by another look at it, pulled his woollen pants up round his thighs. After only a momentary hesitation Potter followed suit, and the pair of them took to the icy-cold water. The pebbly, weed-infested bottom was slippery, but they made the other bank with all their clothing still dry, and rubbed themselves down with handfuls of dry grass before dressing again.

"And now," Head straightened himself after lacing his shoes, "I wonder where he'll lead us. Uphill for a start, obviously."

"When I was thinkin' it out, while we was drivin' here, sir," Potter observed, "I reckoned whoever done it had took a long chance, an' it'd come off. Since he wasn't caught at it on the train, he was all right. But now I begin to think I wouldn't care to have you on my trail, sir."

Head smiled. "All this is elementary, deductions from very obvious premises," he said. "Any country copper would have tried it out."

"I dunno." Potter frowned thoughtfully as he tied the lace of his second shoe and stood up, ready to go on. "I told you when you asked me, I didn't hear anyone drop off the train when the cord was pulled."

"No, but I think he would anticipate that cord being pulled, and would have pulled it himself before Westingborough if it had not been done for him. I think he had a door at the end of the coach opened and closed again, with himself outside, before the train stopped, even, and he either bolted for the fence as soon as it was safe to drop, to get out of the light from the windows, or else hid under the side of a coach till the train went on again. What I cannot understand yet is his crossing the rivers with so many acres of good hiding in the woods on the other side, but it begins to seem to me that he knows the district, and had some definite point in view—one he knew he could reach before dawn.

"Well, I reckon you know where we are now, sir. I don't," Potter confessed. "Two—he had nearly four hours before daybreak."

"Keep behind me—you won't find it easy going through these woods," Head admonished. "Sure you wouldn't rather go back to the car?"

"No, sir. This is a new game to me, somethin' to remember."

"But not to talk about, yet," Head pointed out, as he went on.

The trail was fairly easy to follow, though, as on the other side of the river, no clear footprint showed. Whoever had preceded them had been careful to tread on last year's ridged and heaped leaves, dead branches, protruding tree roots—anything but soil capable of retaining an impress, and it was evident beyond question that he had had light of some sort to guide him. He had gone diagonally up the hillside, heading away from Crandon, and, Head realised, maintaining a direction which would eventually bring him out on the old coach road from Westingborough to Crandon, on which, of course, he would leave no tracks.

A half hour or so after crossing the river, when the ascent had warmed them both from the chill of the water, they dipped down into an irregular sort of gully, worn in the soft soil by winter rains, but quite dry, now, and with a foot or more depth of dead leaves in its bed. Here the recent disturbance of the winter's accumulation was plain to see: whoever had made it had taken no trouble at all over masking his progress. Where two old oaks, one on either side, thrust a network of roots into the gully, and, arching over it, almost hid the sky, the one who had come this way in the night had halted and lighted a fire, clearing the dry leaves to prevent the conflagration from spreading, and feeding his fire with dead wood, of which plenty was at hand in the bed of the gully. There was a thin spiral of smoke, and the smell of a wood fire left, even now, and Potter, halting beside Head, stared at it.

"Well, I'm blest!" he exclaimed softly.

"If he got wet in the river, it dried him," Head remarked. "But I don't think that was his reason for making it. We'll see, though."

He climbed out from the gully, cut a small sapling with his pocket knife, and, returning, utilised the stick as a poker, with which he pulled away the ash and bits of charred wood from the site on which the fire had been built. He raked at it assiduously, while Potter watched, not comprehending, until there appeared the shrivelled and charred soles of a pair of boots or shoes, and a tiny object which Head picked up, but dropped again instantly, since it was still too hot to hold. He pulled the spoiled leather clear of the ashes with his stick, and picked up the tiny thing again, changing it from one palm to the other as it cooled.

"A button!" Potter ejaculated. A brace button!"

"Also, a pair of shoes," Head pointed out. "Almost unrecognisable, but perhaps not quite. There should be more buttons, though."

"You mean—that naked bloke's suit, sir?" Potter asked.

"Maybe." Head went on raking over the ashes with the end of his stick, and pulled four more buttons away from the site of the fire to cool, one after another. "I don't think he anticipated being followed on this trip," he added. "Else, he'd have cut those buttons off the trousers before burning the suit. And it looks as if that is all we'll get. The others were bone buttons—they'd burn to ash."

In spite of the assertion, he was not content with what the stick would reveal, but squatted over the site of the fire and raked over all the ash with his hands, gingerly, because of the heat that still remained. Out of that final examination he gleaned a short collar stud, blackened by the fire and useful only as indicating that clothing had been burned here, possibly, other than the garment to which the five buttons had belonged. The most rigorous search failed to produce anything else, and eventually Head gave it up and lighted himself and Potter cigarettes.

"We'll follow on, now," he announced.

"What about your car, sir?" Potter inquired.

"We may get back to it, or I may have to send for it," Head answered with indifference. "I'm following this track as far as I can see it."

It led them out on the right-hand side of the gully, a little beyond the site of the fire, and, Head noted, never once did the one whom they were tracking leave a definite footprint which might have been measured to give the size and character of his footwear. Apart from that, he had made no attempt to hide his trail, probably realising that it would have been useless to do so, for the disturbance of drifted leaves that had lain for months could not be concealed.

He had travelled, after leaving the gully, parallel with the crest of the ridge, as nearly as the tangled undergrowth would let him. A full two hours after crossing the river, Head and Potter came out to the old coach road between Westingborough and Crandon, a sunken lane over which the trees on either side almost met, and so little used, now that the new and better-graded road had been cut over Condor Hill, that tiny tufts of grass showed on the pebbly metalling, which retained no footprints.

"Bloodhounds?" Potter half-suggested.

"No—we couldn't give them a scent to follow," Head dissented. "Our own is laid over the trail through the woods. No. We'll go downhill to the junction with the new road, and take a bus back to Westingborough. I'll send a man to collect the car when we get back."

* * *

Without so much as looking into his own room at the police station, Head entered the sanctum of Superintendent Wadden and saw, on the superintendent's desk, the mid-morning cup of coffee—a very large cup—with biscuits in the saucer, and Wadden in his swivel chair at the back of the desk, replacing the spoon in the saucer before he looked up.

"Nice, fine weather," he observed. "I've never known a drier March as nearly as I can remember. Here! Hands off my biscuits!" For Head had taken one before seating himself on the corner of the desk. After he was seated, he raised the charred pair of soles by the string with which he had tied them together, and deposited them on the desk. Then he felt in his pocket with his biscuitless hand and produced five fire-marked buttons and a blackened collar stud, which he trickled on to the desk while Wadden stared, and moved cup and biscuits out of Head's reach.

"Mr. X," Head remarked, "was wearing brown trousers."

"I don't remember my algebra," Wadden retorted.

"Mr. X," Head said patiently, "got into talk with Thane between London and Watford, and got Thane to accept a cigarette. That was why he was able to reduce Thane to total unconsciousness with ether without Thane's knowing that he was being doped. If anyone caught you asleep, chief, and shoved an ether pad under your nose, you'd waken momentarily before you went off, and Thane, by what he tells me, didn't waken."

"Hence," Wadden observed, "he is now in skinnis naturalibus, or whatever the original Greek for it is. Carry on, sar'-major."

"You sound quite cheerful," Head said, and managed to snatch another biscuit before Wadden, reaching out, deposited the cup and saucer on the floor beside his chair, and then blew a full-sized gale as he sat up in the creaking swivel chair and glared at his inspector.

"Cheerful!" he echoed. "Oh, yes! Cheerful! Head, I made a nice layout of my glasshouses on paper last night, and positioned the boiler-shed, and pretty much got everything ready to compose my resignation and find a place where I can start growing tomatoes under glass, and this morning we're faced with yet another full-fledged murder case, handed to us by train since our own people ain't bloodthirsty enough. Full-blown and full-grown, and you've got Mr. X all pat and labelled already. All right! Go ahead. I'm cheerful, am I? Hellish cheerful! Get on about the ether pad—I'm listening. What about the ether pad?"

"Mr. X was wearing brown trousers when he handed Thane that doped cigarette," Head pursued. "Was he wearing those same brown trousers when he burned the pair that belonged to these buttons, or was he wearing the murdered man's clothes, and did he burn the brown trousers?"

"You can search me," Wadden said. "Was he, or did he?"

"The fire has taken all the colour out of the buttons," Head said.

"Why didn't Thane do the dam' murder, and then strip himself and pull the cord?" Wadden demanded. "How d'you know he didn't?"

"I don't," Head confessed. "Except that, if he did, why did somebody else get into Squire Hastings' wood the other side of Condor Hill, build a fire where it couldn't possibly be seen, and burn enough to leave these five buttons and collar-stud—still hot when I found them and this pair of soles? If Thane did it, where do these things come in?"

"A tramp got a new suit, and burned the old one," Wadden suggested.

"Said tramp got off that train when the cord was pulled, and waded through the river to get into Squire Hastings' woods," Head pointed out.

"Which is damn silly, to quote Euclid again," Wadden commented. "Where did he go after that —after he'd built his fire, I mean?"

"Out to the old coach road," Head answered. "From there, he might have gone back to Crandon, or come on here to Westingborough, or taken the footpath down the side of the hill to Carden, and in any one of the three cases he wouldn't leave any tracks. So I came back here."

"Does that junk tell you anything?" Wadden inquired, and nodded at the shoe-soles, buttons, and collar-stud on his desk.

Head picked up one of the buttons and handed it over. "Have a look at the inscription round it," he said. "Mr. X ought to have cut those buttons off before he burned the trousers. They were metal with an enamel covering. The rest of the buttons on the suit would be bone, I think, but these—well, have a look for yourself."

Wadden scrutinised the button, turning it round to decipher the letters until he had the whole inscription complete.

"Ragun Nath, Jelalapur," he read, and looked up inquiringly.

"Quite so—and they all bear that name and address," Head said. "Question, now. Are these Mr. X's own trouser buttons, or did he get so wet crossing the river that he burned his and put on the pair he took off the murdered man? For myself, I'm inclined to say 'yes' to that."

"Umm-m!" Wadden considered it. "Which means that any description you may get of X won't apply, as far as clothes are concerned."

"Loosely fitting brown trousers—tweed, most probably," Head said.

"Anglo-Indian, either X or the dead man," Wadden suggested. "Narrows your field pretty considerably, Head."

"Perhaps," Head said dubiously. "I seem to

remember dropping in at the Carden Arms for lunch a year ago—just a year ago. There were five lobster-nosed and bad-tempered strangers staying there for what Cortazzi calls 'ze feesh,' all talking flies and casts and not caring one hoot whether anyone listened or no. And about six families in the district have sons in the Indian army, and another six or seven are connected with the Indian civil—Woods and Forests or something of the sort—and hate the Army people like poison. Reciprocally, of course."

"Ye-es," Wadden agreed thoughtfully. "Montague and Capulet were bosom friends by comparison. And Anglo-Indians like Carden. Y'know, Head, I'm going over to Carden or somewhere round that way myself when I do retire and start growing tomatoes under glass. Condor Hill keeps off the east winds, and the air's softer, better in every——"

"We were discussing this train murder," Head interjected sourly.

The superintendent blew, a long, steady exhalation, but made no other protest over the reproof. His brows wrinkled thoughtfully.

"Bit of a godsend, that naked gent pulling the cord for him, wasn't it?" he questioned after a period of silence.

"I think he expected it," Head said. "I think, too, that if the naked gent, as you call him, hadn't obliged, Mr. X would have pulled the cord himself before the train got anywhere near

Westingborough."

"Probably," Wadden agreed. "Feeling he couldn't afford to land on a platform and give up a ticket—especially with that spare suit."

"Which he may be wearing himself at this moment," Head observed, "and we haven't the faintest idea what it was like. Near on two hundred people got on that train at Euston, and I've drained the guard dry of information of every sort. Also Thane, who gave me the brown trousers and saw no more of the suit, because Mr. X wore a rainproof."

"D'you acquit Thane?" Wadden inquired after a silence.

"Enough to feel we ought to let him have that suit case and the rainproof found in the murdered man's compartment," Head said. "We can keep track of Mr. Thane till we feel satisfied about him."

"Meaning what?" Wadden asked.

"Just suppose he met the murdered man in London, and found out that the murdered man was named Thane and had landed back from Peru yesterday and meant to come on to Westingborough," Head suggested. "Suppose he meant to assume the name and identity of Thane, and had an accomplice to leave the train and burn the missing suit—five thousand a year is worth a good deal of careful planning, and obviously this crime was planned to the last degree. Thane had been abroad since he was ten years old, and according to this Thane there's nobody in England capable of recognising him. He might rake in a considerable fortune and get away with it before the imposition was discovered, if he were careful and quick."

"Ordinary robbery wasn't the motive," Wadden reflected. "Seven one-pound notes, and twenty-three and fivepence in silver and coppers in the dead man's pockets might have been left as a blind——"

"In Thane's pockets, if he's telling a true story," Head interposed.

"Is he?" Wadden looked up with a doubtful expression.

"I'm inclined to believe him," Head said.

"Any special grounds?" Wadden asked, after another pause.

"Mainly that the two cigarette ends in the first-class compartment are a different make from those in Thane's packet—if that packet had belonged to him with the pocket in which it was found—and none of the missing book-matches from the book were on the floor of the first-class compartment. Which looks as if Thane himself used the missing cigarettes out of the packet, and lighted them with the missing matches, before the coat was moved into the other compartment. The two cigarettes in the first-class compartment were probably lighted with an automatic lighter."

"Possible, but slender," Wadden commented

thoughtfully.

"Then, don't forget, I found a key in Thane's compartment which fitted the suit-case," Head pointed out, "and there was the third-class ticket —a big mistake, leaving that in the pocket."

"M'yes," Wadden commented again. "Head, he was a strong man."

"A mighty strong man," Head agreed. "He had two hours between Tring and Crandon, and in that time, assuming Thane's story is true, he stripped an unconscious man, and stripped and then dressed a dead one—dressed him in a way that made it look as if he had dressed himself, not merely dragged the clothes on to him. But there again—he didn't put any underclothing on his victim. No undervest and pants, remember."

"Some men don't wear 'em," Wadden pointed out.

"It'd have been more convincing if he had put them on," Head said, "but he wasted no time— and what he did must have been hard work. That slashing the face to prevent identification must have been an afterthought, done after he had finished redressing his victim."

"A thoroughly dirty dog," Wadden observed. "Why, Head?"

"If we get that, we get half our case," Head rejoined.

"Identity of the murdered man might give you motive," Wadden reflected. "It wasn't plain robbery—no thief would take all that trouble over it. Besides, he'd have killed Thane as well."

"And perhaps not," Head said. "He wanted a nice clean suit to put on the corpse. A tremendously strong man, with brown eyes and a rather purplish nose and close-clipped brown moustache. A nice smile, and good teeth—I'm quoting Thane on the man who gave him a cigarette. Yellowish complexion, probably lived abroad for some time. Might have been in the forties, and possibly younger. Well-spoken, strong hands—they had to be, too—and strongly built as far as his overcoat showed him."

"Dressed how?" Wadden asked.

"Thane says a dark grey, fleecy overcoat, loose brown trouser legs showing from under it, heavy-soled shoes, and a brown soft felt hat. But that was before he stripped his victim to put Thane's new suit on him and Potter couldn't tell me how the murdered man was dressed in his own clothes. Mr. X may be wearing them, and to ladle out that description of his clothes might be totally misleading."

"What do you do next?" Wadden asked abruptly.

"Have another talk with Thane," Head answered, "and then find out if anyone is missing anywhere—though there are always people missing, everywhere. The identity of the murdered man might give us the murderer, though how anyone is going to identify that ——" he broke off, and shook his head as he remembered what he had seen.

"Strangled, and those three slashes," Wadden completed for him. "No. I'd say his own mother would be hard put to it to recognise that."

"We'll have Thane in, I think," Head said. "In some way, I feel convinced he's connected with it, quite apart from that suit of his."

CHAPTER IV

Thane *is* Thane

HE sat in the chair at the end of Wadden's desk, attired in Head's overcoat, from under which the blanket that Samuels, the stationmaster, had lent him appeared with a certain toga-esque effect. Head lounged in careless lack of interest by the side of Wadden's chair, and the superintendent himself, his fierce eyes directed at their guest, leaned back in the chair, so that his three chins showed distinctly over his uniform collar. Thane crossed his bare legs, and appeared quite at his ease.

"I wonder if either of you two kind gentlemen could oblige me with a cigarette?" he asked. "Just to round off your hospitality."

Head offered his case, and with "Thank you very much" Thane took one. Wadden blew, gently, but perceptibly.

"Nothing else you'd like?" he rasped out, as

Thane, taking a light from the lighter that Head flicked for him, drew and exhaled.

"Quite a few things—superintendent, I believe. Oh, yes, quite a few things," Thane answered equably. "But this was most urgent." He held up the cigarette before taking a second draw at it.

"And whaddye think we're going to do with you?" Wadden demanded.

"I've no idea." Thane exhaled a second cloud, luxuriously, before he answered. "I don't think you can throw me into the street like this. Public decency, and things of that sort. What are you going to do with me? Have you made up your minds yet?"

"Have you any idea as to what to do when you leave here?" Wadden asked. "That is, assuming we let you go—don't detain you on suspicion of being connected with the train murder last night."

"I'm connected with it all right," Thane said deliberately. "That dead man had my suit on him, as I told you when I saw the body——"

"When did you last see him, before last night?" Wadden interrupted.

"Never, to my recollection," Thane answered with decision.

"You didn't know him in Jelalapur, by any chance?" Wadden persisted.

"Jelalapur." Thane repeated the word with a sort of musing curiosity. "Jelalapur. Sounds like

India, to me—the termination of it, I mean. And, as I told Inspector Head in that compartment— I am from Peru. If you meant that for a catch, superintendent, it didn't."

"Obviously," Wadden snapped. "You're pretty cool, aren't you?"

"So would you be, with no more than a blanket and an overcoat," Thane answered imperturbably. "But see here! I don't know that corpse from a steak off a dead guanaco—and if I had known him in his lifetime I think what was done to him renders him quite unrecognisable, even by anyone who knew him well. That being so, I don't see how you can detain me on suspicion. I've had plenty of time to think, you see."

"And come to what conclusion?" Head asked, speaking for the first time since Thane's entry to the room.

"Well, for a beginning, do you think Sir Bernard Ashford would be available by telephone?" Thane asked in reply.

"I know he is," Head answered. "Do you wish to call him?"

"I think he's the one man capable of proving that I am who I say I am," Thane told him. "That is, if he kept a certain letter. You see, I wrote him from Peru about six months ago, telling him my mother was a relative of his, and suggesting that I might call and see him when I got to England. I never received a reply. But I suggest, now, writing as much of that letter as I can remember here, in your presence, and if he kept the letter the handwriting should be fairly good evidence of my identity, I think. Especially the signature. What do you think?"

"And if he did not keep the letter?" Head asked.

"In that case," Thane said, "it looks as if I've got to go around in this blanket and your overcoat till I can get an answer back from the British consul in Lima, with a copy of my signature and a photograph of me. For apart from Sir Bernard I haven't a hope in this country."

Head took off the telephone receiver, and listened.

"Oh, Wells," he said. "See if you can get Sir Bernard Ashford, and put the call through here to me if you can."

He replaced the receiver. Thane looked up at him.

"There'll be an inquest on that strangled man, won't there?" he asked.

"Obviously," Head answered, with an ironic tinge in the word.

"Yes. And just as obviously, you'll want me as a witness. Do I go like this, or do you fit me out with a nice new suit?"

"Being so infernally cool anyhow," Wadden snapped, "I think you'd better go as you are. It'll back up your story of being caught stark naked by that guard, and save us expense at the same time."

"I think," Head put in, while Thane stared at the superintendent, "that we'll advance you the sum of eight pounds three shillings and fivepence, which was found in the pockets of the suit you claim as yours. An equivalent of that sum, not the actual money, because everything that was found on the dead man will be required as exhibits, for the present, including the suitcase you also claim, and the overcoat and hat."

"Extremely nice of you," Thane said calmly. "Then, as soon as that telephone is free, I'll spend part of my new capital in a call to any ready-made outfitter you may have in this town, and get him to come along and help me back to respectability—eight pounds of respectability ____"

He broke off, then, for a buzzer announced an incoming call on the telephone. Head took off the receiver and listened.

"Westingborough police, Inspector Head speaking," he said. "Can I speak to Sir Bernard Ashford, please?"

* * *

The girl with the receiver at her ear shook her head slightly, as if the speaker at the other end could see her.

"I'm afraid not, Mr. Head. Miss Loretta

Ashford speaking. My father is not in, just now—
we don't expect him back till lunch time."

"About one o'clock, that will be?" she heard.

"Yes. Meanwhile"—she remembered an
occasion on which Head had been good to her
—"can I do anything for you, Mr. Head?"

"That's very good of you, Miss Ashford. We've
got a man here who claims he is a distant relative
of yours. Nothing against him, but he will be a
witness at an inquest we have to hold, and there
is a certain amount of trouble over proving his
identity. He claims he is Mr. Leo Ashford Thane,
and that his mother was Sir Bernard's cousin. He
also claims that he wrote to Sir Bernard from
Peru about six months ago——"

"I remember the letter," she interjected.

"That's good, Miss Ashford. Could you lay
hands on that letter?"

For a few seconds she reflected. Then "I don't
see——" she said.

"As a specimen of his handwriting," Head told
her. "We have no evidence, so far, that this man is
Leo Ashford Thane."

She heard a distant murmur of expostulation,
the words indistinguishable except for an
irritable "damn it all!" Smiling, she spoke.

"If you'll hold on for a minute or so, Mr. Head,
I'll see."

Knowing the ways of the household, where
things like this were concerned, she ignored
her father's desk, and hurriedly sorted over the

contents of her mother's escritoire under the dining-room window. Eventually she returned to the telephone and took up the receiver.

"There, Mr. Head? Yes. Postmarked Lima, last September. I have not looked at the letter, but it's inside the envelope. What do you wish us to do? Do you want the letter sent to you?"

"We want it, Miss Ashford, with as little delay as possible."

"I see." She reflected through a brief pause. "I'll bring it over myself—I've nothing to do this morning. To the police station?"

"If you'd be so good."

"I'll turn the car out and be there in an hour."

Replacing the receiver, she went to her room, moving rather listlessly—in her way of moving, as in all else, was a suggestion that she was very little interested in what she did. Less than an hour before, she had looked forward to marriage and happiness: one afternoon had changed everything, left her looking down at the dead face of the man with whom she had hoped to find the summit of life, and, worse, knowing it best that he should be dead. By this time, the resilience of youth had changed her from bitter resentment over the tragedy to a grey and rather ironic acceptance of the fact that life must go on, however devoid of aim she might find it.

The full-length wardrobe mirror, as she put on hat and coat before it, showed her a tall figure, rounded to womanhood yet still slender;

soft brown eyes under dark hair, the healthy complexion of one used to an outdoor life— she was the best horsewoman in the district— and finely modelled features, except for a mouth a trifle too large with lips that set sulkily, in these days, yet gave an impression of resolute strength. When she went out to the garage for the car and faced her father on the way, the relationship between them declared itself, for he too had just such a mouth, just such sensitive, delicately-moulded nostrils. There was something of racehorse breed about them both.

"I'm just going to Westingborough," she announced. "That cousin of yours has turned up at the police station, and they want a specimen of his handwriting for identification. So I'm taking his letter."

"Your cousin, rather than mine," Sir Bernard corrected her, "but a distant one. Police station, eh? How did he explain that?"

"He didn't," she answered. "Inspector Head spoke to me. I don't know—you'd think, coming all the way from Peru, he'd have at least a passport. I suppose—do you wish me to invite him here?"

"I'll rely on your good sense, my dear. Vet him and decide for yourself, and remember we shall have Bernard with us some time over the week-end—I don't know exactly when the boat docks."

"Tilbury—Saturday noon. I looked it up in the shipping list this morning," she said. "Though why Bernard couldn't have come overland from Marseilles as he did for his last leave——"

"Your brother is practising economy," Sir Bernard observed with a slight smile. "You can run down and meet the boat, if you like."

"Can I?" Momentarily, she looked pleased. "Take the car, you mean?" This concession from his rigidly economical way of planning all things surprised her not a little, but then her expression changed again. He had made the suggestion, she realised, for the sake of the son he idolised, not for her: the life at Carden Hall, with all its stringent economies, was designed by the father to make things easy for the son when he should come to his inheritance.

"Why, yes," he answered thoughtfully. "After India's dusty plains, he'll be pleased to see a little of the English countryside on his way here. Meanwhile, if you mean to get back for lunch, and especially if you fetch this man Thane with you, there is not too much time."

"You wouldn't mind if I did bring him back with me, then?"

"My dear, I leave it entirely to you. If you approve of him, welcome him for me and invite him. Otherwise—well!"

He opened the garage doors for her, and then left her, going thoughtfully toward the house. During the last few months, he had reflected often over the problem of her future: now, he considered, if this man Thane were presentable,

Loretta was young enough to forget the tragedy of last year. With her settled to marriage with a man who virtually owned a copper mine, there would be more for Bernard...

In those three words, "more for Bernard," was the sum of the baronet's life, the end to which he devoted all things.

* * *

Superintendent Wadden raised his eighteen stone or so out from his chair as Loretta Ashford was shown into his room. Outside the police station, Potts, representative of the *Westingborough Sentinel*, waited hopefully. If Miss Ashford of Carden Hall were in this thing, it looked like being Big, and Potts could make a bit out of a certain London press agency as well as doing his own stuff, until they sent a man to cover it.

"Ah! The letter." Wadden looked at the envelope Loretta handed to him. "Very good of you to fetch it over to us like this, Miss Ashford, and I think, since he claims to be a relative of yours—perhaps you'd like to sit down for a bit." He nodded at the chair by the end of his desk, and withdrew the letter from the envelope, unfolding it and placing it beside a sheet of writing on the desk. "Yes. Yessss." He breathed the sibilant through his teeth. "Not much doubt."

"You mean, this proves his identity?" she

asked, seating herself.

"I think so. Yes. No doubt at all, really."

"Could I see him?" she asked, as Wadden went on gazing at the paper.

"Could you—well, I'm afraid not, just yet, Miss Ashford. He—well, he's not exactly what you'd call visible, to a lady."

"I am afraid I do not understand, superintendent," she said stiffly.

"No. Naturally, Miss Ashford. Sacred mackerel!" He blew, but with a certain restraint in presence of Sir Bernard Ashford's daughter. Why must Head run away just now—I'm not much good at this sort of thing. Yet it'll all have to come out, of course. Y'see, Miss Ashford, this Mr. Thane had a bit of an adventure last night, and now all he's got in the world is a blanket the stationmaster lent him, and Inspector Head's spring overcoat. He's put a whole outfit on order, ready-mades from Parkinson and Williams, but till it gets here he's—well, Adamish."

"But——" she began, and left it at that while she gazed at him.

"Garden of Eden, with the blanket for a fig-leaf," he said rather desperately. "Y'see, Miss Ashford—there's no harm in telling you—a man was killed on the train that Mr. Thane was travelling in, and he was drugged and stripped, and his clothes put on the man who was killed, to prevent identification. It'll all come out at the inquest—hullo! Whaddye mean, Jeffries, butting in like that?"

"The parcel for the man in Inspector Head's room, sir," Jeffries, in the doorway, answered. "Is it to be taken straight to him?"

"Sacred mackerel! D'you think it's to be taken up on the roof? Get along with it, man, and don't ask any more silly questions!"

The door closed again, with Jeffries outside.

"You mean—there was murder, superintendent?" Loretta asked.

"I'm afraid so, Miss Ashford. Inspector Head is looking into it."

"And—and Mr. Thane—he is not implicated, is he? I mean, your having him here in the police station——" she broke off, questioningly.

"Oh, no! Oh, no! That is to say, his suit—they drugged him, it appears, and took—stole everything. But this letter proves he's what he claims he is—especially the signature. Yes, he's the man all right. Very good of you to bring the letter along like this."

"He is quite free to go when—when he is ready?"

"Why, yes," Wadden answered. "His evidence will be wanted at the inquest, but apart from that he's free to do as he likes."

"And," she persisted, "the parcel your man spoke of just now—it will be the clothes Mr. Thane has ordered, I suppose?"

"That is so, Miss Ashford," he agreed. "A—well, what you might call a temporary outfit. Just enough to go around in."

"I think I'll wait to see him," she decided. "That is, if I'm not in your way here. If I am, I can wait in the car."

"Not a bit—not a little bit," he assured her. "I'm waiting till Head comes back, and doing nothing in the meantime."

A preliminary tap, and then the door opened. Wadden looked up.

"Come in, Head. Miss Ashford has come along with that letter. He is Leo Ashford Thane all right —just have a look at this."

Loretta, answering Head's greeting by a slight inclination of her head, rose to her feet and went to gaze down at the two sheets of paper laid side by side on Wadden's desk as Head, rounding the other end of the desk, went to inspect them, so that they stood one on each side of the superintendent. The girl nodded after only a brief glance.

"Unmistakably by the same hand," she remarked.

"Yes," Head assented, "but I'm afraid it will take more than that to release the money he told us was waiting for him."

Loretta looked an inquiry at him.

"A draft for four thousand pounds, on Barclay's head office in London, Miss Ashford," he explained. "He lost the duplicate which he was to present—lost it with other things last night. And now—well, I don't know what steps he'll have to take to get the money."

"That will be rather awkward for him," she remarked, "I—I was waiting to see him, as soon as he can be seen," she added after a pause.

"Yes, I concluded you were," Head said. "If you don't mind my asking, Captain Ashford is in India, isn't he?"

"At present, he is on his way home on leave," she answered. "He arrives on the *Pathankot* on Saturday, at Tilbury."

"I see. I believe he is Indian Army, isn't he?"

"He is." The reply was rather stiffly given, as if she rather resented such apparently unnecessary questions. "Indian cavalry."

"Do you mind my asking where his regiment is stationed?"

"Not at all." But she spoke even more stiffy, now. "It is a small station near the north-west frontier, named Jelalapur."

CHAPTER V

Not Coincidence

THE superintendent leaned back in his chair with a barely audible Phooo! of relief when Loretta Ashford's and Leo Thane's footsteps ceased to sound along the flagged corridor outside the room.

"It'd take dynamite to make that feller jump," he observed.

"Did you compare his nose with Miss Ashford's?" Head asked.

"He wouldn't let me take it off," Wadden retorted acidly.

"It's what you might call the Ashford nose," Head reflected aloud, ignoring the sarcasm. "Like hers, like Sir Bernard's. Sensitive, fine nostrils, an almost unmistakable family trait."

"Brought over by the Conqueror, and planted on 'em," Wadden suggested. "Fined down, generation after generation, so's they can smell the difference between Irish bacon and genuine Wiltshire. Why worry?"

"And Captain Bernard Ashford is on his way back from Jelalapur," Head remarked, again ignoring Wadden's heavy satire.

"Where they stamp their trouser buttons," Wadden said. "Head, is that a coincidence, or is it a coincidence?"

"No," Head answered, and left it a single-syllabled reply.

Again the superintendent blew, long and gently.

"Either way, it'll break old Sir Bernard's heart," he said.

"You mean—we both reach the same conclusion, chief?"

Wadden nodded.

"Isn't it obvious?" he snapped out. "Oh, why didn't I hand in my retirement at the end of last year? I'd have had the glass-houses up and the tomato plants in by now! Instead——"

He broke off as Head seated himself on the opposite side of the desk, took a sheet of paper from the rack, and began pencilling on it. Having finished, he swung the paper around so that Wadden could read what he had written.

"Umm-m! Better prepay reply, hadn't you?"

"Not necessary. That signature, 'Police, Westingborough,' will bring a reply. Besides, I don't know whether you can, with Marconigrams. Wells can telephone it through, and we should have a reply to-day."

"It begins to look like a quite simple case," Wadden remarked. "The sort they call open and shut among the dollarocracy."

"They all look like that, at the beginning," Head commented, rather sourly, and, taking up the paper on which he had written, rose to go.

"And your first move?" Wadden asked.

"No, it will be about the fourth, or fifth," Head answered. "If you see any reason to get in touch with me, chief, I'm lunching at the Carden Arms. I'll be back in time for the reply to this."

"The buttons might be coincidental, you know," Wadden reminded him.

Holding the door for his exit, Head faced about momentarily.

"Have you ever seen a pig's wing feathers, chief?" he asked derisively, and went out without waiting for a reply.

* * *

Having maintained silence after seating himself in the car beside Loretta, until she turned out of Market Street into London Road and accelerated on the way to the bridge over the Idleburn, Thane spoke.

"You're very kind to an absolute stranger," he said.

"In what way?" She did not turn her head to put the question.

"Suggesting that I should come back home with you."

"You have my father to thank for that, not me," she said coolly.

"Very good of him, then," Thane said, just as coolly. "I suppose—we're relations, but I don't even know your first name."

"And both yours were at the end of that letter of yours," she observed. Very distant relations, too."

"But you wouldn't object if I called you cousin?"

"No. If it pleases you." Utter indifference sounded in the reply.

"Cousin what?" he persisted, smiling at her profile.

"Oh, just cousin," she answered, and kept her gaze on the road.

"Fine car, this, cousin," he remarked, when the bridge was behind.

"It has been," she returned. "It's eight years old, now."

"Then I'd say it was brewed in a good vintage year. Not that I know much about them. I've been where the roads are not kind to cars, and now it looks as if England is going to disappoint me."

"Then you'd better go back," she observed calmly.

"Don't you like me, cousin?" he asked, with amusement in his voice.

"I was thinking of your disappointment," she

retorted.

"Going back wouldn't cure it," he said. "Since my father died, I've spent most of my life among the Andes, and it's wild, in a good many ways. I came back hoping to find England all settled and quiet, as I'd been led to believe, and the very first thing that happens to me on getting back is that my clothes are stripped off me and put on a murdered man. Which isn't the peace and quiet I expected, exactly."

"And what were you doing while it happened?" she asked.

"Nothing. I'd been carefully drugged to prevent me from doing anything. And now the clothes I'm wearing are all I have."

"Some of my brother's old things might fit you till you can get more," she said. "He'll be back home the day after to-morrow."

"Probably I can last out till then. But would his fit me?"

She turned her head, then, to look full at him. "When you came into the superintendent's office," she said, "I thought for a moment that you were Bernard—my brother. I haven't seen him for over four years—he's in the Indian Army —but the likeness is very strong."

"Strong enough for you to tell me that first name, cousin?"

"Loretta." With the one word she turned her gaze to the road again.

"Unusual, and attractive," he remarked. "I'll

risk being thrown out of the car by saying it's like you, cousin."

She changed down to third gear for the ascent of Condor Hill, and made no reply while the car ground up into the cutting. They came out to a view of the valley in which Carden was set, and the far-stretching perspective beyond the roofs of the village, clear in the spring sunlight.

"Couldn't we stop for a bit?" Thane asked. "I'd no idea England was like this. I mean—if you have time, of course."

She steered on to the parking width beside the road, and braked to a standstill. "I thought you'd lived in the Andes," she remarked.

"Bigger, wild—more magnificent in its own way," he said, "but the—the ordered peace of this, the matured beauty of it. There is no comparison. No sea, no snowline—look at the way it fades into haze beyond that dark belt of evergreens. But it's familiar to you, though."

"Some scenes, like some memories, never grow old," she said.

"I wonder what hurt you?" he observed after a silence.

She released the brake, and the car moved on. "Perhaps I hurt myself," she answered. "Though I don't know why you should think——"

"It's easy," he said in the pause. "You're all fenced round, cousin Loretta, as if you were absolutely determined that nothing—nobody should ever get near enough to hurt you again."

"You forget," she said coldly. "An absolute stranger, you have no right to talk to me in that way."

"I'm sorry. Please try to forgive me. You see, I've lived where people of our own race are so few and far between that you don't practise reticence when you meet them—if you like them on sight, I mean."

He waited through a silence that lasted nearly to the foot of the hill. Then she turned her head to smile at him momentarily.

"I do forgive you," she said, and added —"cousin."

"I'm not nearly as disappointed as I was," he observed.

Beyond the Carden Arms, she turned the car in at the gateway that gave access to the Hall, and Thane noted that the driveway was rutted and grass-grown, while dead branches from the elms and beeches that shadowed it on either side lay rotting, only just clear of the car's mudguards, at intervals. They rounded a curve, and he saw the frontage of a square, grey stone Georgian house. A grey-headed man stood under the portico.

"That is my father," Loretta said, "and we are not late for lunch."

* * *

A full half hour after Loretta Ashford had gone down the western side of Condor Hill,

Inspector Head followed as far as the Carden Arms, having had to wait until the man who had been sent to retrieve the car had returned with it to Westingborough. So far, Head had made no definite plan over the case: when, with Potter, he had come out to the old coach road and known that he could not hope to trace any farther, he had known, too, that the man he sought might have gone from that point either to Westingborough, Crandon, or Carden: there was little chance of getting trace of him if he had gone to either of the two towns, but if he had headed for Carden it might be possible to obtain news of him. Sergeant Plender, who helped motorists to keep the speed limit through Carden Street, and in other ways was responsible for maintaining order in the village and its surroundings, might have a tale to tell, but he, as Head knew, went over to Gunwell on Thursday mornings to see that all was well there. Lunch at the Carden Arms and a talk with Cortazzi, the naturalised proprietor of Italian extraction, might yield a line worth following, and in any case would fill in time until the sergeant became available.

Cortazzi himself, whose genius in management had raised the Carden Arms from the status of an average village inn to that of a residential country hotel, came to open the door of the entrance lounge as Head descended from his car in the forecourt. Behind him, the lounge showed empty, evidence that any who might be staying in the place were already at lunch. And Cortazzi, Head saw, was not his usual self: he looked apprehensive. His greeting, too, was far from normal.

"Mr. 'Ead, I could not 'elp it," he said. "Per'aps I was not vairy polite to 'im, but 'e was not polite to me. 'E call me damn Dago."

"Most reprehensible, Cortazzi," Head commented, not knowing in the least who had thus spoken, or what it was about. "But are you quite sure you couldn't help it? Honestly, now?"

"Every Saturday night, when I 'ave enough people stay 'ere, we 'ave ze dance," Cortazzi said, "'an' larst Saturday I 'ave sixteen—all ze rooms fool—I am quite fool. I 'ave too five people come from Todlington for ze dance, an' because zey was not resident I close ze bar at ze proper time. An' ze noise was no more zan any time before. It was ze radiogram—zey put on ze records. Per'aps zey laugh a little, but what is it to laugh? One o'clock, all ze dance fineesh, an' all go to bed. An' Sunday 'e come an' call me damn Dago, an' say 'e complain to police because 'e cannot sleep. An' I say go to 'ell, as I would say to any man which call me damn Dago. I could not 'elp it, I tell you."

"Twenty-one of them," Head observed. "You cleared the dining-room for this dance, I suppose?" He might get the identity of the complainant without disclosing that he did not know it, if he asked for a few particulars: Cortazzi was obviously ready to go on talking defensively.

"Yaas, Mr. 'Ead. Always we 'ave ze dance in ze dining room. 'E say 'is bedroom face ze window of ze dining room, an' it do not, because it ees sideways—'is 'ouse is a little more back from ze road zan ze hotel, but ze dining room windows look ze same way as ze back of 'is 'ouse. I say 'e is vegetarian, 'e is killsport, 'e is lunatic, an' when 'e say 'e face ze dining room 'e is damn liar too. An' it ees seventy-one yard from ze dining room windows to ze fence which divide ze 'otel lawn from 'is garden, because I walk it to see after 'e come to grumplain."

"Quite probably we shall be able to smooth Mr. Foster down so that you hear no more about it," Head said consolingly, knowing that Sergeant Plender had not yet reported any complaint by the vegetarian killsport. "Meanwhile, am I too late for lunch?"

"I make it especial for you myself, Mr. 'Ead," Cortazzi assured him. "An' ze cocktail—*de la maison*? Yaas? I order 'im for you?"

"Here—not in the dining room," Head assented. "And see if you can get me a table to myself in there, will you?"

"I see to it, especial," Cortazzi promised.

While he kept that promise, Head moved along to the fireplace at the side of the lounge, and thus obtained a glimpse of some of the people in the dining room, since the top half of the door between it and the lounge was glazed.

He had passed on beyond their view, and had his back to the fireplace, when Cortazzi returned with the cocktail.

"By the look of that dining room, you're still full," he observed.

"Two go, three come—I am fooler," Cortazzi answered. "It ees ze feesh, an' a few ze goluf also. But most for ze feesh. Zere is a Colonel Thomas, 'e catch a salmon fourteen pound, an' I buy it. So just now I tell ze chef, an' you 'ave ze salmon steak especial, Mr. 'Ead."

"Colonel Thomas, eh? One of your regular visitors?"

"Two—three year now, 'e come 'ere for ze feesh," Cortazzi said.

"And those two big dark men in the corner by the left-hand window—are they old acquaintances of yours too?" Head inquired.

"Ze left-'and—no. Oh, no, Mr. 'Ead! Ze young one, 'e is come to buy 'orses, 'orses for ze polo. 'Is car is in ze garage, vairy fast car. An' yesterday 'e tell me 'e want a room for 'is friend, which 'e fetch in ze car zis morning. So I tell 'Arry 'e take 'is bed in ze room with Jules, because all ze proper rooms is fool, an' so I make room for zat other big man. Why 'e is 'ere I do not know. Per'aps for ze feesh, an' per'aps 'e buy 'orses too. I do not know. If you see zat man Foster, Mr. 'Ead, tell 'im you know 'e call me damn Dago."

"I'll bear it in mind, Cortazzi," Head promised, and put his empty cocktail glass on the mantelpiece. Then he went to the shelf outside Cortazzi's little office at the back of the lounge, and gazed down at the open register. The last name inscribed was that of "Ernest L. Rynewald," described as British with "London" and no more as his address.

This information was contained on the last line but one from the bottom of the double page. Scanning the rest of the names, Head came to the second from the top—"Mirza Ali Ajhodia Khan," with the nationality left blank, and, for address, "Khelankot, India."

An open and shut case, Wadden had called it! Head beckoned to Cortazzi, and as he approached pointed at the second line from the top.

"Is that your polo player?" he asked.

"Yaas, Mr. 'Ead. Zat is 'im. An' zat"—he put a finger on the line on which Rynewald had signed —"is 'is friend, which 'e go to bring zis morning, an' I put 'im in 'Arry's room because I am fool."

"What time this morning?" Head asked.

"Per'aps an hour before ze lunch bell, or a leetle more. 'E say—Mr. Khan say—'e bring 'is friend from Crandon."

Harry, the younger of the two waiters, looked out from the dining room doorway with—"Mr. Head, your lunch is ready, sir."

All in the hotel was his to command, Head reflected as he seated himself at the table that had been laid for him just inside the dining room door: Cortazzi knew the wisdom of keeping

on the right side of the police, and either Head
himself or Wadden could be assured of the best
of everything when they put in an appearance
here. But he wished, now, that he had asked
for a table nearer the window: Mirza Khan
and his friend Rynewald were talking earnestly,
continuously; Rynewald had a purplish nose,
a yellowish complexion and a close-clipped
moustache, and appeared about the age of the
man Thane had described as having given him a
cigarette between London and Watford. He was,
as nearly as Head could see at that distance,
a big man, but fined down to a muscular
athleticism—strong enough, by the look of him,
either to undress or dress anyone limp in
unconsciousness—or in death. And arrived by
car that morning—was it in truth an open and
shut case, as Wadden had said?

Mirza Khan did not fit Thane's description:
he was too dark, too slender, though apparently
as tall as his companion, and too young. A
fine-looking man, black-haired, dark-eyed, with
an almost tallowy yellow complexion: either
Khelankot was somewhere in the hills to north
of India, or else Mirza had kept out of the
sunlight, for many Europeans had darker skins
than his. A princely-looking man—but then,
Head had heard enough Anglo-Indian gossip to
remember that even a Pathan horse-dealer looks
like a king, and that among the Indian frontier
tribes may be found some of the handsomest

men on earth.

The salmon steak was delicious. Anglo-Indians—yes. Squire Hastings' son had been killed on the frontier; Bernard Ashford was the last male of a family that had sent men into Indian services since the days of the old John Company; Foster, who had resented the noise of the hotel dance, was retired from the Woods and Forests department, and there were others retired from Indian service who had settled in and about Carden, for Condor Hill sheltered this valley on the east and north-east, and thus it had a climatic value for men whose blood had been thinned by life in the East, especially at this time of year. "This last, perhaps, accounted for the high percentage of men from the tropics who resorted to the Carden Arms for golf and fishing and—in its season—hunting. Of the dozen or so men lunching here, half looked as if they had dried under hot suns, and two or three more had gone stout and apoplectic, appearing rather like the rough and tough old Joey Bagstock in whom Dickens typified a certain class of Anglo-Indian at the end of his career.

Nearly all men. Much talk at the table immediately behind Head of a new patent gaff, its merits and demerits, and of flies, Wickham's Fancy and all the rest, apparently. Very interesting to the three men who maintained the conversation, but not to one who, like Head, was no fisherman. In front of him, the broad back and high shoulders of a man almost bald on the top of his skull, and, facing both her companion and Head, a smallish, dark, vivacious-looking woman who wore very valuable rings and a bar brooch of emeralds and diamonds at her throat, a platinum-set alternation of sparkling facets and green clarity worth not far short of four figures, Head estimated: even the small diamonds at the ends of the bar were two-carat stones, and the centre emerald must be four carats or more. An unwise display, in such a place as this.

She looked rather bored, when her companion moved so that Head could see her face beyond him. Once, for a moment or two, her very dark eyes lighted with interest, and for that brief while they were arrestingly beautiful; her mouth, too, was tempting, passionate—the sort of woman who might cause trouble among men, Head decided. Toward the end of his lunch, when she and her companion rose to leave the room, he saw that the man was tall, deep-chested, brown-eyed, and bloodlessly, yellowishly pale—another ex-empire builder, by the look of him, apparently strong both of will and body, and rather grim in his expression. Head caught the eye of Harry the waiter, and summoned him to his side by a slight gesture.

"Those two who just went out, Harry—who are they?" he asked.

"Colonel and Mrs. Thomas, sir. They come

every year about this time."

"Is he on leave, or retired, do you know?"

"No, sir, I don't know. I'd say retired, though, else he wouldn't get here so regular, would he? Must be well over fifty, too."

"That Mr. Rynewald—ever seen him before?"

"No, sir. Only got here this morning. Dunno anything about him."

"I see. And how long have the Thomases been here?"

"He's been here a fortnight, sir. She arrived with him, and then went away for a few days. Got back this morning, same train as Mr. Rynewald, I guess. Anyhow, she got in nearly as soon as he did."

"And that man on the left of Rynewald—the one with a purple nose sitting all alone at the next table?"

"Major Fitton, sir. Same regiment as young Mr. Hastings who got killed in India. Goes up to Squire Hastings' place a lot. Miss Sheila, they say —people will talk, you know, sir. He's on leave."

"Well built man," Head suggested.

"I wouldn't care to come up against him in a row, sir."

"It would be most unwise. Now, I think, a small dig at that Stilton cheese I saw, then coffee, and I haven't asked you anything, Harry."

"Thank you, sir. Leave it to me, sir." And Harry went off to fetch the cheese and put the coffee on order.

Was it such an open and shut case? Here in this dining room alone, at the very beginning of his investigation, Head had noted three men who fitted to Thane's sketchy description of his travelling companion, and, if Colonel Thomas had not been so pale, he would have made a fourth. That Major Fitton was friendly with the Hastings family, and the trail Head had followed that morning had led through Squire Hastings' woods.

Plender might have some information that would aid, and then there was the man Foster. A talk with him might yield the position of Khelankot in relation to Jelalapur, if nothing more. But, first——

Having finished his coffee, Head sought the glass-walled telephone box in the lounge, and rang through to Westingborough, asking to be put through to Wadden. The superintendent came on the line.

"Head speaking, chief. Any reply to that Marconigram yet?"

"It's here, laddie. Remarkably quick, I call it. And you were right—there was no coincidence about the buttons."

"Read it out to me, will you, chief?"

He waited, the receiver held to his ear. Then he heard—

"Captain Bernard Ashford disembarked *Pathankot* Port Said. Purser, *Pathankot*."

"I was afraid of it," Head said.

"And now, what next?" Wadden asked.

"Lines of inquiry worth following here—I'm speaking from the Carden Arms. Then, to get Sir Bernard Ashford to identify the body of his son, and find out how that son filled in the time between Port Said and getting aboard that train last night."

"Head, I haven't been idle, on that," Wadden told him. "I've been on to Dean and Dawson at their London office—Piccadilly. They tell me he could have left at Port Said, crossed to Alexandria, got on a flying boat and made England in two days, while the boat'd take eleven or twelve to come round and dock next Saturday. I asked first about overland through France, and then if there were any quicker way still. And they told me about the Port Said trick."

"Which means I've got to try to find out what he did with that spare week or so after he left the boat."

"More than that, laddie. You've got to find out, all of it. And then you've got your case."

"Good-bye, chief. I'll be back——"

"Here, wait a minute. You're sure about Sir Bernard?"

"The nose, chief—the Ashford nose. The murderer didn't disfigure that."

"God help him! Sir Bernard, not the murderer. And you'll be back, you say——?"

"With him—Sir Bernard, not the murderer—as soon as I can finish what I want to do here in

Carden and get to him."

"Go to it. If I think of anything at this end——"

"I know. Good-bye for now, chief."

He hung up and emerged from the box.

CHAPTER VI

Views of a Killsport

IT always happened like that, Head told himself with a feeling of intense irritation as he came out from the telephone box and cast a glance over the occupants of the entrance lounge.

In one case he could recall, the main line of approach to a solution consisted in establishing the identity of a woman, resident in the district, probably red-haired, and named Lilian. The voters' list had yielded more than four hundred Lilians, and nearly an eighth of them had been red-haired. In another case a white-robed figure had been glimpsed in the darkness at a time material to the solution of the case: three women wearing white, and who might have fitted as to time and place, had been found—and no one of the three had been the wanted person. Here, as soon as it appeared probable that the case had an Anglo-Indian foundation, Anglo-Indians simply sprouted in Carden, and four of them who looked more or less like the man Thane had described would, on investigation, probably prove to be entirely unconnected with the murder. Yes, it always happened like that.

Probably because he had not, until now, had occasion to consider the subject, it had not occurred to him that so many people from abroad either lived or came to stay in Carden. The police district of which Westingborough was the centre, and over which he conducted investigations for various reasons, was far-reaching, and, although he had a good general idea of all its villages and towns, it was impossible that he should know all its inhabitants, to say nothing of the sportsmen of various sorts, and their womenfolk, who made the Carden Arms their headquarters for a few days or weeks during the year. He knew people like Sir Bernard Ashford, chairman of the Westingborough petty sessions, of course, but, concerned as he was with many kinds of lawbreakers, from mere poachers to burglars and people addicted to criminal assaults, he had to learn the setting of such an unusual crime as this. Sergeant Plender might or might not be able to furnish useful information: he would be able to give particulars of residents in the place, but probably knew no more than Head himself about these birds of passage whom Cortazzi housed.

Mrs. Thomas sat besides the lounge fireplace

in a big armchair, and the colonel perched on the arm of the chair, with his arm laid behind her neck and his hand on her shoulder. She gave Head a long look of curiosity as he stood cogitating outside the telephone box, and he decided anew that she was a remarkably attractive woman, a disturbing personality. Her husband, apparently, was very much in love with her, probably far more than she was with him, judging by their respective attitudes. It seemed that she endured rather than appreciated that hand on her shoulder. Major Fitton stood with his back to the pair, looking out through the window into the forecourt; Rynewald and Mirza Khan were together, looking out through the glazed entrance doors. Two ladies, apparently spinsters of means and addicted to fancy work, had settled themselves in armchairs near the dining room doorway, and were both busy with silks and needles while they talked about "dear Jane" with exasperating semi-audibility. One of the Joey Bagstocks stood near the foot of the staircase while he reduced a very long and very black cheroot to ash. The rest of the visitors had disappeared.

Head decided that the identification of the murdered man could wait awhile, for the quest of the murderer was more important, and Wadden was arranging the inquest for noon of the following day, which gave plenty of time. In addition to that, Head found himself funking the business of facing Sir Bernard Ashford and telling him that his son was, almost certainly, the victim of this deliberate, coldblooded crime. It had to be done, of course, but might be delayed in the interests of justice on the murderer. Probably all these reflections occupied a minute at the most, and then he went out and, leaving his car for the time, gained the road and entered the gateway of the house next to the Carden Arms.

A slender, elderly, dried-up-looking man turned from examination of a rambler rose by the doorway of the house, and scrutinised his caller in a way that indicated suspicion, if not instant dislike.

"Mr. Foster, I believe?" Head suggested.

"That is my name. You are not trying to sell me anything, I hope?"

By way of reply, Head held out his card. Foster scrutinised it in a way that indicated short sight, but did not take it.

"Ah!" he said, with a sour inflection, and left it at that.

"I have been talking to your neighbour, Cortazzi," Head explained.

"The damned, impudent scoundrel!" said Foster, quite calmly. "A nest of hooligans, that place, inspector. It should be closed down."

"Quite a number of them either serving in or retired from Indian service," Head rejoined. "And I don't think the term hooligan applies to that service, as a rule. What, actually, is your complaint, Mr. Foster?"

"My complaint? The loss of at least one night's sleep every week," Foster answered, still in that quiet, unemotional way, at variance with the words he used. "Do you know what this nation's bill amounts to for alcoholic drinks in the course of a year, inspector?"

"I do not, nor do I see how it concerns your complaint against Cortazzi," Head told him.

"Ah, but it does. That bill represents the major part of the taxation under which you as well as I suffer, and if it were not for the share in it of those people in that infernal hotel, I should not be robbed of my sleep. Excited by alcoholic liquors, the people in that hotel turn it into a bedlam, and I suffer. Alcohol is a curse, and its effect reacts even on such as myself, who abhor it. That is my complaint."

"Do you wish the police to take action?" Head asked.

"I have considered that, and decided against it," Foster answered. "The damned Dago would be fined, possibly, and the nuisance would not be abated in the slightest degree. I can get nobody else to take action with me, I find. And I am selling this property, leaving the neighbourhood before the end of the summer. No, I do not wish to take action."

"I see. You don't know any of the—er—hooligans at the hotel?"

"I do not. I fail to see why it should interest you if I did, unless they have been violating the law in some way. They are probably military men, inured to bloodshed and violence. I was in the civil service, the Woods and Forests department. A totally different thing."

"Yes, of course of course," Head agreed placatingly. "I wonder, Mr. Foster, whether you ever visited a place called Khelankot in the course of your time in India. Not that I've been there myself, but——" he broke off invitingly. But Foster shook his head and frowned.

"Khelankot is not a place, inspector," he said with pitying superiority. "It is a state, ruled by an independent prince, and a highly enlightened one, too. I did once visit it, when on short leave."

"Did you meet or hear of anyone named Mirza Ali Ajhodia Khan?" Head inquired, having memorised the rather tricky name carefully.

"I did not meet him," Foster answered, quite as loftily as before, "and I fail to see why, under pretext of having seen that ruffian Cortazzi, you should subject me to this inquisition. It cannot be consonant with your duty, I imagine. I may say I know the name you mentioned, as that of a younger brother of the present ruler, who came to Oxford to get his degree and by this time has probably gone back to his own country."

"On the other hand, he is at present staying with Cortazzi," Head demurred. "That is, unless there are two of the same name in Khelankot."

"Staying——" Momentarily, Foster evinced the limit of surprise, but then he recovered his calm. "But why—why is he there?"

"Buying polo ponies, I understand," Head answered. "There are breeders in the district, as perhaps you know." He had wakened Foster to an interest in Mirza Khan, he saw, and meant to make the best of it.

"Yes—yes." Foster appeared thoughtful over it, though his voice maintained just as level an inflection as when he had called Cortazzi a damned Dago and talked of hooligans. "And he is very wealthy, I know."

"Got a man named Rynewald to help him, apparently," Head observed.

"Rynewald?" Foster appeared still more interested. "But he——"

"What?" Head asked, as the sentence remained incomplete.

"I was going to say—no, he would not be interested in polo ponies, I think. I—I met him. A—a sort of technical adviser to the government of Khelankot. For such industries as there are in the state."

"Arrived at the Carden Arms this morning," Head told him.

"Ah! Then there must be something—I met him, as I said. Something—but I don't see— perhaps I shall recall myself to his recollection, if —if I chance to meet him away from that bedlam of a hotel."

"Do you see much of what goes on there?" Head inquired.

"See much?" Foster grew frigid at such a query. "Inspector, I detest the place—I am giving up this house mainly because of it. What should I see? Do you suggest that I spy on the place?"

"It never entered my head that you would. Merely that you might be conscious of arrivals and departures." He had in mind that, if the man he had trailed through Squire Hastings' woods had come on to the Carden Arms somewhere about dawn, and were one of those to whom Thane's description of his companion in the train applied, Foster might have seen him. But Foster shook his head in a decided negative.

"I take no note of anything to do with the place," he said. "And why you should interest yourself in it like this, or come here to pump me about it on the pretext of the complaint I made to that impudent foreigner Cortazzi, is more than I can understand. Since I do not intend to make a charge against the man for disturbing my rest as he does, I am afraid I must wish you good-day, inspector."

Head left him, then, and, as he went in search of Sergeant Plender, still leaving his car in the hotel forecourt, he reflected that Rynewald fitted into the case only in so far as that he had arrived at the Carden Arms at a time that would permit of his having been on the train with Thane and the murdered man. Apart from that, he did not appear to fit, for whoever had dropped off the train and made his way up through the woods must be fairly well acquainted with the district. The name Rynewald, Head felt sure, belonged to no family living near here, and one who held the post of technical adviser to the government of an Indian state was not likely to have taken such an unerring, straight course in the darkness as had that one who had burned clothes in the gully. Rynewald *might* have done it, but on the face of it this was unlikely.

Plender, doing nothing just outside the Greyhound inn, halfway along the village street, since it was the hour of bar closing, saluted at sight of Head, and went on eyeing the dozen or so of habitués emerging from the doorway of the public bar. He had his watch in his hand, too.

"Been gettin' a bit slack over closin' here, sir, so I thought it wouldn't do any harm if Atkins knew I was keepin' an eye on him."

"Quite so, sergeant," Head agreed, and, pausing beside the watcher, saw the bar door closed and heard the bolts shot. "What do you know of Captain Bernard Ashford? Would you recognise him on sight?"

Plender looked rather surprised at the abrupt query. Then he nodded an affirmative. "The dead spit of old Sir Bernard, sir," he said. "Especially the nose—you can't mistake that, if you know Sir Bernard."

"No." Head remembered Thane's profile, and

how Loretta Ashford had said that she had almost mistaken him for her brother, at first sight. "What do you know about Captain Ashford, if anything?"

"I don't know exactly how you mean, sir. I did hear he's just about due home on leave again. This week, I believe it is."

"You were not stationed in Carden when he last came on leave?"

"No, sir." Since Head indicated that he wanted to walk back toward the Carden Arms, Plender fell into step beside him. "They say here he's quite a nice gentleman."

"Do they say anything else?" Head asked. "I want all you can tell me about him. You've heard about that train murder last night?"

"Why, yes, sir. Not much, only that—but you don't mean to say——" He broke off, and stared at Head as they walked on.

"That I want to know everything you or anyone can tell me about Captain Bernard Ashford," Head completed for him. "Everything."

"Yes, sir, but do you mind my askin'——"

"I do," Head interrupted, "because I don't know myself, yet. I'll do the asking. Everything about him. Habits, friends and acquaintances, whether anyone disliked him—everything. Since you heard of his being due home on leave, it's evident he's being talked about to some extent."

"Well, sir, mainly how things'll be different at the hall when old Sir Bernard drops off and this one comes to the title. They say the old man's pinched and squinched every way he could, so his son should be able to have a good time when it comes his turn. Even made the daughter go short, they do say, because the son is everything to him. How true it all is I don't know. And they say the captain is altogether different, free-handed, a bit extravagant, and every penny Sir Bernard can save'll be none too much. So I've heard 'em say, round here."

"Do you know what form the extravagance takes?" Head asked.

"Horses and women, they say," Plender answered. "And if you can find anything more extravagant, sir, I'd like to know what it is."

"I couldn't tell you, sergeant," Head remarked. "Any special horses, or any particular women, to your knowledge?"

"It's not exactly what you could call knowledge, sir," Plender confessed. "We have a woman in twice a week, to help the missus turnin' out rooms an' that sort of thing, and her sister is parlourmaid at the hall. Now and then she lets things drop, and the missus tells me. The old man lets a word drop now and again, and he told Lady Ashford once so the woman's sister heard him—told her he wished the captain'd marry, because then women wouldn't cost him so much. I don't know what women Sir Bernard meant, of course. Then the horses—that bay stallion Miss Loretta rides about on sometimes.

The captain bought it when he was home on leave last time, paid three hundred and fifty guineas for it. At least, Sir Bernard paid it, and they say he was pretty sick about it, too. Had a real row with the captain, and said it couldn't go on."

"But you can't place any of the women?" Head suggested.

"No, sir. They'd be out there where he is, I expect. I never heard of any what you'd call expensive ones he took a fancy to round here. I did hear he was sweet on that Miss Bell at Condor Grange for a bit—the one that got killed in a motor accident—but she wouldn't be what you'd call really expensive, I'd think. And it didn't come to anything."

"Obviously," Head agreed, remembering the tragedy of Sheba Bell. "Nobody else connected with him as subject for scandal?"

"A bit of talk about a Mrs. Jevons—her husband is one of Mr. Houghton's tenants, farms about a hundred acres out along the marsh road to Crandon. They say he hung round there a bit too much for Jevons' last time he was on leave, but she'd hardly be what *she'd* call expensive, either. This is pure gossip, you know, sir."

"Exactly what I want," Head assured him. "What sort of man is Jevons? Physically, and temperamentally too?"

"Quite pleasant spoken, sir, though I'd say he's got a devil of a temper if he did let fly. Big, weatherbeaten-looking man, and I'd say by the look of his nose he's partial to a drink or two."

Another, possibly quite innocent, subject for investigation, in case he might have been Thane's companion at the beginning of his journey!

"And Mrs. Jevons?" Head asked.

"Dark, good-looking woman," Plender answered. "Quite young, and a bit of a hothouse plant to look at her. Too towny for a farmer's wife, I'd say. Years younger than her husband. No children, either."

With that, Head reflected, Jevons appeared rather less innocent. A resident in the district, he would know his way about Squire Hastings' woods, and from the point where his trail had ended could easily escape observation as he made his way to the farm on the marsh road.

"Plender, I want you to get hold of Potts."

"The newspaper man, you mean, sir?"

"No, not him. Your champion poacher—the one who makes Squire Hastings' life a misery over lost pheasants. Go and see Potts."

"Yes, sir?" Plender sounded dubious over it.

"You've got to assure him," Head said slowly, "that if he did happen to be out after fur or feather last night, we're pleased, not annoyed. Hint to him that we're after far bigger game than pheasants, and if he saw anything that might help us, he'll be well paid for telling us about it. Especially do I want to know if he saw anything in Squire Hasting's woods—anything or anybody

—or along the old coach road that goes over Condor Hill, at any time after two o'clock this morning. Tell him, if he saw anyone at all after that hour, and can identify whoever it was, I'll gladly pay him five pounds. And wherever he was last night, or whatever he was doing, we shall take no action against him."

"I get it, sir. The murderer hid in the woods."

"Don't tell Potts that—don't tell him anything, but ask. If he were not out, or out anywhere but in the woods, don't mention them."

"Right you are, sir. I'll go after him."

"At once, Plender." They had reached the Carden Arms, and halted in the forecourt. "If you get anything at all from him, ring through to Westingborough and report it immediately—I shall be back there by the time you've found Potts and persuaded him to talk."

He got into his car as Plender saluted again and went off. Then at a thought he called the sergeant back.

"Do you know anything about a Colonel Thomas and his wife, Plender?"

"I believe he's staying here now, but I haven't seen anything of her, yet."

"Know any more about them?" Head persisted.

"No, sir. Rather a couple of love-birds, by all accounts."

"Major Fitton—does that name convey

anything to you?"

"Going to marry Miss Hastings, sir, I heard. He got home on leave in time for the shooting up at Squire Hastings', and he's due to go back pretty soon, now. Staying here, he is."

"That's all for the present, thank you, Plender. See if you can get anything out of Potts, and report at once if you do."

Fitton, past question, would know his way about those woods, Head reflected as he turned in at the gateway to Carden Hall. But why should he, about to marry Sheila Hastings, murder another officer of the Indian Army? It did not make sense.

Abruptly Head saw how he could dispose of his batch of possible suspects at the Carden Arms, and turn to investigating Jevons and any others who cropped up provided with possible motives and opportunities for the crime, together with knowledge of the locality to facilitate escape.

* * *

"An amazing story, Thane. A perfectly incredible story!"

Sir Bernard Ashford stroked his carefully-trimmed white moustache as he reflected over it, and gazed at Thane much as he would have gazed from his chairman's seat on the bench of magistrates at a defendant whom he had just asked what he had to say. Thane inclined his head in assent.

"Wild," he said. "I came home to England for peace and quiet, and get—that! Drugged and stripped, and my clothes on a murdered man. The senselessness of it! Why? Why strip and rob me?"

"That four-thousand-pound draft," the baronet suggested.

"How did anyone know I had it? Besides, any attempt at cashing it would land him on the murder charge. He must know that."

"You had no other money, you say?" Sir Bernard asked thoughtfully.

"Eight pounds and a shilling or two. That very courteous inspector at Westingborough advanced me the amount, or I wouldn't have had a rag on me when Miss Ashford called at the police station, let alone been able to take advantage of this very generous invitation of yours, sir."

"I wonder what was Head's object in advancing it?" Sir Bernard mused.

"Wanted to get rid of me?" Thane made half a question of the statement. "The other one—the big man with half a dozen chins—seemed as if he didn't care what happened to me, I thought."

"You saw very little of either of them, I gather," Sir Bernard observed. "The superintendent—the big man—is a very capable administrator, but Head—his mind is generally two jumps ahead of a steeplechase winner, and it's impossible—but all that is beside the point. Four thousand pounds is quite out of the question, as far as I am concerned, but I should be glad to write you a cheque for, say, two hundred or so, until you can recover the amount of this draft of yours."

"I wouldn't dream of it, sir! I can manage somehow—go to the Peruvian consulate in London, and get him to cable our consul in Lima, or whatever happens to be the best way of proving my identity and ownership of the money. I'm very grateful to you for suggesting it ____"

"My dear Thane," Sir Bernard interrupted him, "from what you have told me, we are the only relatives you have in the world, and your uncanny likeness to my son is proof enough of your identity for me. I insist on writing you a cheque for two hundred pounds, to tide you over until you can lay hands on your own money— and I gather that that is not all you have in the world. The draft for four thousand, I mean."

"Not quite." Thane smiled as he answered. "I managed to play level with the financial jugglers when it came to forming a company to exploit my copper discovery, and can count on about five thousand a year."

"Would that I could!" Sir Bernard observed sadly. "Land is nothing but an excuse for taxation, in these days, and I have to economise in every direction to assure an inheritance for my son. I'll write you a cheque now, open and payable at Westingborough, before I forget it."

"Well, it's more than good of you," Thane said, and, as Sir Bernard rose and went to a desk in the corner of the room, he too got to his feet and went to the window, to see, on the lawn outside, Loretta, engaged in an inspection of a spaniel's forepaw. The dog lay on its back, a ludicrous carcase begging for sympathy after the way of spaniels, and Thane saw that she laughed as she released the paw and gave the animal a push, at which it got on its feet and regarded her solemnly.

"Shamming," Thane said to himself, and smiled as Loretta glanced his way. But then, as she turned her head the other way, he frowned, for from behind shrubs that had masked him Inspector Head drove his car into sight of Loretta and of the dining-room window as well.

"Here you are, Thane," Sir Bernard said, coming toward the window. "You can repay it just as suits you. When you get your draft, say."

"I'm more than grateful to you, sir." Thane turned to take the offered cheque. "By the look of things, though, your Inspector Head can't leave me alone—he knew I was coming here. I wonder —they told me the inquest is not till to-morrow. More questioning, probably."

The two men, gazing through the window, saw Loretta go to the side of the car, and saw, too, that Head took off his hat and sat bareheaded to speak to her. He stayed only for a question and its reply, and a statement as to his purpose in coming to Carden Hall.

"Do you mind telling me if Sir Bernard keeps a chauffeur, Miss Ashford?" he asked.

"Say that the gardener looks after the car, and can drive it at need," she answered. "As a rule, I drive it. Why do you ask?"

"Because I want the man to drive it over to Westingborough and back, with Sir Bernard in it," he answered. "And I wish to see Sir Bernard."

She gave him a long, steady look. "Is the mystery too deep to be revealed to me, inspector?" she asked caustically.

"So deep, Miss Ashford," he answered sombrely, "that I hate what I have to do as much as I hated it on a certain Sunday afternoon last year. The fact that I dare to mention that to you may impress on you that I must see Sir Bernard—and I don't wish you to drive the car, please."

She started back, momentarily, when he spoke of a Sunday afternoon, for, as he knew, that day had marked black tragedy, for her. But then some form of intuition came to her: he was trying to prepare her for—what? She made a curious little beckoning gesture with her hand.

"You were good to me then," she said. "Come to the house—I'll tell my father you wish to speak to him."

He followed her in, and saw the baronet's

spare, tall figure in the dining-room doorway. Loretta halted facing her father.

"Inspector Head wants to speak to you, father," she said.

"I thought perhaps he wanted Mr. Thane again," Sir Bernard said. "Will you come in here, inspector, and tell me what it is that you want?"

Entering the room, Head felt afraid of the task before him. Yet it had to be done. He saw Thane, faced about before the window to look at him.

"About what happened to Mr. Thane last night, sir," Head said, and found his voice strange in his own hearing. "And—and the other man."

"The murdered man, do you mean, inspector, or the murderer?" Sir Bernard asked. "You have not come already to apply for a warrant?"

"No, Sir Bernard, not that. Not anything so— so satisfactory to myself. Nor to you, I fear. What I have to tell you will mean a very bad shock, and I—well, I don't know how to prepare you. I want you to turn out—to turn out your car, and come to Westingborough to identify the murdered man. For certainty. I am sure, but for certainty."

"You... want..." Sir Bernard made a long pause after each incredulous word. "Man, what do you mean?" he fired out fiercely, abruptly.

"We learned, sir, that your son is due home on leave on the *Pathankot*," Head said, forcing the words out.

"Well, what of it? He arrives at Tilbury the day after to-morrow. Yes? What of it?" Anger in the questions hid fear, perhaps.

"Captain Ashford left the *Pathankot* at Port Said, sir," Head said steadily, "and that is why I—I want you to come to Westingborough."

Time ceased to have any significance while he stood facing the rigidly erect figure of the old baronet. He heard a choked sobbing from where Loretta, in the doorway, realised the significance of what he had said, and saw Thane move swiftly toward her. They disappeared from his sight in the hall, and he heard her voice—

"Go away! Oh, go away! I don't want you—I don't want anyone!"

Stillness again. After certain eternities Sir Bernard Ashford went and leaned on the back of a chair by the window.

"If you will order the car for me, inspector, I will come with you to Westingborough," he said, quietly and steadily.

CHAPTER VII

Trial by Thane

LOOKING out from the dining-room window again, after Sir Bernard and Head had gone, Thane saw that the inspector's car stood in the drive, a small, evidently old, but well-tended two-seater, its hood down, and the well-worn upholstery of the driving seat contrasting with that beside it to declare that the car seldom carried more than its driver. The fact of its standing there indicated that Head meant to return with the baronet—as, of course, he would. More questioning, for a certainty.

He, Thane, could not stay here now, as Sir Bernard had suggested. They would not want a stranger in the house. Fortunately, he had that cheque for two hundred pounds, which would enable him to fit himself out completely and carry on while he proved his identity and got at his own money. Go to Barclay's head office and ask there what steps he ought to take to recover the amount of the draft on them, cable the consul at Lima, another cable to de Vega, the manager of the mine... get hold of a lawyer and let him do it all....

The opening of the door put an end to his reflections, and he saw Loretta just inside the room, gazing across at him.

"Won't you come to the drawing-room?" she asked. "Tea is ready."

"Why—yes, thank you," he answered, and crossed toward her. "I didn't think—I mean, I didn't want to trouble you——" he left it incomplete, being unable to find an end to the sentence, and followed her across the entrance hall to the drawing-room.

"The servants don't know," she said. "If they did—well, the normal ways of life must go on. Even afternoon tea. Do sit down."

He complied as she seated herself behind the tray, and saw her as quite composed again. The hand that held his cup out to him was perfectly steady, as was her voice when she spoke again.

"I want to tell you how very sorry I am for my rudeness to you," she said "When—when the inspector told my father——"

"Just forget it, please," he interrupted. "A stranger like me had no business to bring himself to your notice at a moment like that. I understand quite well—I'd have resented it myself, probably."

"But we can't look on you as altogether a stranger," she said.

"I shall be very glad if you won't," he told her. "And after this is all over, I'd like to come here again and see you, if I may."

"You mean—but my father asked you to stay," she said, puzzled, "and you told him you would, I thought. Do you mean——?"

"Well, I can't stay here now, surely," he explained. "It was before—before he knew what he knows now that he asked me."

"But don't you see—he'll wish all the more that you should stay, now. I wish it too, for his sake. Somebody—someone belonging to us as you do, to arrange, help him—there will be so many things to do. But—your own affairs, of course. I'd forgotten——"

"No," he interrupted again. "It wasn't that. A feeling that I should be—that neither he nor you would wish it——"

"Quite wrong," she interposed in turn. "I wish it, for his sake, and I know he will be glad of your help, too, if—if it is not asking too much of you. Bernard—my brother—meant everything on earth to him, and I'm afraid he will be terribly broken by this in reality, though he would never let anyone see it. And—and when I overheard what the inspector told him, it was not the thought of my brother that made me break down as I did—and be so rude to you—not nearly so much that as the knowledge of what it would mean to my father. Not that I didn't care anything about my brother, but——"

She broke off, as if unable to find a way to express what she would tell him, and he took a sandwich off the tray and waited.

"Best to tell you all of it, to make you understand," she said at last. "There was a Mr. Chalfont whom I met, and who had an invention which would have made him very rich indeed, if he hadn't been financed for it by another man who would have taken all the profits. That other man was the hard type who insists on all of the pound of flesh—a moneylender, in reality, though he called himself a financier."

"I believe most of them do," Thane observed. "Anything but, in fact."

"Anything—yes, though, I understand. When this invention was perfected and ready to be put on the market, the moneylender came to see Mr. Chalfont and his friend named Wilson, who was working with him all through. Came to take it from them, in fact. All of what happened will never be known, but that they killed the moneylender because he would not alter his terms, although the invention was worth a hundred and more times what he had paid them for it. Killed him, and hid the body."

"I don't see where you or Sir Bernard come in," Thane remarked.

"You will, soon," she told him. "Inspector Head took up the case of the missing man—

it was not known that he was dead, of course, since they had hidden the body—and went to arrest them on a Sunday afternoon last year. They had hidden the body under the floor of a wooden shed they used as a workshop, and that Sunday afternoon the shed caught fire with Mr. Wilson inside. Inspector Head and his men got there in time to see Mr. Chalfont break into the blazing shed and stagger out carrying his friend's body, and Mr. Chalfont was so badly burned himself that he died that afternoon. Inspector Head called it the bravest act he had ever seen, that facing almost certain death to attempt the rescue."

"The greater love," Thane observed gravely. "Still I don't see——"

"Mr. Chalfont and I were to have been married less than a month after that day," she said quietly. "And as I told you at the top of Condor Hill, I think—some memories never grow old."

"I begin to feel I know you, now, cousin Loretta," Thane said after a long silence, "and I'm honoured by your confidence."

"Thank you, cousin Leo." She smiled momentarily. "But my reason for telling you all this. Both my father and mother were opposed to my marrying Mr. Chalfont—bitterly opposed. I had never meant much to them in comparison with my brother, but after that day—it brought them both near to me, in a way nothing else could have done. Especially my father. Then, just before Christmas, my mother died, and that brought my father and me still closer together. I've grown to share in his plans for Bernard, to look forward to this home-coming for his sake—he was going to persuade my brother to resign his commission and take over the estate—every day has been full of plans of what we shall do and what shall happen when Bernard comes home. And when I heard what the inspector said, realised—it struck me through him, what this must mean to him. He's old, and he had that one great interest in his life. Taken away, like this. I am afraid for him—afraid! Won't you—stay and help?"

"I'll do anything on earth for you and for him too," Thane said gravely. "I thought—but if you wish me to stay, I'll stay, of course."

"Things he would not ask of me—things a man can do. And he likes you—he told me so. Your likeness to Bernard—and yourself."

For a while they said no more. Loretta broke their silence.

"I'm glad you told him—told him of what had been done to Bernard, I mean—before he knew it was his son. He'll have to—have to see——"

"Loretta——" Thane rose to stand beside her, and laid his hand on her shoulder—"stop making mental pictures and pour me another cup of tea. I'll stand by you as well as him as long as either of you need me, and remember, that inspector may have been mistaken."

She shook her head. "If there had been any chance of it, he would not have asked my father to go," she said. "If ever you get to know Inspector Head, you will realise he would not make such a mistake as that."

"I thought him a bit above the average myself," Thane observed as he took the refilled cup and went back to his chair.

* * *

"Do you mind if I take your arm for a moment, superintendent? A—er—a twinge of gout, perhaps. I am—er—not young."

Instead, Superintendent Wadden took Sir Bernard Ashford's arm, and helped him out from the mortuary at the back of the cottage hospital, while, on the other side, Head watched carefully in case his aid too should be needed. When, round at the front of the hospital, Wadden would have turned toward the entrance, Sir Bernard resisted.

"I will go straight to the car," he said. "It is my son's body—since you know that, you do not need me any more."

"For your own sake, Sir Bernard," Wadden said. "They keep brandy here, and I'm sure you need it, after—my God, I've never done a more awful day's work than this, and I'll pray you to forgive me for what we had to ask of you, sir. What we had to ask, not wished to ask."

"I understand. Very well, then—inside for a moment. And of course you'll want me to tell you all I can about him."

"I'll leave that to Head, sir, and I know he'll spare you in any way he can. Yes—in here, sir, and I'll get the brandy for you."

He went out as Sir Bernard, half-supported now by Head, dropped into an armchair in the little waiting-room and looked up.

"Spare me? Why should he talk of sparing me, inspector? A brutal crime has been committed, and it is my duty to assist you in any way I can. Have you ever known me fail in my duty, inspector?"

"Never, sir, nor would anyone who knows you consider it possible. But I am driving back with you—there is plenty of time."

Sir Bernard gazed across the room with unseeing eyes.

"When he was quite a little boy," he said, in scarcely more than a whisper, "he fell and cut his knee on a flint, the left knee. On his last leave he showed me the scar one day and asked me if I remembered. A scar shaped like a capital T, just above the kneecap."

"It is the only mark anywhere on his body, sir," Head said.

"Eh?" He looked up suddenly. "Oh, yes, though. I—I just thought of it, inspector. Not to tell you, but—thought of it."

Then Wadden entered again, bearing a glass

which he held out.

"There you are, sir, and I don't mind owning I had one myself."

"Er—yes. Thank you, superintendent." He took the glass and drank its contents, and after a few seconds a shade of colour returned to his face, which, since he had looked on his son's body, had been awfully, deathly white. "You are most considerate," he added, as Wadden took back the glass. "I—er—I think I will go, now."

He made no demur over Head's taking his arm to lead him out from the hospital and help him into his car, while Wadden, after a word with Head to learn when they might expect to confer together on the case, went back very thoughtfully to the police station. The gardener who at need acted as chauffeur had driven out from Westingborough, along the Idleburn valley road, and on to the top of Condor Hill before either of his passengers uttered a word, for Head knew what the shock to this old man had been.

"Have you—ah—any idea, inspector?"

"Too many, sir, I'm afraid. I want to get Mr. Thane to help me."

"Yes. Yes, of course. You have your own ways of working, I know. Over the—yes, the identity of —of the one who killed my son."

"I should consider that you have a right to know everything I know myself," Head said, "and, up to the present, you do know it."

"Er—thank you, inspector. And anything you

wish to ask me, at any time—I shall be at your service. At any time."

"Thank you, sir. Not yet, though. Perhaps not at all."

For, apart from all other considerations, he could see that it was only the limit of effort by the man beside him that prevented an utter breakdown. Sir Bernard was putting up a gallant show, but it was show and no more. His twitching hands and compressed lips told their story.

Beyond the foot of the hill, they turned in at the hall gateway.

"I thought to have this drive repaired," Sir Bernard said, gazing straight before him and speaking as if to himself. "But not now."

The car drew up by the Georgian portico, and Loretta came out and opened the door. Head gave the baronet a hand while he got out.

"Come in, daddy, and let me take care of you."

"Er—yes. Thank you very much, inspector. Loretta, Thane has not gone, I hope?" He looked past her into the open doorway.

"No. He would have gone, but I told him you'd wish him to stay."

"Yes, I do. He might—he is a relative, you see. Ah—good-bye, inspector, and do not forget. At your service at any time."

"Thank you, Sir Bernard. Before I go, might I see Mr. Thane?"

"Certainly. Loretta, will you tell him the

inspector is waiting?"

They went in together, and Head saw that the suddenly old man leaned heavily on his daughter's arm. He waited in the portico, and after a minute or two Loretta came out to him.

"Please come inside, inspector, and forgive me for leaving you out here. If you'll wait in the dining-room I'll find Mr. Thane for you."

Again Head waited, the brief time until Thane came to him.

"I thought there would be a further inquisition for me, inspector," he remarked, "though I can't think of anything else useful to tell you."

"Neither can I, here," Head remarked rather drily. "But I want to see Cortazzi, the proprietor of the Carden Arms, and get him to reserve me a table for two in his dining-room to-night. And I want you to be the other one of the two, and tell me if you recognise anyone who may happen to be dining there. In case you didn't notice the hotel on your way here, if you turn toward Westingborough when you get to the road, it is on your left, just at the foot of the big hill."

"I remember it," Thane said, and added nothing to the remark.

"Dinner is at half-past seven. Can I expect you then?"

"You can. A sort of—well, trial by Thane, call it."

"Or a process of elimination," Head suggested.

"Call it what you like. But supposing he knows I recognise him? I haven't a gun of any sort—will you bring one?"

Head smiled.

"Not necessary," he said. "This is England, not Peru."

"Which gives me no confidence, after the welcome to England I had last night," Thane retorted. "But I'll leave it to you, inspector, and since this one suit is all I have, I won't dress. Seven-thirty."

"A few more minutes before, if you don't mind."

"Yes, and the cocktails on me. Seven-twenty, then. I'll be there."

* * *

"Y'know, Head——" Superintendent Wadden spoke with no preface at all as Head entered his room at the police station, "I don't think anyone ever faced a loss that broke his heart with a finer courage than old Sir Bernard. Did he hold out till you got him back home?"

"He did," Head answered. "A proof that breeding counts for something. His daughter has it too, I happen to know."

"The son, now—what about him?" Wadden asked.

"Well," Head answered reflectively, "I've come to the conclusion that you couldn't throw a stone in Carden and miss an Anglo-Indian, meaning by that someone connected with the Indian services. Unless you happened to hit the full-blooded Indian staying at the Carden Arms."

"Like that, is it?" Wadden observed. "For the same reason that they put that about barking like a dog in the cockerel riddle. Well?"

"That man Thane is going to eliminate the improbables for me—I'm dining with him at the Carden Arms for that purpose to-night," Head explained. "You shall 'ave ze table especial, Mr. 'Ead"—he mimicked Cortazzi—"an' I make ze dinner especial for you an' your frien'."

"And thus we use up the county funds," Wadden mused aloud. "Well, they shouldn't ship us cases by rail. Whaddye make of it, Head?"

"Nothing, yet. I've not collected enough premises—"

"No, no, man!" Wadden interrupted with some asperity. "I mean the impossible way it was done—that business of stripping Thane and putting his clothes on the corpse. And by the way, are you wise to go giving Thane dinners, taking him into your confidence like this?"

"I acquit him entirely," Head answered with decision. "He had nothing whatever to do with the murder of Bernard Ashford."

"On your own head—I mean, it's your case. But whaddye make of that? Sheer lunacy? I don't see any other possible reason, myself."

"A puzzling feature, but not necessarily the

act of a madman," Head demurred. "Miss Ashford remarked on Thane's likeness to her brother."

"I don't see that that's got anything to do with it," interposed Wadden.

"No? One suggestion for you, then. Suppose that Mr. X, looking for Ashford to kill him, found Thane first and mistook him for Ashford. Gave him a doped cigarette, intending to strangle him when he had gone off, but discovered before he went off that he was not Ashford. Mr. X then found Ashford, doped and strangled him, and then thought it would be a brilliant idea, since he already had Thane doped, to destroy all traces of his victim's identity by stripping him and putting Thane's clothes on him, also mutilating his face to prevent the features from being recognisable—but forgetting to mutilate that ultra-characteristic nose which set me thinking, remembering Sir Bernard's and Miss Ashford's faces as I did, as soon as I saw 'Jelalapur' on that button. If Mr. X had destroyed that mark of resemblance, Ashford's body might have gone to its grave unidentified—and Mr. X hoped and believed that it would."

"But he took one hell of a lot of trouble, Head."

"He had two hours to fill," Head pointed out. "Don't forget, Thane was well on to falling asleep doped by the time the train left Watford and Mr. X left him alone in his compartment—to go along and find Ashford and—this is guessing

—get him to accept a similar cigarette. Get him practically unconscious in some way before strangling him with the cord, in any case, for as you know yourself there isn't a bruise or sign of struggle on the body. He'd planned to leave the train after Crandon, which is guessing again, based on the straight and certain track he left through Squire Hastings' woods to the old coach road. So far, I'm restricted to guessing, because I have no evidence except the trouser buttons, no suggestion of motive, no anything."

"Never mind. Go on with your guessing, laddie."

"Well, two hours to fill. Thane might wake up and realise the cigarette had been doped, and come looking for the doper. Therefore, return to him, and complete the doping with ether. Perhaps it was then the idea of stripping Thane and destroying the dead man's clothes came to Mr. X—I don't know and probably shall never know, unless he confesses after being sentenced. But I don't see him as the confessing sort."

"He's coming to trial, then?" Wadden inquired ironically.

"Chief, he's given me the best hope of all for that—the superiority complex that's fatal to so many murderers. If he hadn't it, he'd never have risked strangling a man in a railway coach, and still more would never have risked that bizarre exchange of clothes. But in making the exchange, he not only—as he thought—destroyed the dead man's identity altogether, which he did not, but prolonged Thane's unconsciousness until Thane wakened enough to pull the communication cord. If he had not done that, Mr. X would have pulled that cord on the Crandon side of Westingborough, I feel sure. He meant to escape through those woods, and dispose either of the murdered man's clothes, or his own, by burning them. Together with whatever baggage Ashford had with him."

"Wouldn't he think, with that resemblance between Thane and Ashford that Miss Ashford noticed, that Thane might identify the body?"

"He'd talked to Thane, learned that this was his first day in England after years in Peru— Thane told him that much. Further to that, if Thane had known Ashford, on whom Mr. X was keeping close watch, you may be sure, X would have seen them meet somewhere, somewhen. He saw that they got on the same train without taking any notice of each other. Thane didn't know Ashford was on the train, Mr. X thought he had disfigured the body beyond recognition— what more could he ask?"

"Ah! What?" Wadden echoed, rather grimly. "And you're going to try to find Mr. X's other name in Carden, or somewhere round about here?"

"The murderer knows this district," Head answered indirectly. "Call it a fifty-fifty chance that he lives in this district. The way he planned and carried out that crime—for he must have planned it very carefully, chief—leads me to credit him with too much sense to move or change his normal way of living directly after the murder. It would invite suspicion, and he has brains enough to realise that."

"He took one hell of a risk, anyhow," Wadden reflected.

"Not with Thane doped—he and the murdered man appear to have been the only other two in that coach, after Tring," Head pointed out. "It was one chance in a million that anyone would come through from the coaches in rear, and if the guard did go through the train, he'd have seen all the tickets and wouldn't intrude in a compartment that had its blinds down. The risk is much smaller than it appears on first thought of it."

"Motive?" Wadden inquired after a silence.

"Sir Bernard was once heard to say he wished his son would marry, because then his women wouldn't cost him so much," Head answered. This is via the back stairs and Plender, whom I saw to-day."

"Don't forget that Plender is a leetle given to assuming a good deal on next to nothing," Wadden warned him. "Which is not to say Sir Bernard didn't make that remark. You might verify the recent movements of a chap named Jevons, a farmer on the Castle Garde estate, for one."

"I've got him marked for investigation," Head assured him.

"You would!" And Wadden blew, heavily. "And that explanation of yours, about leaving Thane all stark—it's so specious it might even be the right one. I dunno, Head. Thank heaven my job is wages and reprimands and indent forms, until I can see my way to resigning and starting to grow tomatoes under glass. While your job— well, this may not be a woman case at all. He might have been seconded for secret service, and got bumped off for something he was carrying. Anything at all."

"What do you know about Jevons?" Head asked after a pause.

"A bit of talk I happened to hear when Ashford was home on leave last time. All it amounted to was that Ashford and Jevons' wife had been seen somewhere together. A Crandon tea-shop, I believe it was. Nothing more than that, and how wild Sir Bernard'd have been if it had got to his ears. You know what local gossip is."

"I do—precious beyond rubies, in a case like this. Or perhaps not. And if I stay talking any longer, I shall be late for my appointment with Thane. See you in the morning, chief."

"Or to-night, if he identifies Mr. X for you," Wadden suggested. "S'long, laddie, and good luck to you."

CHAPTER VIII

Mr. X Remains Mr. X

THE dinner gong at the Carden Arms began its clanging as Cortazzi himself emerged from the back of the entrance lounge, with cocktails for Thane and Head. Thane, taking his, put back on the tray that Cortazzi held, an empty glass for, having had to wait for his host, he had made a solitary test of "ze cocktail de la maison," and found it good.

"Ze table, she is ready, Mr. 'Ead," Cortazzi announced. "Ze one I say you shall 'ave. I tell ze two ladies which do ze needlework it is only for ze one meal I move zem, an' zen I run away, because zey both go on talking about it, although I give zem ze terms especial."

"What are the names of those ladies?" Head inquired, remembering their discussion of "dear Jane" after lunch.

"Ze Miss Tomsongs." Thus Cortazzi

pronounced it. "I do not laik unmarried ladies of zat age. Zey should be dead."

With that emphatic pronouncement he faced about and darted across the lounge to open the dining-room door for Mrs. Thomas, who had descended the staircase with her husband following her. Head observed the smile with which she rewarded the slight service, a captivating, even alluring smile. She was beautifully gowned—rather too beautifully for a country hotel like this—in closely-fitting, shining pearl grey, and wore the diamond and emerald bar on her corsage. Thane stared at her so openly that Thomas, following her and revealing himself as a fine figure of a man in his dinner-jacket kit, noticed it and returned a resentful, even vindictive look, as if to ask what the devil the man meant by it.

"What a woman!" Thane exclaimed admiringly, when the door had closed on the pair. "What a smile—and those marvellous eyes!"

"Wait till you see ze Miss Tomsongs," Head advised ironically. "But did you notice her husband, and the smile he did not give you?"

"I did. But I don't see why he should resent anyone admiring his wife. Jealousy of that sort is silly, I think. Who are they?"

"A Colonel and Mrs. Thomas, I understand. Indian Army, retired."

"I see-e," Thane commented thoughtfully. "Which is why you asked me if I noticed him, of course. Not my man. Not unlike, facially, but much too pale. My man had a purple nose, and the colonel's is hardly pink. There—just going in! Who's that? The older one of the two, I mean—not the young foreigner with the black hair."

"That," Head told him, "is a man named Rynewald, also from India. And the one you call a foreigner is native Indian."

"Are they all from India, the people in this hotel?" Thane asked with a hint of irritation.

"I believe ze Miss Tomsongs are not," Head told him. "But what made you ask about Rynewald? Does he look like your man of the train?"

"A little, I think," Thane answered. "I'm not sure. I'd like to get him talking, if possible—or hear him talking to somebody. So far, all the men who have gone in are dressed, and I don't feel too happy over dining in my one suit. We shall be conspicuous in day clothes."

"You want to see Rynewald animated," Head suggested, ignoring the rest of his companion's observations.

"I do. You see, inspector, all I saw of my man was loose brown tweed trouser legs, a rainproof coat, and a soft hat pulled down over his eyes —and I didn't take much notice of him at that. Saw no need to notice him, then. Didn't look at him overmuch. I remember his purple nose and brown eyes, and I believe he had a small brown moustache, but I am not sure about that, even, now. I *think* he had one. And by Jove! Here's one more like it, even, than the one you say is Rynewald!"

Major Fitton came down the stairs, attired in well-fitting brown tweed—just to make it more difficult, Head reflected—with eyes that declared themselves brown even at a distance, a big nose reddened by weather or other causes, and a small toothbrush moustache. He nodded pleasantly at Head and Thane on his way to the dining-room.

"Hope you're dining, to keep me company," he said. "Otherwise, I shall be the only one who hadn't time to dress."

He went on without waiting for a reply. Thane shook his head.

"No," he said. "Not that sort of voice at all. Rule him out."

"Unless he affected a different sort of voice," Head suggested.

"He was not the man," Thane stated with decision.

"Finish that drink and let's go in," Head urged. "Our table gives you every chance to see any others who may come in to dinner. And by the way, it would be better if you did not call me 'inspector' so that others can hear. I think, if you listen, you'll find the principal subject of conversation will be the murder. The news of it has got here by now, I expect, and it will make good dinner table talk."

"Thus even murders have their uses," Thane

observed.

Cortazzi himself, superintending the service in the dining-room, preceded them across to the table in the far right-hand corner, drew back the chairs, and bowed as only men of his nationality can as Head indicated that Thane should take the seat which gave him easy view of all the room, faced outward from the corner. A pair of the stout and choleric guests, following into the room, had to pull their own chairs out, for both the waiters were busy. Head, on Thane's left, faced directly toward Rynewald and Mirza Khan, and Rynewald faced him and Thane.

"I 'ave ze claret which I recommend, so good as ze Lafitte, signori," Cortazzi announced, "or I 'ave a *nuit* Burgundy vairy good, an' I theenk you 'ave ze Amontillado especial wiz ze soup—yaas?"

"What do you say, Thane?" Head inquired.

"I am entirely in your hands," Thane answered.

"Then we will have the sherry with the soup, Cortazzi, and the claret. And do not speak my name for other people in the room to hear."

"I remember zat, Mr.—— I remember it, signor. An' ze dinner is especial for you—I make it especial. Now I put ze claret to warm."

"Cortazzi's meals are always especial," Head observed after Harry had put down the soup and Jules had followed with the sherry. "But who is interesting you over there by the door?"

"The two just come in," Thane answered. "By

the way they're glaring over here, they must be the Eves turned out of this Eden—this table we're at, I mean—and they waddle exactly like ducks, both of them."

One of the sudden and unaccountable silences that sometimes occur in such a gathering as of that dining-room fell then, and into it sounded the words of one of ze Miss Tomsongs, just then seating herself—

"And they say he hadn't a stitch on him, my dear."

She realised too late that the remark had been audible to everyone, and coloured deeply as a little ripple of laughter sounded from other tables. Mrs. Thomas, mirth in her eyes, met Thane's gaze across the room.

"They've got the news, as you said," Thane observed. "I suppose I could create a sensation by telling them I was the one without a stitch."

"Can you recognise anyone at all who might already know it?" Head asked, as he saw Colonel Thomas look their way steadily. The colonel, who had to turn his head rather far to see them, had evidently noted the direction of his wife's gaze, and resented Thane's returning it.

"I cannot," Thane answered. "That colonel over there ought to buy his wife some yashmaks, if he objects so much to people looking at her."

"Didn't you say you'd spent all your life in Peru?" Head asked.

"Yes, since I was ten. Why? Oh, I see, though!

But I bought some picture postcards in Port Said. That's how I got hold of the word."

Until Cortazzi had poured the claret and left them, they said no more. Head remembered Wadden's question as to the wisdom of inviting Thane to dinner, and reflected that the word 'yashmak' was not one that would drop so readily from the lips of a man, unless he had lived in the east. There might be nothing in it, of course, though Thane had obviously realised it as a slip. Then Head caught Mirza Khan's voice—

"Preposterous, surely. Why strip the other man of all his clothes? There is no sense in it. Mere robbery one could understand."

"To prevent him from following, perhaps," Rynewald suggested.

"That railway guard has sprung a bad leak," Thane observed to Head. "Otherwise, how would they get the news as soon as this?"

"I don't think it was the guard," Head dissented. "Tom Adams, the ticket collector who was on duty at Westingborough, has a brother Bill, postman at Todlington, which is the next village to Carden."

"It is now too late to murder either Tom or Bill," Thane remarked gravely. "Else, I think I would ask you to excuse me."

"Did that voice you heard just now tell you anything?" Head inquired.

"Nothing definite." Thane frowned annoyedly. "Conditions are so different. He comes nearest, and yet I wouldn't accuse him. Here we've got shaded lights, evening dress, practically no noise except people talking, and there I had the rumble of the train in tunnels, my man's face shaded from above and half his forehead cut off by the hat he'd pulled down—I believe he meant to disguise himself—and quite possibly he altered his voice to speak to me. It was not any of the others in this room, and I doubt if it were that one either. Possible, but unlikely."

"If I had had your experience, I think I should be able to identify the man responsible for it," Head remarked rather acidly.

"Which means you regard this dinner as a waste of time," Thane suggested, with a rather rueful smile.

"Far from it. These—acquittals, call them—of yours set me free to follow other lines of inquiry. With the one exception—and I attach very little importance even to that—I can ignore these people, now."

"And about your being able to identify in my place—do not forget that you have trained your mind to observation, and as far as people are concerned I have not," Thane said. "When I tell you the man I saw was big, do not forget that I have lived most of my life among small men— the *mestizos* of the Andes are much smaller than the average here to-night, or than the average I have seen since landing in England. A big man is an exception there, and very nearly the rule, here. Dress that man you call Rynewald in loose brown tweed trousers and an overcoat and pulled-down hat, and I'll either acquit him finally or identify him. But not unless you do that. I cannot be quite certain, though I have heard his voice, now. He might have changed it to talk to me."

Head crumpled his table-napkin beside his plate. "We will sit over coffee in the lounge, I think," he said, "and choose our chairs before the rest finish and get outside. Then you can continue your observation."

Thane shook his head as he stood up. "If you want to get away, do," he suggested. "If I observe till midnight, I can tell you no more."

Head led the way out. "Does that mean you want to get away?" he asked, and saw Colonel Thomas eye him and his companion as they passed.

"Not a bit. I've put myself at your disposal for the evening."

Out in the lounge, Head chose two armchairs between the entrance and the window, backed against the outer wall of the hotel, and thus yielding a view of all the apartment. They had settled themselves and were waiting for coffee when Colonel Thomas held the dining-room door for his wife and followed her out. They heard her say—in a way that indicated determination—"I will, then," and perhaps disagreement with her husband, and them to Head's surprise, she advanced directly toward him and Thane, while Thomas turned toward the staircase and stood there as if waiting for her. Both men stood up at her approach.

"I hope"—she addressed Thane—"you will forgive my husband and myself for staring at you during dinner. I know it must have seemed very rude of us. Do you mind my asking if you are related to a Captain Ashford? You are so very like him, which was why we kept looking at you."

"Why, yes, madam," Thane answered, rather confusedly. "I—er—he is a distant relative of mine. I'm staying with his people."

"How very remarkable! Our meeting you like this, I mean. You see, we knew Captain Ashford in India—he was a lieutenant, then. My husband was second in command of his regiment until he retired."

"Well, that is rather a coincidence," Thane said lamely.

"Yes, isn't it? And I understand"—she turned to Head with an engaging smile—"you are the famous Inspector Head?"

"My name is Head, madam," he told her coolly.

"Making inquiries about this murder we're hearing about," she suggested. "Such strange stories are being told, too. Most thrilling."

"I have been dining here with my friend, madam," Head said curtly, "and I fear the murdered man's relatives would not relish your description of a particularly foul piece of work."

"Oh!" His reproof bit home, as he saw. Then —"I'm so sorry—do forgive me, won't you?" and she turned away and put her hand on her husband's arm. They heard her say—"If we have our coffee in the drawing-room, Phil, we shall be ready when the others come looking for bridge."

"Thrilling! Ugh!" Head exclaimed as he sat down again. "Merely a new sensation, to a woman like that. And she made me put my foot in it, too. But if she'd seen what it means to Sir Bernard—they're all alike, though."

"How did you put your foot in it?" Thane inquired.

"I might have gone to that husband of hers and got useful information as to Captain Ashford's life in India, possibly," Head explained. "Squashing her like that has put it out of the question."

"Possibly not," Thane reflected. "How did she get to know who you are, do you think? Had she seen you before this evening?"

"At lunchtime to-day. She or Thomas probably asked one of the waiters. Ah! Here's our coffee. Would you like a liqueur?"

"I'm not keen, unless you insist on having one yourself."

"No liqueurs, then. Lord! Here's another inquisitor!"

One of the Bagstock breed made straight for them, an elderly, tallish man with a purplish face and an equator over which his tightly-fitting vest slanted obtrusively. He achieved an ingratiating smile.

"I understand—that is, my friend told me at dinner—you are Inspector Head, sir. Yes. This —er—terrible crime—have you any clues to the assassin, sir? Such as might be made public, I mean?"

"I expect you know quite as much about the crime as I do," Head answered gravely, "and I might tell you that word 'clues' is one I particularly detest. Beyond that, I can give you no information."

"Er—thank you, sir." Surprisingly, his questioner smiled as if well pleased. "I respect your discretion, and admire it. As much, I expect, as you resent my indiscretion. Woodville is my name, sir—Colonel Woodville. I hope you will pardon my intrusion."

And, before Head could reply, he turned away to join the other of his type with whom he had been dining. They moved slowly together toward the door that, as Head knew, gave access to the hotel drawing-room, and Thane laughed softly as he leaned back and stirred his coffee.

"I liked him," he said. "Another from the shiny East, eh?"

"Undoubtedly," Head said, with a certain grimness. "I am not throwing any stones whatever in this village, even outside the hotel."

"I don't see why you should," Thane observed

meditatively, just as Rynewald and Mirza Khan came into view, and, past surprise, now, Head saw Rynewald approach with a view to speaking.

"I hope you will excuse me for troubling you," he said, in a singularly pleasant voice, but I was told you are Inspector Head, and reside near here. My name is Rynewald, and I am connected with some industries in a small Indian state. Could you possibly tell me, Mr. Head, the best way to get to a Mr. Raymond Nevile's home? I have the address in his letter inviting me to call on him, but of course it conveys nothing to me. As to how to get to this house, I mean. 'Long Ridge, Westingborough,' rather leaves a complete stranger to the district at sea.

"It would," Head agreed. "How do you intend to go there—by car?"

"Yes, unless it is within walking distance," Rynewald answered.

"Westingborough is about nine miles, and Long Ridge nearly two more," Head told him. "I would advise you to drive to Westingborough, which is a direct road, and inquire there. If you care to inquire at the police station, which you must pass and can hardly miss, I will leave instructions for full directions to be given you there, Mr. Rynewald."

"That is very good of you. To-morrow morning, about eleven?"

"Full directions," Head assured him with a smile.

"I am much obliged to you, and will take advantage of your kindness."

With that he turned away to rejoin Mirza Khan, and the pair of them took chairs by the fireplace for coffee and cigars.

"Kind of him to come and talk like that," Thane remarked. "You can strike his name off your list absolutely and finally. Very much like my man as far as looks go, allowing for the difference in dress. Yes, very like. But not the man, I am quite certain."

"Also quite certain about Colonel Thomas?" Head asked.

"Quite. Quite certain about that man in brown tweed, too. And nobody else here is as much as a remote possible, I'm afraid. Thank you very much for my nice dinner, Mr. Head, and please don't swear."

"I assure you I'm far from swearing," Head told him, and rose to his feet. "It has been a very pleasant dinner, and you have cleared this piece of ground for me. Now if you will forgive me for seeming discourteous, shall I drive you back to the hall before getting on with things?"

"I'll walk back, thank you. And it's just as well I should get back early, too—Sir Bernard or Miss Ashford may want to see me, knowing I've been with you. In case there's anything to tell them?" He made a half-question of the final sentence.

"Nothing," Head said, "except that I wish to see Miss Ashford some time to-morrow morning. Between ten and eleven, say."

"I'll tell her. Good night, and my thanks for a pleasant evening."

He got his hat and coat and went out. After a minute or two of reflection Head followed him and, getting into his car, drove through Carden to pull up outside Sergeant Plender's cottage, where the sergeant himself answered the knock on his door and recognised his caller.

"Will you come in, sir?" he asked. "The wife's abed—I'm alone."

"What news of Potts, sergeant?" Head ignored the invitation.

"No good, sir. I tried to persuade him to talk, but he was like an oyster. Started to use bad language, till I warned him about it."

"I see. His is the last house on the other side of the road, before you come to where the marsh road branches off, isn't it?"

"Yes, sir—that's his place. He owns it, too."

"Yes. No, I won't come in, thank you. Good night, sergeant."

He uttered those last sentences very gently, very softly, and turned away as Plender answered. Getting back into his car he spoke again, just as softly, to himself—

"If you want a thing well done—

"If you want it done at all, in fact!"

CHAPTER IX

Potts

A GLANCE at the clock beside his speedometer dial showed Head that it was not quite ten o'clock as he drew in beside the garden gate which gave access to Potts' domain, deciding that after Sergeant Plender's visit the poacher would stay at home for a night or two. The little property consisted of a half-acre or so of ground on which Potts raised good vegetable crops, an old, four-roomed one-storied cottage, and two pigsties, one of which housed Potts' sow, and the other such of her progeny as were kept for killing. The sow was one of Carden's subjects for conversation: her litter of nineteen attained fame even to Crandon and Westingborough.

Except for his gardening and the care of his pigs, Potts did no work: his wife went out by day to houses in and about Carden where occasional help was required, and the two children were always tidily dressed and appeared well-fed. Superintendent Wadden, plagued by Squire Hastings and others who preserved game over their persistent losses, attributed more than half the depredations to Potts, but, though both Plender and Constable Hawker obeyed the superintendent's orders to keep an eye on the man, he managed to evade them. Head had caught him once, when out on an entirely different quest, and on another occasion an energetic young constable had caught him on Sir Bernard Ashford's preserves, but poaching was in his blood, and the two sentences he received for those offences made no difference. The Potts family still flourished on roast pheasant and other game.

"Good evening, Potts," said Head, when the door opened and revealed the sturdy, middle-aged, middle-sized man he had come to see, one whose sleek black hair and swarthy face declared the gipsy blood in his veins. "I want a bit of a talk with you, and called to——"

"The sergint's bin arter me once to-day, mister," Potts interrupted with marked hostility. "I up an' told him he couldn't prove a thing on me, an' I tells you the same. An' that's all, so good night, mister."

"Just a moment," Head persisted. "I know we can prove nothing against you, and I don't want to prove anything——"

"Which is what the sergint said, when he

come askin' me where I was last night," Potts interrupted again. "So's he'd know where to look for me next time, huh? I ain't quite such a fool as that, mister."

"Potts, we've caught you twice, haven't we?" Head asked.

"You have, mister. A fourteen days an' a twenty-eight, an' I——"

"And how many hundred times have we failed to catch you?" Head interrupted in turn. "Look here, man, I've come to you for help, not to try to get evidence against you. I want you to be sportsman enough to forget your grudge against us, and I promise that nothing you tell me shall ever be used against you in any way. Is that fair enough?"

"Well, I s'pose it is, mister," Potts admitted reluctantly. "What is it you want, though?"

"Do you mind if I come in for a bit?" Head asked in reply. "I give you my word that anything I see, or anything you tell me, will never be mentioned outside this door in a way that could harm you."

"Well, I reckon that's fair enough," Potts stood back and pulled the door wide. "The missus an' kids are abed. Yes, come in, mister."

Head entered directly into what was the living room of the cottage, by the look of it. An Aladdin incandescent paraffin lamp lighted the room brilliantly, and on the uncovered deal table stood a shallow bowl of water, on which floated bits of envelopes from which Potts appeared to be soaking off some foreign stamps, while other stamps, already peeled off their backings, were drying on a sheet of blotting paper.

"So you collect, do you?" Head observed, nodding at the bowl.

"You can't bring me afore the bench for that," Potts said surlily.

Head turned to smile at him.

"Get out of your head that I want to do anything of the sort, man," he urged. "Bury the hatchet, for tonight. I used to collect myself, till it got too expensive. I've still got two albums, both nearly full, but haven't looked at them for years."

"They'll be gettin' pretty val'able, then," Potts suggested.

"I suppose so. Mostly unused colonials——"

He broke off as Potts went abruptly to the fire in the grate and poked it vigorously. He was smiling when the man faced him again.

"The old saying—one feather or one bone is as bad as the whole bird," he remarked. "But you needn't have taken that trouble. I told you, I'm not here to get evidence against you, or for anything that can harm you in any way. For once, you may be able to help me—perhaps."

"It was a pork bone," Potts lied sullenly. "We had pork for supper."

"Then pick up that pig's rib down by the coal bucket, and put it in the fire, too," Head advised. "What they call small pork, wasn't it?"

With a muttered exclamation Potts spun about, picked up the clean-picked thigh bone of a hare, and thrust it into the heart of the fire.

"I'll skin young Jimmy for that, in the mornin'," he said as he straightened himself. "You got a hawk's eye, mister."

"Neither young Jimmy nor you had any idea I should come into this room," Head pointed out. "Forget it, as I promise you I will. They're not really good now, though. Close season began a month ago."

Potts gave him a long, searching look, and drew an audible breath.

"What *do* you want, mister?" he demanded at last. "What's the game, anyhow? You can't prove a thing. You got no right to touch that bone."

"And it would make no difference if I did burn my hand in getting it out of the fire," Head answered. "Potts, I'll tell you frankly, I'm out to-night after bigger and more dangerous game than you have ever hunted, and come to you because you may be able to put me on the track of it. Murder was done in the last train to Westingborough last night, and I'm looking for the murderer. You've heard of it, I expect."

"Course I've heard of it," Potts agreed. "Mean to say——?" He broke off, his brows drawn together as he puzzled over it.

"Where were you last night, after midnight?" Head asked him.

"Ah-h-h!" Sullen suspicion sounded in the

exclamation, and showed in the man's face. "So's your men'll know where to look for me next time, eh? You led up to it clever, but I ain't bein' caught by it."

"You are not," Head agreed quietly, "for I have given you my word that nothing you tell me shall be used to harm you in any way. If you were so placed last night that you saw and can give me any description at all of the man I want to find, I'll put down five pounds here and now. I think you know me well enough to know I don't break my word."

"Yes, you're straight enough, mister." Potts sounded reflective over it. "This here murder—who was it got killed?"

"Captain Ashford—Sir Bernard Ashford's son," Head answered. Since the fact must come out at the inquest tomorrow, as he well knew, there was no harm in revealing it here and now.

"Gord!" Potts whispered the exclamation. "Old Sir Bernard!"

"What about him?" Head asked. "Do you know—anything?"

"I was thinkin', mister. I ain't got no cause to love old Sir Bernard, but I do remember—when I come up arter bein' caught on his land, I remember how he got outer his chair on the bench an' went out—wouldn't stop while I was tried, because it might look as if he had it in for me for his own sake. An' I thought then—that's a proper gentleman, that is, one what plays fair.

Fourteen days, they gimme."

"Yes, I remember. Now, Potts, in case it might help me to find the man who killed Captain Ashford, and not for any other purpose at all— did that bone in your fire come out of Squire Hastings' woods?"

"Takin' your word it's all straight, mister— yes, it did."

"You caught it last night?"

Potts gave him an almost pitying smile. "Lord, no, mister! You got to hang 'em longer'n that, else you'd hardly tear the meat off the bone. Four nights ago, that chap was unlucky. I ain't a cannibal."

"No. I ought to have known better. Well, since we've got so far, and you begin to realise it's safe to tell me, were you anywhere near Squire Hastings' woods last night? I don't care what you caught, if you were—it doesn't interest me. What does is what you might have seen."

"No, mister, I warn't there last night. I warn't so very far away from where I was when you caught me, that night arter the big storm."

"Westingborough   Parva?"   Head's disappointment sounded in his voice.

"Aye, mister, round that way. Miles off from Squire Hastings."

Miles from the old coach road, with all Westingborough between him and the man who had come through the woods, Head knew. His sigh of disappointment was audible.

Potts leaned over the bowl of water on the table, lifted one of the bits of paper with his fingers and, taking up a pair of tweezers, pulled the stamp off the paper and put it down on the blotter.

"No use to ye, mister," he observed unconcernedly.

"I want to find a man who crossed the river and went up through those woods between two o'clock this morning and dawn, Potts," Head said frankly. "If you can show me that man, the five pounds is still yours."

"I shan't earn it," Potts averred decidedly. "I don't tell nobody where I go, an' I don't ask nobody where they go. Safest, that way."

"Well, thank you very much for breaking that rule in my case."

"Eh?" Potts slid another stamp off its backing and put it on the blotting paper by means of the tweezers. "What rule, mister?"

"You told me where you went," Head pointed out.

"Not so's you could track me there, except that it warn't on Squire Hastings' ground nor nowhere near it, last night," Potts dissented.

"Quite so. As a bit of advice, why not stick to stamps and leave the fur and feather alone? It's a risky business, you know."

"An' that's why, mister." Potts gazed squarely at him to reply. "A risky game—'tain't what the birds are worth, but the fun of it. My missus often says just what you said then, but I just couldn't stop it if I tried, not if you was to catch me with 'em in my pockets every night for a month, like you caught me that time arter the big storm. 'Course, you're right about the stamps. They'd pay better."

"Even stamps like these?" Head pointed at the bowl.

"Lord, no! Chicken feed, that is, mister, stuff I just put away for my boy Jimmy to play with— learn him to take to stamps. Here, if you ain't in no hurry, I'll show you what I mean."

Turning his back on Head, he went to an old-fashioned sofa under the window of the room and, feeling under its upholstery, returned to the table with a lambswool-lined case from which he took a loose-leaf album. He put this down on the table quite near the bowl, opened it and turned a few pages, and then glanced up at Head.

"There!" he said, with a note of exultation. "How's that, mister?"

It was a corner block of six black penny stamps, the left-hand top corner of a sheet with full margin, as fresh and new in appearance as when the stamps had been issued. In the corner of the margin the figures "11" were set in a circle, and, lifting the piece by inserting his tweezers under it, Potts revealed that the original gum was intact.

Bending down to examine it, for a few minutes Head utterly forgot the purpose of his visit, for here was something that few collectors had ever seen, let alone owned, as he knew well.

"Yes, but—how, Potts?" he asked.

"On the straight, mister—absolutely on the straight," Potts assured him. "It were this way. I asks people sometimes if they got any old stamps, the way you do when you collect, an' I had a few finds that way, though not like this. An' I happened to ask old Barnsley the saddler one day, an' he said it was curious, because he'd always kep' a letter what his father'd always kep', because of what happened about it. When old Barnsley's father was a boy, he told me, he was sent away to boardin' school, an' his father—old Barnsley's grandfather, that'd be—got disappointed because his son didn't write home as often as he'd liked him to. So he wrote to tell him about it, an' put them stamps inside the letter for the boy to write back to him—an' before the boy used one o' them stamps, his father which was old Barnsley's grandfather died. So old Barnsley's father always kep' the letter with the stamps inside, just as he'd got it, an' old Barnsley kep' it too. I asked him to let me see it, an' you c'n guess my eyes bulged when he did. An' I told him them stamps was worth quite ten shillin' now, an' he said bless his soul was they an' you'd never think people could be such fools as to pay it, an' the end of it was I give him eight shillin'—for a block o' six plate eleven black pennies, mint with margin showin' the plate number."

"Yes, absolutely on the straight," Head observed ironically.

"Ev'rybody know what old Barnsley is," Potts declared defensively. "Damned old skinflint—do his own mother in the eye for tuppence, he would. 'Sides, he was happy about it. So was I. I shew that block to Fletcher, the chap what keep the big antique shop at Crandon, an' he said he'd give me five quid for it, so I larfed. He bid up to sixty quid, an' then I come away with it. I'm keepin' it till the centenary, an' then takin' it to auction. It's known where most of the plate elevens is, but this block is extra—it ain't on record nowhere."

While he talked, Head's gaze shifted from the treasure to the bits of paper floating in the bowl—and remained on it. After a brief silence, Head pointed with his forefinger at one particular stamp.

"And where did you get that one, now?" he asked.

"That? Oh, they're common enough—common as dirt, mister. The missus got it, as a matter o' fact, when she was doin' a day over at Jevons' place—she allus keeps her eye open for foreign stamps for me, the missus do. An' it seems like Mrs. Jevons got someone write to her from there, because my missus picked five or six o' these outer the wastepaper basket from first to last, when she emptied it. All like that one, they are—two annas, an' the same postmark."

"No value, of course," Head remarked. "Quite common, as you said."

"Aye, but some o' these used ones get rare, sooner or later, so I keep the lot. In envelopes—I don't trouble to mount 'em, only go through 'em sometimes to see if I got anything worth while."

"A very sound policy, Potts. Well, I'm very much obliged to you, especially for that sight of the plate elevens. You've got a very great rarity there. I'll be getting along, I think, and thank you very much."

"Don't mention it, mister—as long as you don't. To the sergint an' all them others that go lookin' for me, I mean."

"I told you, this is strictly between ourselves. It doesn't mean that I shall not run you in if I catch you, though."

"I know." Potts grinned at him. "I reckon you're a sport, mister, though you did stick the bracelets on me that time you caught me."

"Perhaps I'll trust you to come along without them next time."

"Ah, well, mister, it's all in the day's work, ain't it?"

"Quite so, Potts. Give and take, call it." Head bent over the bowl for a final look. "Yes, India, two annas, and the postmark dated six weeks ago, with the word 'Jelalapur' quite distinct. I won't keep you any longer from what you intend doing." He straightened up and turned away from the table as Potts closed the album on his greatest treasure. "Good night, and thank you, Potts."

"Good night, mister. I'd earn that there fiver if I could, but I can't. Quite enjoyed our talk, I have. Mind the step, mister."

* * *

"It's that little bit of luck that counts for more than hours of strenuous work, laddie," Wadden commented the next morning after Head had told his story. "And Potts' wife has had about half a dozen of those stamps with the same postmark, you say he told you?"

"Which means," Head answered slowly, "Mrs. Jevons has had far more."

"Does she get up in the morning and meet the post or is her old man the sort that don't care what happens?" Wadden inquired.

"All this establishes, chief, is that somebody writes to Mrs. Jevons from Jelalapur, not that there's anything suggestive or illicit about the correspondence. There is that rumour, of course, about Captain Ashford and Mrs. Jevons meeting conspicuously—or suspiciously—while he was on his last leave, but even if you put the two things together——"

He reflected over it. Wadden blew, gently and long.

"No news of that four-thousand-pound draft,

Head," he observed.

"Nor will be," Head asserted. "Robbery wasn't the motive. All Thane's papers went to ash in the gully in the woods. The change of clothes on the corpse was to make absolutely certain that no trace of identity remained, perhaps to mislead by giving him Thane's identity. Supposing Thane had not been able to identify himself by his handwriting and his likeness to the Ashford family? We should have concluded—and Mr. X hoped we would—that he was telling us those clothes were his in order to claim the identity of the man he had murdered."

"You're dead sure of Thane?" Wadden asked after another silence.

"I'm dead sure of nobody till I've identified Mr. X," Head answered. "So far, Thane has given me no cause to suspect him."

"Except that he pulled the communication cord to let Mr. X off the train," Wadden pointed out. "Was it a one-man job, for certain?"

Head thought over the suggestion, and made a little gesture of annoyance. "We know nothing, as yet," he said. "Now I think of it, you'll probably have a man with a car calling here this morning, one who answers to some extent to Thane's description of his man in the train. His name is Rynewald, and he will want to know how to get to Long Ridge to see Raymond Nevile. Also, he's some sort of technical adviser to the government of Khelankot, which I've looked out in the atlas, and Iessabad, the capital of that state, is about seventy miles from Jelalapur. I think Rynewald merely comes in to make it more difficult, the sort of coincidence which has no right to happen, but if you could be somewhere about our front door about eleven o'clock, and he does make the inquiry as he told me he would, you might find out all you can about him. He arrived at the Carden Arms yesterday morning, and spoke to me last night."

"Oh, yes!" The superintendent blew, hard. "I'm to cool my tail on our front doorstep, on the mere chance of his inquiring here?"

"I'm due over at Carden Hall at eleven o'clock," Head said.

"And Payne-Garland is opening the inquest at two, you know."

"At which we say nothing about what I found in the woods," Head suggested. "I see the Universal Agency have sent Percy Butters down to cover this—Potts of the Sentinel got wind of a naked man in the train, and that will put the murder on the front page of every paper in the country. Therefore, I think, tell Payne-Garland we don't want too much emphasis laid on Thane's story—I'll instruct Thane as to how much to tell. Let Robert Potter tell all his story, and Bennett and you can detail all that's necessary about finding and examining Captain Ashford's body—I expect Sir Bernard will give evidence of identification. And then adjourn

—'Members of the jury, no useful purpose will be served by carrying this inquiry any further to-day'"—he imitated the coroner's measured, precise way of speaking. "You won't need me, chief. As soon as I've finished with Miss Ashford, I'm going on to find out where Farmer Jevons spent the night before last. Oh, and I nearly forgot! Those shoe soles I rescued from the fire—where are they?"

Wadden pointed at the cupboard in the corner. "Top shelf," he said.

Head went to the cupboard, and returned with a brown-paper package which he opened on the superintendent's flat-topped desk. He took out and put away in his pocket the cord with which Captain Ashford had been strangled, and then, after picking up and scrutinising carefully one of the charred and brittle-edged shoe soles, repacked them.

"To what intent and purpose?" Wadden asked, since Head made no move to put the package back in the cupboard.

"Expert opinion, chief. We know from Thane that the corpse had his shoes on. If this pair was made in England, it helps us to assume that the murderer did not trail Ashford all the way from Jelalapur, though it doesn't prove anything. And if these are Indian, they are probably Ashford's. Mr. X must have got his own shoes very wet when he crossed the Idleburn, and I think it very probable that he changed into Ashford's shoes

and socks and trousers when he built that fire in
the woods, but at the same time Ashford's shoes
may have been too small for him, and he had
to retain his own. If possible, I want an opinion
as to where these were made, and the size and
shape of the wearer's feet."

"What about Bennett producing that cord at
the inquest?"

"Fake one like it for him, if it must be
produced. I particularly do not want this piece
produced for anyone to see, yet."

"Signed his name on it, did he? Head, since
boy sprouts started sprouting, everyone knows
how to tie every sort of knot there is."

"Is that so?" Head's tone was caustic. "Very
well, chief. Without looking at the knot on this
piece, tie me a slip-knot that will slip one way
and merely tighten itself if you try to slip it in the
reverse direction."

"Laddie, boys hadn't begun to sprout till long
after I grew too old to wear short pants and
a long walking stick. I'm a prehistoric survival
from a better age, and as soon as you've finished
this case I'm going to retire and start growing
tomatoes under glass——"

"It's time I started for Carden Hall," Head
remarked, just before the door closed on him.

CHAPTER X

Secret Service?

A ROLLS-ROYCE saloon went out from the forecourt of the Carden Arms, chauffeur-driven, just as Head's car reached the level at the foot of Condor Hill. He was too far off to identify the passengers behind the chauffeur, but near enough to see two big trunks on the grid at the back, and to make a mental note of the car's registration number. Although it was already past eleven, he turned off the road when he reached the hotel, stopped to pencil the lettering and number of the Rolls in his note-book, and then entered and sought Cortazzi.

"Who was that just left you, Cortazzi?" he asked.

"Colonel Thomas an' 'is waife, Mr. 'Ead. She is not well. Ze colonel 'e say per'aps ze pain is in ze appendix, because she 'ave it before, and 'e do not trust ze bumpkin of ze country, but take 'er to

London for ze examine. An' 'e pay me to reserve ze room till Monday, an' 'e say if she is all right zen 'e will come back. For ze feesh."

"And she will come back too?" Remembering Mrs. Thomas's interest in Captain Ashford, Head felt that he did not wish to lose sight of her yet.

"'E do not say, Mr. 'Ead. An' I do not see 'er all ze morning—she do not come down to breakfast. She do not come down till zey go away."

"Can you tell me what address they left for forwarding letters?"

"Zey do not leave any. I do not theenk to ask 'im."

"You have some address, surely? When he booked to stay here?"

"'E write, zis time—it ees in January 'e write—from ze Continental 'otel in Paris. 'E write so soon because 'e 'ave been 'ere before an' know zis taime of ze year per'aps I will be very fool. Larst year, 'e write from ze Savoy 'otel in London. I do not know where 'e live, if 'e live at all. Per'aps 'e do not live, but stay at 'otels."

"There is a difference, of course," Head observed. "All right, Cortazzi. I'll just have one telephone call."

He called Westingborough police, and, getting Sergeant Wells on the line, gave him the number of the Rolls-Royce and instructed him to find out the name and address of its present owner. Then he drove on to Carden Hall, and saw that Sir Bernard Ashford observed his arrival from the dining room window. And, although Head asked for Miss Ashford, the maid who admitted him conducted him to the dining room, and announced—"Inspector Head, sir."

The maid had had her orders from the baronet, Head concluded, but, he determined, he would see Miss Ashford before he left the hall, for she might be able to reveal more than her father knew of his son's life, and in that son's past, beyond doubt, was the cause of this present tragedy.

"You wish to see my daughter, inspector, I understand," Sir Bernard said. "Do sit down, won't you? I felt that I wished to see you first, to tell you something that may have a bearing on your—your search for the one who killed my son. I wish to give you every aid I can."

The evenly-spoken sentences gave no indication of this gallant old man's bereavement, though his appearance defined it. He looked shrunken, aged by years, though still he maintained his upright, soldierly poise. Head took the chair he indicated, his own face toward the light, while the baronet's remained in shadow as he sat with his back to the window.

"I wish to spare both you and Miss Ashford all I can," Head said.

"I know. We have known you, and your work, quite a long time, inspector, and I may say that we do not regard you as—well, as an ordinary police officer. Your consideration for my daughter last year—but you have not come to talk about that, I know. What I have to tell you goes back five years, to the time of my son's last leave here."

"I shall be glad to hear it, sir," Head assured him.

"I do not know if it will be of any use to you," Sir Bernard said with slow precision. "As, possibly, you are aware, Carden is a favourite resort for people who have lived in the tropics, owing to its sheltered situation. Especially in the spring. Some five years ago, a man named Kindersley stayed at the Carden Arms in the early spring, a middle-aged man, and through a mutual acquaintance I got to know him slightly and found that he had spent most of his life in India, though I could not learn what he had been doing there—I did not ask him directly, of course. I mentioned that my son was a lieutenant in a native regiment, but this Kindersley said nothing of having known him, you understand."

"Quite, Sir Bernard," Head commented. "India is a large territory."

"Yes. So I thought at the time. Kindersley went his way, and my son came home on leave. One day, while we were talking, I mentioned Kindersley's name, and my son asked me to describe the man. I did so. He thought for awhile, and then he said—'If you should meet him again, ask him if he remembers J 35.' I am sure that was the letter and number my son said. 'Ask him if he remembers J 35.' Nothing more."

"I see the meaning of it, of course, sir," Head observed.

"Possibly more clearly than I do," the baronet rejoined. "But that is not quite all. About a week later, apropos of nothing, my son said to me—'If ever you meet that man Kindersley again, do not say anything to him about J 35, and forget I ever mentioned the number.' I promised to do so. I may add that I have never seen this Kindersley since, nor heard of him. He apparently never came near the Carden Arms again."

"And you conclude——?" Head asked, and did not end it.

"I surmise," Sir Bernard amended gravely. "I know that the Indian secret service is one of the most tortuously intricate and widely organised departments in existence. It has its representatives in this country as well as in India itself. Similarly, there are organisations at work in this country, as well as in India, to counter the work of the official secret service. I may tell you, inspector, I have been thinking over those two remarks my son made, thinking over them all night, and determining that I would tell you, in case it might help your search."

"That is very good of you, sir," Head told him.

"I thought"—he paused to arrange his ideas —"that, assuming my son were this J 35, he might have been followed and killed for the sake of some information in his possession—some knowledge, say, that could only be extinguished by his death. It seems to me, inspector, that the awful mutilation of his face points to a reason of this sort for the crime. The assassin or assassins responsible for it wished to destroy all possibility of identifying him, as well as to kill him."

"It is possible, sir," Head admitted thoughtfully. "To give themselves time to get out of the country, or at least clear of this district if they were recognisable as foreigners. Yet——" He broke off, thinking. The track through the woods indicated knowledge of the district: would such assassins as Sir Bernard postulated know their way so well?

"I attach most importance to my son's request —'do not say anything about J 35.' To Kindersley, that is. As if to say that my son was J 35, and had no right to disclose the fact even to one who had evidently retired from the service," Sir Bernard explained. "Absolute secrecy is obviously one of the first principles of that service."

"If this Kindersley has retired—retired five years ago, in fact, he is not likely to be much use to us now," Head observed.

"None whatever," the baronet agreed. "The only point in all this which may be of use to you is that it may be—I do not say it is—it may be an assassination planned and carried out by agents of the disruptive fanatics who wish to destroy British rule in India altogether."

"I am much obliged to you for this information, sir," Head said. "It puts a different complexion on the case. And now, before I see Miss Ashford, might I ask you a question or two?"

"Ask anything you wish, inspector. I am anxious to help you."

"Do you know of anyone who might have —well, might have felt enmity toward Captain Ashford for personal reasons?"

"Nobody at all," Sir Bernard answered unhesitatingly. "You must realise that I know practically nothing of his life in India."

"You know the name of Colonel Thomas, I expect."

"It was a brevet lieutenant-colonelcy, and he retired shortly after it was granted him," the baronet said. "Retired, I understand, in consequence of having inherited a rather large fortune, about four years ago. He was at that time second in command of my son's regiment, and I gathered from Bernard—from my son— that he was not a popular officer. He has stayed here at intervals during the past three years, his wife too, but we made no effort to meet him or his wife. I do not know the man, inspector. In fact, as far as I know I have never seen him."

"Not a popular officer," Head echoed thoughtfully.

"I know that my son disliked him," Sir Bernard said.

"Therefore, you would not want to know

him," Head commented.

"I did not seek his acquaintance, nor did he attempt to establish one with me. I have no idea as to why he persistently chose Carden as a resort for himself and his wife, as he has for three years, now."

"Captain Ashford disliked him, sir," Head suggested.

"I gathered from one of my son's letters that nobody liked him," Sir Bernard replied. "But all that concerns four years ago, at least."

"Was Colonel Thomas married at the time, do you know?"

"Was he—— Oh, yes, I see the implication! His wife travelled out to marry him on the boat that took my son back from his last leave. The marriage took place in Bombay—Thomas went on leave to meet her there."

"She and Captain Ashford travelled out together," Head observed.

"Yes, but—inspector, you need attach no importance to that. I happen to know—as far as my son was concerned—this is in utter confidence and I rely on you to respect it—I know as far as he was concerned there was another attraction at the time. Travelling on that boat with him, too. I have good reason to remember it."

"Nothing came of it," Head half-asserted.

"Again in the very strictest confidence, inspector—I met the lady on the boat at Tilbury

—I went down to see my son off. One of the wittiest, most delightful women I have ever met —she died within the year, unfortunately. Her husband, a Mr. Foster, lives next to the Carden Arms, since his retirement from the Indian civil service."

Head nodded appreciation of the confidence, silently.

"I am, you understand, telling you all that I can, with no reserve on any point," Sir Bernard added. "Neither sparing my son, nor this lady of whom I tell you—keeping back nothing."

"Mrs. Foster was much younger than her husband," Head suggested.

"Many years younger, I should say, having seen him a few times."

"Seen him—that is to say, you are not acquainted with him?"

"The man is a vegetarian, an anti-vivisectionist, a rabid opponent of what he calls blood sports, and he distributes pacifist pamphlets," Sir Bernard answered indirectly. "I have no use for cranks."

"You know of no other contacts Captain Ashford made, either before he joined the Indian army, or while on leave, which might have led to what happened the night before last?" Head asked after a pause.

"None whatever. If my suggestion about this J 35 leads you to your solution, inspector, the political aspect does not alter the fact that the case is one of brutal murder—carefully planned murder, too."

"Nothing alters that fact, sir," Head agreed, and rose. "Might I see Miss Ashford now, to find out if she knows anything that might help?"

"Certainly." Sir Bernard rose, went to the doorway, and pressed a bell-push. "Oh, one other thing—identification will be necessary at the inquest. I shall attend for that, and may see you then, in case you think of anything else you wish to ask me."

He directed the maid who answered his ring to tell Miss Ashford that Inspector Head wished to see her, and then went out. A stranger, seeing him, would have gained the impression that he was a rather grave but unperturbed elderly man of fine presence: Head, knowing him, knew that he was a broken-hearted man, but one who had the strength and courage that would enable him to conceal his tragedy, a figure of real manhood.

Then Loretta entered the room, scarcely less self-contained than her father. She advanced to face Head, and smiled at him.

"My turn, I understand, inspector. What can I tell you?"

"I have yet to find out, Miss Ashford," he answered. "As much of Captain Ashford's life as you can, I would say."

"Yes—won't you sit down?" She seated herself as she asked it. "Well—Winchester, and then Camberley, I believe. Then he went to the regiment—two of my uncles were in it. One leave —the summer of five years ago—and then this. There it is in outline."

"His contacts at Winchester—schoolfellows?" Head asked, seating himself since she had already done so. "Did he follow up any friendships from his schooldays to your knowledge, I mean?"

"I never heard him speak of any," she answered.

"Then the Camberley period. Did any associations grow out of it?"

"He once brought a man named Underwood to stay here for a few days. Miss Underwood, this man's sister, subsequently married a Mr. Foster, who is living in Carden at the present time, a widower."

"I have the rest of that story from Sir Bernard," Head remarked. "That is—your brother was very much attached to Mrs. Foster, I believe?"

"For a time," she answered. "I wonder——" she broke off abruptly.

"Yes, Miss Ashford. What you tell me travels no farther, so far as Captain Ashford's good name is concerned. I want all you can tell."

"That was what I wondered," she said, and again smiled at him. "I think—you see, this is the end of everything for my father, but if the one responsible for this—if it is only one—if that one were brought to punishment, I think it would make a difference to my father. And so—I don't wish to say anything that might reflect on my brother, and yet——"

"It is nearly a day and a half since this crime was discovered," Head said slowly, "and, so far, I know nothing. I tell you that frankly. I may guess one or two things, but guessing never yet convicted a criminal of any kind. Anything you can tell me of your brother's life, his character, or his associations, may enable me to stop guessing."

"I think you had better question me as if I were in the witness box," she suggested. "I'll try to answer fully—everything."

"Thank you. To begin with—forgive me for bringing it in—a rather cruel piece of gossip that came to my hearing. To the effect that Sir Bernard said he hoped his son would marry, because his women were too expensive—Captain Ashford's women, of course. Is that correct?"

"I think my father might have said such a thing," she answered.

"Then—still being brutally frank—Mrs. Foster was one of those women. Do you know of any others, Miss Ashford?"

She shook her head. "He wouldn't tell me," she answered.

"Does the name Thomas mean anything to you?" he asked.

"There was a Major Thomas in my brother's regiment. He retired three or four years ago, and

I believe he comes to stay in Carden every year since his retirement. Why, I don't know, except that the fishing is good, and there is no reason why he shouldn't. Married. We don't know either him or his wife, socially. My brother detested him."

"Told you that he detested him, you mean?"

"Yes. On his last leave. He did not know Major Thomas was going to retire, then. An unpopular officer, my brother said."

"You and your brother got on well together, Miss Ashford?"

"Of course we did! Bernard and I—— Ah, don't!"

She turned her head away from him abruptly, and he sat silent. She turned to gaze at him again, and shook her head, trying to smile.

"I know, inspector—it's just a case, to you. I'll try to make it one too. I won't spare myself, or—or him. What else?"

"To thank you for your help, and for being so brave about it, first of all," he answered. "Then—another name. Jevons. Does it mean anything in connection with your brother?"

She shook her head. "Not in connection with him," she said. "There is a man named Jevons, a farmer on the Castel Garde estate. A surly, evil-looking man. There was a meet of the hounds over that way, and the fox went across his land. Jevons stood in the gateway of a field with a double-barrelled gun—the hounds were hot on the scent—and threatened to shoot the horse of any man who tried to ride across the field—the hedges were too high for a jump. The huntsmen and whippers-in had to go round—and we lost that fox. That's all I know of Jevons."

"And Mrs. Jevons?" he asked.

"I didn't even know there was one," she answered.

"There is," he told her. "Further to that, and not to be repeated to anyone, Miss Ashford, there was some talk of Captain Ashford having been seen with her while he was on his last leave here, in addition to which I understand that she has received not less than five or six letters from Jelalapur, the last of them about six weeks ago."

"And you told me you know nothing, yet," she accused.

"Because that proves nothing," he pointed out. "Proves less than ever, with your description of Jevons as a vengeful, angry sort of man. I deduce—not know, but deduce—that she must have received those letters openly enough for her husband to see them, and they must have been received over a considerable period, which leaves me guessing again."

She reflected over it, and in the end shook her head slowly.

"If he had been—well, friendly with this Mrs. Jevons, he would not have told me or my father about it," she said. "It is not——"

"Not the sort of thing he would tell you," Head

completed for her. "Have you any idea what this man Jevons is like—physically, I mean?"

"Oh, the typical farmer type. He is a big, red-faced man."

(Yes, Head thought, he would be. Another Vallambrosan leaf!)

"Did your brother spend all his last leave here, Miss Ashford?"

"Oh, no! Less than half of it, I should think."

"Was he acquainted with a Major Fitton, who is staying at the Carden Arms at the present time? That is, did he mention the name?"

"Sheila's young man," she reflected aloud. "No, Mr. Head, to the best of my knowledge my brother never met Major Fitton. I have met him, and liked him very much. I think he and Miss Sheila Hastings will make a match of it. He is Indian army, stationed somewhere in Madras."

"Can you mention anyone else—anyone else at all—whom your brother met and knew, either on his last leave or before?"

"He may have met any of the people whom my mother and father know," she answered. "There were the Bells of Condor Grange, and the Hastings and the Neviles and the Enthwaites— Oh, yes, and he got to know Quade, the man who keeps training stables the other side of Westingborough, because he bought Bayard, the steeplechaser I ride, from Quade. But you would hardly call that a social contact. A business acquaintance."

Remembering Quade, a five-foot-nothing, horsey and slangy ex-jockey, Head ruled him out from among those who might have lighted a fire in Squire Hastings' woods, in spite of his wife's reputation.

"You have been very helpful, Miss Ashford." He stood up as he spoke. "A painful question—there was no difference between you and Captain Ashford—nothing to prevent his telling you anything?"

"Nothing, inspector. I forgive you for asking it, because I can realise why. To answer that frankly, he meant everything to my father, and I, not much more than nothing. I knew it, always. But it made no difference between Bernard and me. I loved him too."

He held out his hand, then, and she took it and smiled at him.

"You can step out of the witness-box, Miss Ashford," he said, "and I doubt if I shall ever find a better or more understanding witness."

"Not so very long ago, inspector, you were very good to me," she answered. "My father believes in you, and so do I. That's all."

"I'll go, now," he said, "and try to justify your belief."

* * *

Blowing softly from time to time, and pacing the corridor between the doorway of the room that served as his office, and the entrance to the police station, Superintendent Wadden passed the time between ten forty-five and eleven-ten, and then an open four-seater Aston-Martin pulled up in front of the police station with an abruptness that sent sparks flying from under the rear wheels. The superintendent waited while a tall, red-faced man inquired of the constable on duty the way to Mr. Raymond Nevile's private residence, Long Ridge, and then came forward.

"Fourpence, sir," he said. "We expected you."

The tall man stared at him. "Eh?" he inquired, uncomprehendingly.

"You just tell that feller driving you every time he stops like that, it costs him fourpence," Wadden explained. "Brake-lining, I mean. You can't jam on brakes like that to stop a car for less. Fourpence, I said. It's a low estimate. If he'd taken his foot off the accelerator two hundred yards before he got here, now, and slid up gently——"

"But we only just saw the police station," the other man expostulated. "I told him to pull in, to get direction as to the way to Long——"

"Ridge, for an appointment with Mr. Raymond Nevile," Wadden took up the story. "I know all about it, and you're Mr. Rynewald. Am I right, or am I right? I had warning that you might call."

Rynewald's lips parted in a smile. "Bit of a character, aren't you?" he inquired, sticking both hands in his pockets.

Wadden gave him a steady stare, and the power of those fierce eyes made him uncomfortable. Certain minor offenders had been heard to declare that the superintendent's eyes could read a man's inmost thoughts.

"You are from India, I believe, Mr. Rynewald?"

"Er—yes. I've spent most of my life there. But ——" He broke off, staring doubtfully back at this man with the piercing gaze.

"Yes. In that climate, tomatoes ripen quite freely in the open, I expect. That is, do they, or don't they?"

"I believe so. I'm not a tomato grower. But I wanted——"

"Yes, I know. They don't in this country. Which is why I intend to grow them under glass. Now, Mr. Rynewald, you keep on the way you were going when you stopped here, and take the second turning on the right—the second, not the first. Carry on over the river bridge when you get to the foot of the hill, and the third gateway on your left—you can't see the house from the road —the third gateway, and you drive straight up to Long Ridge, Mr. Raymond Nevile's place. You can't go wrong."

"Ah—thank you. You seem to have been instructed as to what I want to find, officer," Rynewald said, eyeing Wadden's uniform tunic.

"Instructed?" The superintendent blew at him so fiercely that he backed a couple of steps.

"Instructed? I left off being instructed before you were born, young man! Inspector Head informed me this morning that you would come here fretting about the way to Long Ridge."

"Do I look fretful?" Rynewald demanded with some asperity.

"Don't tempt me to commit a breach of the peace, for I won't," Wadden retorted. "I'm not telling you what you look like. Whaddye want with Mr. Nevile, anyhow? And you from India's coral strand!"

"What the hell business of yours is it what I want with him?" Rynewald inquired, though with a twinkle in his eyes rather at variance with the form of his question. He appeared more amused than angry.

"Everything that happens for twenty miles round here is my business," the superintendent retorted. "Especially if strangers are in it."

"That is to say, you've had a murder happen," Rynewald observed, with a satiric inflection. "That always upsets country police, doesn't it!"

"Let me tell you," Wadden snapped back, "we're used to 'em. Murders are what you might call our speciality. When they don't happen among our own people, we get 'em sent—we get 'em by road or rail, like this last one, and it appears to me that people come here specially to get murdered. Or to murder. I'm sick of it! I'm fed up with it! Westingborough was respectable, once, but now—— Oh, Lord!"

"Don't blame me," Rynewald said blandly. "I came here on business, not for crime. And since you've been so kind as to direct——"

"Just one moment—*stranger*," Wadden adjured, with heavy emphasis on the epithet. "What is your business with Mr. Raymond Nevile?"

"You haven't the slightest right to ask me," Rynewald retorted. "I know enough of England and English ways to be sure of that. But I'll tell you, all the same. Nevile dyes have no equal in the world—they are unique. In the state of Khelankot, we weave silks—not in a wholesale way, but as a small industry, say—worthy of Nevile dyes. I want to see Mr. Nevile himself, and see if I can persuade him to let us dye our own fabrics with his dyes, use his processes under licence to show the world what can be done with Khelankot silks."

Wadden gestured him toward the door. "Go straight ahead, Mr. Rynewald," he said. "I've told you how to get there. Call in here as you come back, and ask for Superintendent Wadden. If you get what you went after, I'll buy you anything you like in Westingborough—and they've got three bottles of 'forty-eight brandy left in the Black Lion cellar, I happen to know. I'll buy you all three, if Mr. Nevile coughs up."

"In other words, you think I've come here for nothing?" Rynewald suggested.

"Think? Man, if you'd ever tasted that brandy,

you'd know I'm not thinking! It's not a liqueur. It's a gift from heaven."

"And I'm to have all three bottles, you say?" Rynewald asked.

"You are not. Call in on your way back, and own it," Wadden dissented. "Get off, now—I've got to attend to the business of an inquest, and not too much time to see about it, either."

"I'll call back." Rynewald moved toward the waiting car. "What did you say your name was?"

"Wadden. Just ask for the superintendent, and they'll burn holes in the atmosphere. If they don't, I will. And tell that feller you've got driving you it costs at least fourpence, a penny a wheel, every time he stops like that. Brake lining, tell him. I drive myself."

He watched while Rynewald, laughing, got back into the car, and made some remark to Mirza Khan, who was at the wheel.

As they went off, Rynewald turned his head to call out—

"If I lose, I'll buy those bottles."

Wadden turned back into the police station.

"It's a gift," he said to himself as he went. "That's a sound feller, too. It's a gift."

CHAPTER XI

The Jevons Angle

AT the point where the marsh road branched off to the right of the main highway to Crandon and London, Head, on his way to Jevons' farm on the Castel Garde estate, braked to a standstill and waited. For, coming toward him along the main road, he saw an incongruous couple, Constable Hawker and a smallish boy whom Head recognised as Jimmy Potts, carrying a trunk between them. Jimmy struggled manfully along with his end of the burden, which, on account of the bulky constable's height, slanted considerably, and Hawker, whom Wadden always called his man of weight, tried to adjust his step to that of the youngster. They stopped and deposited the trunk on the grass border of the road beside Head's car, and Hawker held up a broken leather strap while he explained.

"Must of fallen off a car, sir. This youngster

found it an' told me. The strap give way, by
the look of it. Couldn't leave it there, so I got
him to give me a hand. He was goin' to borrow
his father's barrow for me to wheel it along to
Sergeant Plender's place."

Head saw the initials—"P. W. T." on the lid of
the trunk, and remembered the Rolls-Royce that
had gone away from the Carden Arms.

"Lift the lid of my dickey, and put it in there,
Hawker," he bade. "Then you'd better go back
along the road and see if there's another like this
anywhere in your territory. They may have been
strapped on separately, but there were two on the
back of the car. I'll attend to this one."

"Right you are, sir." Opening the dickey,
Hawker deposited the trunk in it. "And the strap
—you'll take that too?"

"Put it in," Head bade. "If you find the other
trunk, take it to the Carden Arms and tell
Cortazzi I'll explain when I bring this to him."

Then, after presenting Jimmy with sixpence,
Head drove on. Either Colonel Thomas would
return to the room he had reserved until Monday
at the Carden Arms, or else, missing his trunk
at the end of his journey, he would institute
inquiries for it. As a third alternative, Sergeant
Wells would get the address at which the
Rolls-Royce was registered, and then it would
be possible to get in touch with Thomas and
tell him his trunk had been found. A fourth
possibility did not occur to Head's mind just

then: he had reverted to thought of how best to approach Jevons and get information about this Jelalapur correspondence.

With the old, battlemented central tower of Castel Garde in sight among its trees, he drew up to inquire his way of an elderly man busy cutting back a thick hawthorn hedge with a billhook. Yes, Jevons' farm was straight on, the second on the right after you passed Mr. Houghton's gateway. Big black barn with a tiled roof—you couldn't miss it.

The car bumped along the hundred yards or less of rutted drive that led to the house. Head stopped and got out, to knock at the green-painted front door set under a trellis on which a rambler rose was well in bud, though there was yet another day of March to go. Inside the house a little dog yapped peevishly, and a woman's voice bade it be quiet. The door opened, and Head had a momentary impression that he ought to know the woman who faced him, though he did not. Something about her reminded him of —of what? The full recollection eluded him. She was not over tall, and was very well-dressed in blouse and skirt: her dark eyes as they surveyed him gave an impression of wistful sadness —appealing, beautiful eyes; an exceptionally attractive woman, still young.

"Yes?" she asked, and her voice was low-pitched, as attractive as her appearance. "What is it you want?"

"To see Mr. Jevons, if possible," he answered.

"A canvasser?" Her expression altered, hardened. "Because we never under any circumstances buy from them."

"A police inspector, madam, from Westingborough," he said baldly.

Again her expression changed, or rather, she tried to render her face quite expressionless: again Head felt that he ought to know her, that he had seen her before, yet knew he had not.

"You are Inspector Head," she asserted rather than asked.

"Quite correct, madam," he answered. "My name is Head."

"Yes. We get so many canvassers. I thought you might be one."

"It is possible to see Mr. Jevons?" he asked bluntly.

She shook her head.

"He is not at home," she answered. "His brother leaves Liverpool for Canada to-day. I expect him back to-morrow."

"Has he been long away from home?" Head persisted.

"Only since Tuesday. But why do you ask that?"

"Curiosity, call it," he said, with an appearance of indifference.

Her dark eyes expressed disdain. "You can hardly expect me to believe that of you, Inspector Head," she retorted incisively.

"One may have reasons for being curious," he said. "Serious reasons."

"Such as—?" she asked. "Why do you want to see my husband?"

He frowned at the direct demand. If Jevons had been absent from his home since Tuesday, he could have been in that train on Wednesday night. "Did Mr. Jevons go direct from here to Liverpool, madam?" he asked in reply to her question, after a brief pause.

"He did not. He met his brother in Birmingham, I understand, and they went from there to Liverpool together. But why—why all this?"

"Mr. Jevons might possibly be able to give me some information I want," he answered evasively, "Since he is not here, though——"

"Perhaps I could give it to you," she suggested, as he did not end his sentence. "What is it that you want to know? Nothing—nothing to do with that murder they are talking about, is it?"

"I am not sure," he said slowly and with an air of reflection, while he watched her steadily. "It might even have a bearing on that."

"Why be so mysterious about it?" she demanded impatiently. "Surely, if you say directly what it is that you want——" But there she broke off, and her full, red lips fined to a thin line. As if some thought had occurred to her, and it were better to say no more.

"At what time to-morrow do you expect Mr.

Jevons?" he asked.

"I'm not sure. Not until the afternoon."

Momentarily, for the second time, her gaze went past him to his car. He could not understand, then, why the first glance she had cast in that direction had caused her to alter her manner, to close her lips in such a decided fashion. Now, as she answered, she gazed at him again.

"Very good. I will call late to-morrow afternoon, thank you. Good afternoon, madam—I won't trouble you any longer, now."

"Nor tell me what it is you want of my husband?" she asked.

"I am afraid not. Good afternoon, and thank you."

And, lifting his hat momentarily, he turned away, facing toward the car. What was there about it...? He was conscious that the woman did not close the door, but stood watching until, turning while he seated himself, he saw her again. Then she drew back into the shadow beyond the doorway, and became an indistinct figure, but still did not close the door. She was watching something, and it was not himself.

He drove away. On the Carden side of Castel Garde, and thus well beyond sight of Jevons' windows, he stopped the car beside the road and, crossing to the off side, surveyed the vehicle with the width of the road dividing him from it. Something about it had arrested that woman's

attention, altered her manner toward him—
made her afraid to question or invite further
questioning from him. It might not have been
the car, but some thought that had occurred to
her, yet the change had coincided with her first
glance past him at the car. And, standing as he
did now, he viewed it from just such a distance
and position in regard to it as had been hers
when she stood on the doorstep facing him.

Just an ordinary old two-seater, with the
dickey opened and that trunk stood on end in it.
And the initials visible on the trunk!

Colonel Thomas' initials, P. W. T. But surely...
How could those initials mean anything to the
wife of a local farmer? Yet there was nothing else
about the car to mark it out from scores of old
two-seaters, except that it was very clean and the
plated parts exceptionally well polished. Why
should those initials——?

He gave it up, and got back into the car
to drive on. An unusually attractive and well-
spoken woman. Clever, too. She would be
difficult, if the case developed in a way that
brought her into it. He had made a mistake, too,
in announcing that he intended to call again. She
would warn Jevons, put the man on his guard.
What did those initials mean to her? Was there
anything to connect her with Thomas? Only a
close intimacy could account for her recognition
of the initials, if they had been the cause of her
sudden decision to say nothing—for the change

in her that he had noted had amounted to that. He was still considering the problem when he drew up in front of the Carden Arms.

"That trunk, Cortazzi, I'm fairly sure it dropped off the back of Colonel Thomas' car a short while ago. I want you to get it off my car and store it till you see whether he comes back on Monday—there's a broken strap, and you can take charge of that too. If he does not come back or make inquiries, I'll get in touch with him about it."

"Yaas, Mr. 'Ead. Jules, tell Fred 'e must get ze tronk out of ze car an' take it to ze Colonel's room, an' to be very queek. An' if you laik, Mr. 'Ead, all ze regular lunch is fineesh, but I make ze lunch especial for you. It take only five minute, ten minute—yaas?"

"All right, then," Head agreed, rather wearily, with a glance round the lounge. Except for ze Miss Tomsongs, busy as ever with silks and needles and semi-audible conversation near the fireplace, no guests were visible. "And get me one of your eye-opening cocktails, Cortazzi."

"I make him myself, especial," Cortazzi promised.

* * *

There was an audible buzz of excitement among the crowd in Westingborough corn-hall when Sir Bernard Ashford, called as witness, stated that he had identified the body which was the subject of this inquest as that of his son. Up to that point, only those directly concerned —Thane might be regarded as one of them— had known the identity of the victim, and Sir Bernard's demeanour as he descended from his car and entered the hall had given no hint that he was personally affected by the tragedy.

He had understood, he stated, that his son had been due to arrive in England on Saturday —the day following that of the inquest—by the liner *Pathankot*, and had had no idea, until his identification of the body, that Captain Ashford was already in the country. Nor had he any idea of when Captain Ashford had arrived, or where he had been between the time of his leaving the *Pathankot* and boarding the train in which he had been found dead. Beyond the identification, and the fact that his son had said he would arrive at Tilbury on the liner when he had last written home, Sir Bernard could give no information about him.

With that, two pressmen stole out to see that the latest sensation in connection with this sensation made the mid-afternoon editions of their respective evening papers.

"Mystery of Victim's Movements," and "Train Murder: Baronet's Startling Revelation," were the respective headlines that resulted.

Meanwhile Loretta, having driven her father and Thane to Westingborough for the inquest, sat waiting for them to join her in the small writing room of the Duke of York, almost opposite the police station in Market Street. The door between the writing room and the main lounge of the hotel stood open, and a faint murmur of voices came to her as she sat gazing out from the window and wished, more for her father's sake than her own, that these hateful formalities connected with Bernard's death had not to be, or at least would end quickly.

Then a voice, deep and resonant, sounded clearly to her from the lounge. Someone must be standing quite near the doorway.

"He's not in," said the voice.

"Then you save your money," said another voice, a higher-pitched, silkier-sounding one. "Shall we try for lunch here? I think it would be too late if we went back, now."

"We can try here. Finish the drinks first. And I should like to see the old boy and tell him. After all, it was a bet, really."

"You mean, he will be back by the time we finish lunch?"

"Probably. He's at the inquest on that poor devil who got murdered the night before last, I expect."

"Poor devil is the correct epithet."

"Ah, yes, but what is behind it? What had that poor devil, as we call him, been doing to invite what he got——"

There Rynewald, the speaker, broke off, for he

saw facing him a white-faced girl with eyes that literally blazed rage. Both he and his companion stared at her in blank amazement.

"I wish to tell you two *gentlemen*"—she put bitter, ironic emphasis on the epithet—"that the dead man you are slandering was my brother. Be so good as to save the rest of your judgment on him for a less public place than this."

She turned her back on them and disappeared from their sight beyond the writing-room doorway. They took up their glasses and moved silently to the other end of the long lounge, and then looked at each other.

"I am not sure that I want any lunch, now," said Mirza Khan.

Rynewald thought for awhile, finished his drink, and put down the glass. "My friend," he said, it has got to be done."

The Indian stared at him. "You do it, then," he said.

"I think you could do it better."

"I am quite certain I could not. No—you."

"Toss for it. Best of three. No, sudden death."

He took a florin from his pocket and spun it up.

"Tails," said Mirza Khan, and then the pair of them bent over the coin on the carpet.

"Heads," said Rynewald as he picked it up. "You go."

Mirza Khan passed his hand over his sleek black hair—quite unnecessarily, for it was glossily smooth—fastened the top button of his lounge coat, and went as the coin decreed. Loretta cast one glance at him as he came across the writing room toward her, and then looked out from the window again, as if he did not exist.

"Madam," he said, "my friend and I wish humbly to express our very deep regret for the pain we have caused you."

"Unfortunately"—she did not look round —"this is a public place. Otherwise, you would not be able to molest me."

"I have no wish to intrude one moment longer than will tell you we are both deeply sorry for our careless words," he insisted gently.

She stood up and faced him. "Then you need not stay one moment longer," she said sharply. "I accept your apology. Now please go!"

Thane entered the room in time to hear her last words. He came swiftly to her side, and faced Mirza Khan.

"You heard that, as I did," he said quietly. "Go!"

With a deep bow at Loretta, Mirza Khan turned and went, to rejoin Rynewald, at whom he shook his head with a rueful expression.

"The next time," he said, "I will look in all the corners before I speak. And if we both incur blame, we will both apologise."

"I don't think any apology could quite cover, in this case," Rynewald observed after a silence.

"How right you are! I need another drink, a large one. Since I made the apology, you will pay for the drink."

In the writing room, Thane gazed questioningly at Loretta.

"Was that devil forcing himself on you?" he asked.

She shook her head. "Listeners never hear any good," she said. "He and another man were talking about—about my brother. Perhaps I was hard on him, though. He must have had courage, to apologise as he did."

"He looked humble enough," Thane observed. "But I've come to tell you Sir Bernard got straight into the car, and is waiting now. I spoke to the superintendent, and he said he would stretch a point and let us go as soon as we'd given evidence, instead of waiting till the end."

She took up her handbag and moved toward the door.

"And there is no—nothing to indicate who ——?" she asked.

"If there had been, I should have told you," Thane answered. "It's early, yet, little more than twenty-four hours since you drove me away from here—since we met. Feels much longer, but ——"

"You mean you are anxious to get away?" She looked full at him.

"Good heavens, no! I meant—I'm glad you admit me as you do, make me feel that I really know you. As if we had known each other longer."

"Don't go away just yet," she asked. "My father is glad of you."

He wanted to ask—"And you?" but kept it back, for the time.

* * *

Rynewald entered the superintendent's room, and stood before the desk. Wadden looked up at him, and nodded slightly.

"It's fifty shillings a bottle, Mr. Rynewald, and he'll only sell two," he said without preface. "I rang through and asked him. Do I pay, or do you?"

By way of reply, Rynewald put his hand in his pocket and brought out a wad of currency notes. He counted off five and put them on the desk.

"If we want Khelankot fabrics Nevile-dyed, we must send them to Raymond Nevile," he said. "Which is out of the question—it would cost too much, and there is the risk of loss in transport."

"There and back—yes, I suppose there is." Wadden reached out and took up the notes. "I appreciate this, y'know. Not every man would have come back as you have. Now one bottle goes home to the old lady, and I'll keep the other here in the hope that you'll drop in and test it when nobody's looking. And I want you to bear witness, if you should be asked, that I never bet. Police superintendents never do."

"I will affirm that, if asked," Rynewald told

him, "but I won't swear to it. I'll go as far as a simple lie in a good cause."

"May you never have it on your conscience," Wadden said solemnly. "Now I'd like you to tell me, if you can spare the time, what is your opinion about this murder I've been attending an inquest over?"

"My opinion?" Rynewald looked his surprise. "What on earth use could my opinion on it be? I know nothing about it."

"You've heard the gossip—you know as much as the next man in the street," Wadden declared. "And with a puzzle like this, the solution may come from an utterly unexpected source—so much so that I'd ask my own grandmother the question I've just asked you, if I still had one. You might let fall the one word that unlocks the puzzle, as might anyone."

"I see the logic of it." Rynewald frowned thoughtfully. "I'd say—or rather, I'd ask—what was the murdered man doing before he got into that train? Whom had he met, and what had he done?"

"And how would you find the answer to your question?" Wadden inquired.

"I don't know," Rynewald confessed after a pause.

"It is a bit difficult, isn't it?" Wadden observed, with the faintest hint of irony in his tone. "Thank you very much for your opinion, though, and also for your absolute certainty that I never bet. If you happened to look in about this time to-morrow, and I'm available, I expect I could lay hands on a corkscrew."

"Many thanks, superintendent—I will see if I can manage to get here. Now I must go—my friend is waiting for me."

CHAPTER XII

Council

THE superintendent frowned at Head, who sat at the end of the desk while Wadden himself occupied the swivel chair behind the kneehole. It being Saturday morning, there was a pile of forms of various sorts on the desk for consideration, signature, and the like, but Wadden had pushed them aside for the time, since they were unconnected with the train murder case. There was also a heap of newspapers, all of which went to justify Percy Butters, the smart young representative of Universal Press Agency, in describing this case as a godsend to the press.

"And supposing both brothers get on that boat for Canada?" Wadden asked. "That chap in the Crippen case got broke for just such a mistake. Not stopping Crippen and le Neve from sailing, I mean."

"He had some justification for stopping them," Head pointed out. "In addition, if Jevons meant to go, I couldn't stop him. That boat would have been in sight of the Irish coast before I could set anything working. And the wireless that caught Crippen still functions."

"I believe the scenery when you get to the St Lawrence river is the sort to write odes about," Wadden remarked pensively, "but if you do get the trip, I shall dock it out of your holiday. No, sit tight, man. The big noise rang through just before you came in, and told me he's coming along for a talk on the reports he got from you and me this morning. And if you're not here it'll be like Macbeth without the witches. Reminds me, that. What did you make of Mrs. Jevons?"

"Have you ever seen her?" Head asked in reply.

Wadden shook his head.

"Possibly, but I don't know her by name. May have seen the woman who is Mrs. Jevons, for all I know. Carry on."

"Very attractive," Head said. "Dark, beautiful eyes, medium height, quite well-dressed, with hair and make-up in keeping, and managed to give me the impression of a woman—a youngish woman, too—of good position and plenty of experience of the world."

"Umph! And Jevons farms a hundred acres on Houghton's estate."

"Yes. She doesn't fit, chief. Then you have those letters from Jelalapur—Potts had no reason for telling me that if it were not true. Then, the fact that she apparently received the letters quite openly, or at least made no attempt to conceal the envelopes. Unless her husband is an utterly incurious fool, that seems to put paid to any idea of a liaison between her and Captain Bernard Ashford."

"You'll know more about that when you bring Jevons back from Canada, if they manage to hold him on the boat for you," Wadden remarked. "You think she's the sort that might have had an affair with Ashford?"

"I think, if she wanted to make such a man as he appears to have been fall for her, he wouldn't stand much chance," Head answered.

Then Jeffries, the police clerk, threw the door of the room wide, and as he announced "Colonel Morrison, sir," both Wadden and Head rose to their feet to face a white-haired, well-dressed man whose gait and bearing proclaimed military service. He nodded greetings, and Head went to the back of the room to fetch a chair.

"Morning, Wadden—sit down—sit down! I felt we could hardly discuss this by telephone, after reading those reports of yours. Ah! Thank you, Head—good morning. Any more developments? Sit down, man."

"Nothing at all, sir," Head answered.

"This Jevons, now—what about him? Does he appear probable?"

"On the face of it, no, sir," Head answered. "I

have yet to see him."

"This afternoon, if he comes back from Liverpool," Wadden added.

"If he does not, he condemns himself," the chief constable observed. "But no man would be fool enough to attempt that sort of flight in these days. That is, no man of the mentality which committed that crime."

Head nodded agreement. "I think of asking that man Thane to go with me this afternoon," he announced. "I think he will agree to go."

"To settle whether Jevons were the one who drugged him," Colonel Morrison suggested. "Yes, I see. And on the face of it, you say, Jevons does not appear probable as the murderer. To put that another way, a little more than two days after the discovery of Captain Ashford's body—call it two days and a half since the murder—you confess yourself entirely at fault and with no definite line of inquiry, Head?"

"I do, sir," Head answered frankly, gazing full at his questioner.

"Yes. Yes. And I would call it the first time, in any of these cases of yours, that you have made such a confession two days after the discovery of the crime. Head, I don't want to be compelled to ask the Yard for a man and spoil your record, but —well!"

"You wouldn't do that before Monday, sir," Wadden suggested.

"No-o." Morrison sounded doubtful over it. "I

suppose I could—but you own you're utterly at fault, Head. Look here! Let's go over it together, now, and see it anything comes of considering it in conference. Three brains may be better than two, and I own that this case is worrying me. Begin at the beginning, and go through all we know."

"We haven't got the beginning, sir," Wadden objected. "That, to my mind, is when Captain Ashford left the *Pathankot* at Port Said. From there, I've ascertained by having inquiries made, he went to Alexandria and then came straight on to England by air. He landed from the air liner and cleared one suit case as baggage at the customs', a week ago last Thursday, and from then on he does not appear anywhere alive. That is to say, as nearly as can be told he went to London. Since he didn't tell his people he was in England, and didn't let them know he was not arriving at Tilbury on the liner to-day, I suggest he dropped his identity for the time, for some purpose of his own."

"You have no hint of that purpose?" Morrison asked.

"Sir Bernard suggests secret service," Head took up the tale, "on the strength of Captain Ashford's having said something on his last leave in this country—five years ago—which might make him secret service."

The chief constable shook his head. "No man in that service ever mentions the fact—or he would not be in it," he said.

"For that reason, I put the theory out of my mind," Head observed.

"And Ashford himself—what have you learned about him?"

"In Sir Bernard's opinion, he ought to marry because his women were too expensive," Head answered. "The merest rumour concerning an acquaintance with Mrs. Jevons, some sort of regard for or intimacy with a Mrs. Foster, who died four years ago and whose husband now lives in Carden, and a suggestion that he was attracted by Miss Sheba Bell, who is also dead now. And these three—friendships, call them—are all five years old. Except that Mrs. Jevons received letters from Jelalapur, where Captain Ashford was stationed, up to about a month ago."

"And almost certainly her husband knew it," Wadden put in.

"Added to which, a correspondence based on a possible intimacy of five years ago is hardly cause for murder," Morrison pointed out. "Can you get anything more definite as to the nature of the correspondence?"

"Short of a search warrant, sir, I don't see how," Wadden said.

"Did this Mrs. Jevons appear perturbed, Head?" Morrison asked.

"Not in the least. We have to remember, sir, that at the time I saw her yesterday she would not know the identity of the murdered man—

that was not disclosed till the inquest, except that for my own reasons I saw fit to reveal it to Potts, the Carden poacher, late last night. It was through him I learned of Mrs. Jevons receiving letters from Jelalapur."

"Then he might have told her Captain Ashford was the victim."

"I think that very unlikely, sir. He collects foreign stamps, and his wife, working at the Jevons', took the envelopes with the Jelalapur postmark out of the wastepaper basket for him. A man like him would have no direct approach to a woman like Mrs. Jevons."

The chief constable frowned thoughtfully. "This, then—about the identity of the victim not being known, I mean—would apply to everyone until after the inquest yesterday afternoon, I take it?"

"Unless the servants at Carden Hall talked— and I am not sure that even they knew it," Head said. "I asked Thane not to mention it anywhere, and I am fairly certain he would not. Thus—yes."

"And what is the 'yes' about, inspector?" Morrison inquired.

"I was thinking, sir—I got Mr. Thane to have dinner with me at the Carden Arms on Thursday, because when I'd lunched there that day it seemed to me that three or four men might fit his description of the one on the train—big men with red noses. But none did."

"Well, where does your 'yes' come in?"

Morrison persisted.

"That, as nearly as I can tell, the murderer believed he had destroyed all possibility of identifying his victim," Head explained. "Until news of the inquest got out, he would believe he had succeeded. Knowledge of failure might make an entire difference to his attitude, and might even make him betray himself by showing fear."

Morrison took out his case and thoughtfully lighted himself a cigarette. Then with—"I'm sorry, Head," he offered the case, and Head took one, while Wadden refused.

The three sat silent awhile.

"Now the next point," Morrison suggested at last.

"The murderer, I think, sir," Head said. "Someone who knows the district, and had somewhere definite to go after committing his crime."

"Amplify that, please. The somewhere definite, I mean."

"Thane pulled the cord for him, and he left the train," Head explained. "A stranger to the district would not have known the depth of the Idleburn, and with plenty of woods for hiding on the other side would not have crossed it in the dark. Then, having crossed, the murderer did not make for the road and easy going. He took a diagonal course through Squire Hastings' woods —I should say that the ascent of the slope guided him—and kept to that course pretty accurately until he came out on the old coach road and I lost trace of him. The reports you have tell you that he burned clothing in the woods, in a gully deep enough to conceal the fire, and I found trouser buttons marked 'Jelalapur.' His track as I followed it is practically a straight line, and he made it in the dark. I think a stranger to the district would either have gone back or forward along the line of railway, taken to the woods on the far side of the river, or followed the river bank for dry crossing somewhere. He would not have risked drowning in the stream by entering it in the dark."

"He would expect you to examine the spot where the train stopped when the cord was pulled," Morrison asserted reflectively.

"Yes, but he knew that if he could reach the point at which he was aiming, unseen, he would be safe," Head added. "Because he knew—wrongly, of course—that he had obliterated his victim's identity, and without that he could not be connected with the crime, unless seen on his way to the place he wanted to reach. And that might be Westingborough, it might be Carden, and it might be Crandon, from where I lost him."

"It might also be Jevons' farm," Wadden observed sourly.

"Well, on probability, you locate your man as belonging to or at least thoroughly familiar with the topography of the district," Morrison said. "Who was absent that night, and so possibly on the train?"

"The population of Westingborough alone is about twelve thousand," Wadden said, as if to himself, and blew softly. "But Jevons—yes."

Head made a little gesture of impatience.

"I shall see Jevons this afternoon," he said, rather sharply.

"Or in Canada, after the boat docks," Wadden said, very softly.

"What I meant was—who with a possible motive for murdering Captain Ashford was in a position to be on the train?" Morrison amended.

Wadden, with Head gazing full at him, silently formed the word—"Jevons" with his lips, and then sighed deeply.

"We seem to be getting nowhere," the chief constable remarked rather irritably. "All you have of the murderer, inspector, appears to be a track through the woods which does not even tell you the size of his feet, certain trouser buttons and a collar-stud and pair of shoe soles which may have belonged either to him or to his victim. Has that pair of soles been properly examined yet?"

"I expect a report from—well, from a specialist in footwear—this morning," Head answered. "I arranged for it yesterday after returning from Jevons' farm—but they may have been Captain Ashford's shoes."

"In which case—but no, of course not. I mean —if they are not, the murderer may still have the pair that belonged to Captain Ashford."

"He wouldn't be such a fool, sir," Wadden protested.

"I was thinking of the difficulty of destroying them," Morrison explained, "and because of that I still say he may have them yet. In a house, for instance, one's servants would notice if one tried to burn a pair of shoes, and sinking them in water or burying them would not appeal to me, I know. I should be afraid they might turn up at any time."

"Worth considering, Head," Wadden remarked thoughtfully.

"Unless the pair of soles I have represents Captain Ashford's shoes, and the murderer kept on wearing his own," Head said. "He might have changed over, because of having soaked his own in the river, but I think it unlikely. Further to that, sir"—he addressed the chief constable —"before going over to Jevons' this afternoon, I intend to go back to the ashes of that fire in the gully, and sift them handful by handful. In case other small bits of metal may be among the ash. Sleeve links, for instance. A front collar stud. Especially sleeve links."

"Since he left one stud, he might have left the links," Wadden said.

"All that is after the fact," Morrison observed, with a recurrence of his signs of irritation. "Before it—there is a week of Ashford's life blank, apparently. Where was he—what was he doing? Why, if he wanted his father and sister to believe he was landing at Tilbury on Saturday —to-day—did he set out for Westingborough on Wednesday?"

"We haven't checked up on it, sir," Wadden said, "but I expect, if he didn't want to account to them for the missing time, he might tell them he'd come overland from Marseilles, and mention a day in Paris if he had one over. But probably we shall never find out that part of it. And our problem amounts to locating him after he landed."

"How will you do it?" Morrison snapped, still more irritably.

Wadden blew, long and softly, and made no other reply.

"I wish I could answer you, sir," Head said.

"There is still Jevons," Wadden observed. "Or rather, up to this present time, there is not. There may be, here or on that boat."

"Not on the boat." Abruptly, as he spoke, Morrison stood up, and the other two followed suit. "If he planned and carried out that crime, he's not fool enough to attempt that form of escape. It seems that we can do no more useful discussion for the present, but I must say, Head, I have never before known you utterly at a loss as you seem to be now. I attach very little importance to this Jevons line of inquiry, in spite of the woman's receiving letters from India. That might mean anything, and might be entirely unconnected with Captain Ashford. If you will ring me about this time on Monday, superintendent, I shall be glad to hear what you have to say. I wish you better success by that time, Head—good morning to you both."

When he had gone, Wadden seated himself and stared across his desk. He pursed his lips, but realised the occasion as too serious for blowing. "Laddie, you know what that means. He's giving you till ten-thirty Monday morning to take your hat off and hand over the rabbit. If you haven't found the burrow and dug it out by that time, the finest brains in the country are going to be turned on the problem, and your name is just plain mud. And then, in goes my resignation, but tomato growing wouldn't be the same. Forty-eight hours from now—you've *got* to do it, somehow! The old man's a sport—play up to him!"

"How?" Head asked. "Give me a line to follow."

"Grr-r-r! Fly off out of this and grub in the ashes!" was the reply.

* * *

An elderly, spectacled, half-bald man leaned on the counter of his shop, and tapped the sole of the burned shoe that he had not dissected.

"You'll see, Mr. Head, I've made my examination of only one, in case you want the other one perfect for somebody else to try his hand. Belong to this here train murder, I expect, don't they?"

"They might have a bearing on it," Head admitted.

"Ah! I thought as much. Well, I'll tell you all I can, the way you asked me to see what I could make of 'em, Mr. Head. Hand-stitched, and the very finest and best hand-stitching at that. You see, Mr. Head, in our line of business there ain't so very many of what you'd call artists left, nowadays. Machines have done away with them—youngsters, too, haven't got the patience or the love of their job that us old 'uns had. Why, I remember—but that's not what you want to know. A man of my sort—and you've got to go some miles to find anyone I'd call a fellow craftsman—a man of my sort, knowing work when he sees it, can tell you this is hand work, not machine, though if you went to a shoe-store manager of the modern sort he'd probably tell you it is machine. See?"

"Explain it all," Head bade, and smiled at the old man's enthusiasm.

"Like this. A machine works dead evenly. Your eye couldn't tell that the stitches along here are not dead even. Mine can, because I've stitched leather all my life. This was hand done, but by one of the best of us old-time craftsmen, not by a cobbler. I'd say that pair of shoes cost four or five guineas, unless they were made for sheer love."

"Made by whom?" Head asked. "In this

country, or abroad?"

"You might find men do do stitching like that abroad—I don't say you wouldn't—but then we come to the leather, sir. These heel pieces. Have a look at that, Mr. Head! Not waste stuff, such as they put in the intermediate heel layers of cheap shoes, but—there! That stamp. The crown, and the crossed hammers under it. That's the Mallow trade mark, which goes on to every hide tanned by Mallows. Every hide perfect before they accept it for tanning—Mallow leather, the finest in the world."

"And supposing they exported a hide or two to India?" Head asked.

"Then none of it would ever be used for intermediate heel layers," the old man retorted promptly. "I've had Indian-made stuff through my hands. People like Foster of Carden come to me, when they want good stuff and good work, and I've done their repairs. You see, sir, there's no wear in intermediate layers in a heel, and so they can be made up of anything, as long as the edges show good. No Indian shoemaker doing handwork on a pair of shoes would waste Mallow hide—he'd reckon it a waste—in a part where there's no wear, no matter how much he charged for the finished article. No, sir! He'd fill in with scrap, and put a Mallow layer to take the wear. You might get as good stitching as this out of him—I don't say you wouldn't, because they're wonderfully clever with their hands, but when you take the stitching and the exclusive use of Mallow leather together—London made, sir, and the very best of London make at that. Not a doubt of it. The very best, Mr. Head."

"Give me a few names to try," Head asked. "Possible makers."

"Well, Mr. Head. Well! I'd say Peto, of south Molton Street. Then there's Gibbs in Jermyn Street, Madderley, somewhere just off Cavendish Square—I forget the exact address. Torrens and Barr—no, they're not quite up to this class of work and leather. Fledgeley in Sloane Street. Calman—he's Knightsbridge. Winter is in Maddox Street, and you'll find Farman—no, he's moved out of Conduit Street into New Bond Street, and probably isn't keeping to the old-time quality. And I think, Mr. Head, that's all there are of the old-time individual shoemakers. Yes, I know them all! Many's the clout over the head I had from old Mr. Peto when I was an apprentice in his shop, for what he called spoiling good leather. We were taught in those days that work is a noble expression of the best that is in us, Mr. Head, whether it's on a shoe or a statue in marble. I think, sir, if you work through the names I've given you, you'll come to the end of the men who might have stitched Mallow leather into this sole."

Head finished inscribing the list of names the old man had given him in his notebook, and put both book and pencil away. These shoes had been made to measure, possibly by one of the makers his informant had named. Captain Ashford had not been near London for five years. Although the shoes had been of superb quality, it was unlikely that Captain Ashford had worn them or any others for five years—besides, if he had done so, the original stitching of the soles would not have remained. He would have had them re-soled, in India, almost certainly. There was the trouble with all this reasoning. Almost certainly!

Following that reasoning: whoever had made the fire in the gully had believed, when he saw the embers, that the shoes had been wholly reduced to ash, instead of covered by it. And, since probably—only probably!—these were not Captain Ashford's shoes, they were those of his murderer, who put them in the fire to don the dry pair which he had taken off his victim's feet. What had the murderer done with Captain Ashford's shoes?

"I am very much obliged to you. You left one uncut, in case I felt like consulting another expert. But after your very expert information, I think I shall be able to keep the other sole intact. For the trial, I hope. Thank you very much. Good morning."

And, feeling reasonably confident that the murderer had burned his own shoes, Head emerged from the little shop, entered his car, and went to investigate once more the remains of the fire in the woods—which, by the way, yielded no more than he had already found. Meanwhile, all unsuspected by him, Percy Butters of the Universal descended on the elderly artist in shoe leather, and the result of his interview appeared in nearly every edition of the London evening papers, since his agency catered for them all.

INSPECTOR HEAD HAS A CLUE
TRAIN MURDER: SHOEMAKER INTERVIEWED
Naked Man Tragedy: Clue in Shoe Shop

Thus they revelled. Superintendent Wadden, recipient of London papers direct off the train, blew, and the force of it moved his door an inch or two. He noted the acknowledgment to "Universal" at the end of each paragraph about Head's visit to the shoemaker.

"Butters again! That young man is working up to a gory end. I'll be in at it—damned if I won't!"

He was a little consoled by the fact that the elderly artist in leather had not revealed the object of Head's visit to his shop. All Butters had to tell the world was that Inspector Head was following up a line of inquiry in connection with which he had paid a visit to a shoemaking establishment, which dealt mainly in hunting and sporting footwear and numbered most of the prominent people of the district among its patrons, and that, on leaving the shop, the well-known detective had hurried off to pursue his inquiries elsewhere. Important developments were expected over the week-end.

Knowing the developments the chief constable threatened to bring about, Wadden ground his teeth over that final prophecy.

CHAPTER XIII

Still at Fault

"AND now what?" Thane asked, as Head drew on his hand brake in front of Jevons' farmhouse late on Saturday afternoon. "Do I sit here in the car, or get out and come to the door with you?"

Before Head could reply, the door opened and a big man stepped out from under the trellis and advanced to the side of the car. A bad-tempered man, Head decided at sight of him, broad shouldered and apparently immensely strong, and with a decidedly purplish nose. He laid his large hand on the top of the door that Head had been about to open, and looked across at Thane and then back at the inspector.

"I know you by sight, Mr. Head," he said, "and my wife told me you would call about this time. But I don't know that gentleman."

He spoke evenly, coldly, and with a hint of a question in the final statement. As if he resented this witness to any interview. Thane, after one good look at him, settled himself in his seat and gazed straight before him, as if he were no longer concerned over what might happen.

"Quite so, Mr. Jevons," Head answered him. "He is——"

"One minute!" Jevons interrupted him, and the fingers on the edge of the car door tightened their grip as he spoke. "I know exactly why you've come to see me—what you want, and everything about it."

"That will save us quite a lot of trouble, probably," Head predicted calmly, as he took a cigarette from the case Thane offered.

"Perhaps Mr. Jevons would like one too," Thane suggested.

"I would not," Jevons said. He took a lighter from his vest pocket and flicked it to give Head a light, while Thane lighted his own. "I might resent your coming here like this, Mr. Head, but I don't. You have your duty to do, and I realise it. About Captain Ashford's death."

"My calling on you may or may not be concerned with that," Head told him, as calmly as before. As long as the man chose to make revelations of his own accord, there was no need to question him.

"And my whereabouts on Wednesday night," Jevons pursued, with a shade of satisfaction in his tone over being able to tell the police inspector his purpose here. "That's what you want to know, isn't it?"

"Well?" Head asked, and let the one word serve as encouragement.

"Well, shall I bring you my bill from the Midland Grand hotel in Birmingham for Tuesday and Wednesday nights, or do you want me to go to Birmingham with you to prove I am the man who stayed there those two nights? Because you might think I'd got that bill as alibi and hadn't stayed there myself. I'll go with you—if you compensate me for the time it takes—and then you can be absolutely sure."

"I accept your word for it, Mr. Jevons," Head said. "You need not even take the trouble to show me the Midland Grand bill."

"Then"—there was a hint of gathering anger in Jevons' voice—"what reason had you for coming here to question me? Why suspect me?"

"As answer to that—how did you know, as you obviously did, that you might come under suspicion in something which concerns Captain Ashford?" Head asked, gazing squarely at Jevons as he spoke.

"How did I——?" The halting echo betrayed not a little confusion. "Why, I knew you'd be investigating the murder, didn't I? I knew I was away at the time it was committed—away from home, that is—and knew you came and asked for me yesterday. Why"—he regained confidence as he stated his reasons—"I naturally put two and two together, as soon as my wife told me you'd been looking for me!"

"Naturally?" Head echoed with a thoughtful inflection. "Why should you connect yourself with Captain Ashford? I might have wished to inquire about someone you know, and who also knew Captain Ashford. I might not have been in the least interested in your own movements. Why should I assume that you have any connection with or interest in Captain Ashford?"

"I—well—my being away when the murder was committed," Jevons stammered. "I thought —thought if I accounted for myself——"

"Thought that I did associate you with Captain Ashford," Head suggested in the pause, still gazing hard at his man.

"Why keep harping on his name like that?" Jevons demanded angrily.

"Possibly because I am trying to find all the people who were associated with him in any way—in any way." Head repeated the words and thus gave them significance. "Even if only by correspondence."

"On that, he saw Jevons' lips shut tightly, as had his wife's lips when she had glanced at the car. They opened again to emit—

"I had nothing to do by the man, by correspondence or otherwise."

"Do you know anybody who had to do with him, in any way at all?"

"No."

The denial was definite. Much too definite,

Head felt.

"Man—or woman?" He kept on gazing steadily at Jevons.

"No, I tell you!" There was real anger in the reply. "You took my word over where I was on Wednesday night. Why keep on pestering me about this? How should I know anything at all about him? He didn't live here, and when he was here, he wouldn't make friends in my class."

"And yet I've heard it said that he did," Head remarked.

"Well, I know nothing about it," Jevons declared harshly.

"In that case, I won't trouble you any longer." Head pressed his starter button and engaged gear. "Good day, Mr. Jevons."

He turned the car about.

After it had emerged from the entrance gateway to the farm, Thane spoke.

"Not the man, in any case," he said. "What were you aiming at when you kept on at him like that—or ought I not to ask?"

"Proving to my own satisfaction that the man is a liar," Head answered. "Not an efficient liar. He loses his temper too easily."

"He seemed a bit worried, to me," Thane observed. "When you began hinting that he must be connected with Ashford in some way, I mean. I can tell you with absolute certainty that he was not the man I saw in the train, but I suppose you've unearthed some connection——"

He broke off, evidently hoping that Head would enlighten him.

"I'm very grateful to you for coming to clear him off the list of suspects," Head said. "Now I'll run you straight back to the hall, and get along to attend to some correspondence. How is Sir Bernard?"

"I would say he's got more courage than strength, and there is a big difference between the man he was when I first saw him and what he is now. I'm staying on for a few days yet—funeral arrangements and things of that sort I can save him. And save Miss Ashford, too."

And your own affairs?" Head asked. "Your identity, and money matters? You are leaving them for the present, I suppose?"

"On Sir Bernard's advice, I went to his solicitor," Thane explained. "A regular Tulkinghorn type in Westingborough. Named Barham. Stuffed with family secrets, by the look of him. He accepted me on Sir Bernard's word, and is going to arrange everything for me."

Head turned the car on to the hall drive, and went on to draw up before the pillared portico. He had just a glimpse of Loretta at one of the ground floor windows as he drove away, to pull up again before the Carden Arms, where he asked for Cortazzi.

"Ah, Mr. 'Ead! You stop for ze dinner? I make it especial for you!"

"No, I hope to dine at home to-night, Cortazzi.

I want to ask you a question or two about Captain Ashford——"

"Ah, ze poor gentleman—an' ze poor father!" Cortazzi interjected. "Mr. 'Ead, when 'Arry tell me about it, you could 'ave blow me down wiz a fezzer. It ees vairy shocking, vairy terrible. I feel sad."

"Just when did Harry tell you about it?" Head asked.

"Before ze breakfast yesterday—Noh! It was in ze dining room, after ze breakfast is begin. Yaas. 'E say 'e 'ear it from a man name Potts, of which sometaime I buy ze trout. Ze man Potts come to ask——"

"Buy trout from him, do you?" Head interrupted interestedly.

"Yaas, Mr. 'Ead. Because sometaimes, 'e say, 'e buy ze trout sheap, an' make a leetle profit by sell to me. Vairy fresh, 'is trout."

"They would be," Head observed. "You knew Captain Ashford?"

"I see 'im. Four—five year ago. I read in ze paper it is five year when 'e come on leave, but it do not seem so long. Yaas. No."

"You mean you saw him here in the hotel, then?" Head asked.

"Yaas, Mr. 'Ead. I remember 'e come in 'ere—in ze lounge—for ze drinks, an' 'e 'ave frien's come in too. Two men—I do not know."

"What sort of men? Young—old—can you remember anything of them?"

"Like 'im, I theenk. They talk much an' laugh. Young, they was, like 'im. Frien's of 'is. I do not remember more. Per'aps 'e only come in that one taime, per'aps two taime or three taime more. I do not remember. An' I see 'im an' 'is sister on a 'orse, ride past sometaime."

"Did you ever see him with any woman except Miss Ashford?"

"Not any uzzer, Mr. 'Ead. Noh. You theenk a woman kill 'im in ze train? But ze woman would not take ze clothes off ze uzzer man——"

"You don't know what they'll do, Cortazzi. I won't keep you any longer. And remember—a still tongue about my questioning you."

"No 'otel-keeper talk what 'e is asked, Mr. 'Ead. Else, 'e do not keep 'otel long. Me, I say nozzing at all. Goodnaight, Mr. 'Ead."

* * *

"That car you asked me to inquire about, Mr. Head. Here's all the particulars. I had to make quite a few inquiries." Sergeant Wells held out a sheet of paper which Head took. "Registered to Edward John Smith, at that address, and when I got busy on it I found that Edward John Smith calls himself the Crompton Hire Service. Runton Mews is off a turning out of Queen's Gate, by the map, and the man in charge of the car was another Smith—Albert James, his names are. He turned back in with the car last night—hire finished, they reported."

Head gazed at the written particulars. "Yes, thank you, sergeant," he said. "Anything said about a trunk fallen off the back of the car?"

"Nothing, sir. I expect we'll hear about that in other ways, if at all. You left the trunk at the Carden Arms, you said."

"That is so. Yes, it will probably be a police inquiry."

Thought of the trunk set Head's mind working on another line. He looked into Wadden's room, and found the superintendent still busy over forms with a fountain pen. He began closing the door again.

"Come in, man!" Wadden adjured. "Did he sail on that boat?"

"He did not, and according to Thane he is not our man," Head answered, advancing into the room after closing the door. "Not the man of the train, that is. Therefore, Scotland Yard, because I don't think it will be possible to get what I want before ten-thirty on Monday."

"I might get an extension," Wadden said doubtfully. "That is, if you've got a promising line to haul on. What do you want?"

"Trunks," Head answered. "Trunks and trunks. The dead man's heavy baggage, the not-wanted-on-voyage stuff, which would come through to Tilbury on the *Pathankot*. He'd have left it for forwarding."

"What damned fools we are!" Wadden

observed softly. "If I'd told the old man about that hope this morning, he might have given us longer. Lord knows what we might find! Photos, letters—Head, you've hit it! The story of my life, by Bernard Ashford. Diaries—anything!"

"It will come through to Carden Hall—or will it?" Head asked.

"Where else would he want to park his heavy stuff, man? Of course it'll come through! Monday or Tuesday, Patter Cartison—any old forwarding agents. And we're on velvet from that moment! What's that in your hand—that paper? Anything to do with the case?"

"No. I asked Wells to get me the address of Colonel Thomas' Rolls Royce, thinking it would be Thomas' own address—because he dropped a trunk off the back of the car when he went away from the Carden Arms, and I delivered it back there and told Cortazzi to keep it for him. And that, chief, although it has nothing to do with the case, was absolutely providential, for when Wells handed this slip on to me just now it set me thinking that Ashford couldn't have taken his trunks by air, and they may give us all we want about him. Apparently Thomas doesn't own a car, but can afford to hire Rolls Royces when he wants them—in any case, he hired this car, complete with chauffeur. And I'm grateful to him for losing his trunk, for if he hadn't I'd never have thought of this."

"Shows how inconsequent details may have

big meanings," Wadden commented. "Do we advise Thomas care of the hire people that you found his trunk and left it with Cortazzi to be called for?"

"We do not, chief—we don't take the trouble. Thomas reserved his room at the Carden Arms till Monday, and in addition to that you're certain to have an inquiry for the missing trunk through the usual channels by Monday at the latest. I wonder how soon I can get at Ashford's lost?"

"Having missed it off the boat, you can't intercept it between there and final delivery," Wadden said thoughtfully. "Whoever he instructed to handle it will be clearing it through the customs' on Monday morning, I should say, and then pushing it straight along. Tuesday, probably."

"What about Colonel Morrison and Scotland Yard?" Head asked moodily.

"Laddie, I'll gamble on it. I'll go as far as to describe this idea of yours—this bright idea of yours!—as a clue, if you ain't careful. Moreover, I'll call you a sleuth when I'm talking to him. The sleuth is following up a clue. Smile, Head—we're not dead yet!"

Head leaned over the desk and took off the telephone receiver.

"That you, Wells? Carden Hall, and say I wish to speak to Mr. Thane!"

He replaced the receiver. "I can't ask Sir Bernard, chief—he'd think it sacrilege for us to examine his son's belongings. I want Thane to put it to Miss Ashford, and for them to arrange it between them without the old man knowing anything about it. Best that way."

"Far the best," Wadden agreed. "Lord, why didn't one of us think of this before? You might have been down at Tilbury to go through the stuff there, and have your case in shape by this time, if we had thought of it. Instead, Providence has to arrange to bust a trunk off the back of a car to make you think of the trunks that matter to us."

"And even then I didn't think of it," Head said. "Not till Wells handed me this, and put trunks in my mind again—that will be Thane."

He took off the telephone receiver and put it to his ear.

* * *

"I think, my dear, I will got to bed, early though it is. Say good-night to Mr. Thane for me, will you? The inspector appears to be having a very long conversation with him—you can tell me about it in the morning, if you think it worth while. I am very tired, to night."

Loretta went to the door with her father, and kissed him good-night. Then she returned across the big drawing-room and put more coal on the fire, to stand gazing down into it until Thane came to her.

"I can't help admiring that man," he said, as she gazed inquiringly at him. "He wants to go through your brother's baggage when it turns up, because he thinks there might be something in it to help his inquiries, so he asked me to ask you to help him over it, because the idea of his doing anything of the sort might give pain to your father.'"

"I see." She reflected over it. "Yes, Inspector Head is the sort of man who would think of that. What did you tell him?"

"That I'd ask you, and ring him at ten to-morrow morning, the time he said would suit him. What shall I tell him then?"

"Tell him"—she paused to think—"that if it will help in any way, he can do what he likes about it. Tell him I appreciate his thought in not going direct to my father. And—I expect they have ways of finding out—if he can find how the baggage is coming here, and can stop it to make his examination in some way so that my father shall know nothing about it, I shall be grateful to him. As I am already."

"As you are already," Thane echoed slowly.

"I said that to you, not to him," she said, and turned to gaze down into the fire again. "He was kind when kindness meant much to me."

"How long have you and I known each other?" Thane asked abruptly.

"Quite two days." She looked up at him to answer. "Why?"

"Long enough for me to speak rather plainly?"

"As plainly as you like. Relatives are entitled to quarrel."

"The last thing I would wish is to quarrel with you," Thane said seriously. "Merely a quotation from an old song—'The past is the eternal past.' A very old song—my mother used to sing it when I was a very small child. But it is. And you're quite young, cousin Loretta."

"Meaning——?" Again she glanced up at him, momentarily.

"The most obvious meaning," he said. "You cannot live all your life in the past that makes you grateful to Inspector Head. Think of it! Ten years, even—are you going to consecrate even that length of time to what is not and can never be? If so, you'll waste the years."

"I may not consider it waste," she rejoined quietly.

"Consider, then, that it would be living to yourself," he said. "It would narrow you down to a tiny little peep hole on life—not on life at all, but on a yesterday that is part of the eternal past. And the greatest voice that ever spoke said—'Let the dead past bury its dead,' I believe. Cousin, I'm with you in this new tragedy, wanting to help you and your father through it and see you both come to the memory that means acceptance of the will behind things. And in these two days I've seen how that older tragedy colours your life— darkens it. Wrong."

"It runs in us Ashfords—we cannot forget," she said.

"I'm an Ashford too—look at my nose if you think I'm claiming too much," he bade. "But I've learned—you've *got* to forget! Or change the nature of the memory, not live in it, but get up over it and make it something sacred, perhaps, a help for to-morrow rather than a dwelling-place that keeps you in yesterday. The very little you've told me is enough to make me realise that the man you meant to marry was one worth all you gave him, capable of the limit of self-sacrifice for his friend. Do you think he would wish you to go sorrowful all your days? Wasn't he more the heroic figure who would go laughing into disaster, and hope to look down from his Valhalla and see you laughing because he'd been so splendid? Forgive me if I say too much about him. I feel——"

"Oh, you're right!" She turned and grasped his arm as she interrupted him. "Laughing down from his Valhalla—but I couldn't see it before. Of course he is! And—and—yes. Just that."

Thane reached up his free hand and took hers, smiling at her.

"When this—this present trouble—is all over, I wouldn't like to think it meant the end of all things," he said. "I mean, if you're really going to laugh, I should like to help."

"It isn't time, yet," she reminded him, sombrely.

"No, it isn't. But when it comes?"

"Help me then as you're helping now, cousin Leo. Good-night—I'm going to bed. Put the screen in front of the fire when you feel like leaving it."

CHAPTER XIV

Trunks

ON Sunday morning, unless some matters of urgency demanded his attendance at the police station in his official capacity, Superintendent Wadden usually strolled in as might any casual visitor at a little before ten o'clock, not in uniform as on week-days, but resplendent in civilian attire which emphasised his bulk, and with an unsympathetic bowler which revealed a dark red line on his forehead when removed. On that first Sunday of April, he appeared at the usual time and looked into the charge room, where, since it was Wells' Sunday off, Harrison, the junior sergeant, sat industriously reading his Sunday paper.

"Morning, Harrison. All quiet as usual?"

"Quite, sir. Three drunks from last night in the cells."

"Three, eh? Anything interesting in that rag

you're reading?"

"I was looking over the account of the case—the train case, sir."

"Ah! I haven't seen that one—only respectable papers come to my house. I'll just have a look at yours, if you don't mind."

Lacking anything of greater importance—there were only two wars and an international treaty worth calling news just then—the paper had made a splash over Mystery of Naked Man, Unparalleled Ferocity of Train Murderer, Ghastly Fate of Baronet's Son, and a series of cross-heads in the columns devoted to the crime. Among them Wadden fastened on "Possible Political Aspect," beneath which he read—

"It is not beyond the bounds of possibility that this brilliant young officer lost his life while engaged in carrying out some task laid on him when, ostensibly, he set out from India on leave. Though the fact is not generally known, the least advertised of our Services is recruited in part from Army officers whose special gifts fit them for duties more onerous and in times of peace far more dangerous than those which fall to the lot of the majority. While there is nothing as yet to justify a definite statement to the effect that the murder is due to such a motive, the bizarre nature of the crime and effort at disfiguring the victim beyond recognition render possible a political aspect of the tragedy. In the present unsettled state of Eastern politics, anything is possible, for, as has been demonstrated on more than one occasion, there is in existence a fanatical organisation whose members stop at nothing."

Reaching the end of this allegation, which was also the foot of the last column devoted to the crime, Wadden blew heavily and folded the paper, but did not hand it back. He put on his bowler.

"Lend me this for a few minutes, Harrison."

"Certainly, sir. I've just about finished with it."

Emerging from the police station, Wadden crossed the road, entered the Duke of York—where, he knew, such reporters as might be covering the case would have their quarters—and sought the dining room. There he found Percy Butters, Universal Agency's representative, breakfasting late and alone, and, marching up to Butters' table, he put down the paper beside the young man's coffee cup, his thumb on the paragraph he had just read. Butters shifted his cup, and looked up at his visitor.

"Morning, superintendent. Anything to hand out to me?"

"Read that!" Wadden adjured grimly. "Where I'm pointing."

Butters glanced down at the paragraph. "Seen it already," he said.

"Did you send it in? Is it your people's doing?"

"Lord, no! I send 'em facts, not guff like that. Have to dress the facts up a bit and swell 'em out, of course, but Universal don't hand out pies with no meat in 'em, like that one, supe."

"Which of your feller-scavengers down here did it?"

"Have a heart, supe. We're the best in the world, all of us. Scavengers! No, no! I've heard us called a few things, but——"

"Which of you sent that muck from here?" Wadden interrupted.

"None of us. Have another look at it, supe. Y'see they've leaded all they dare—it looks thin, that tripe, right from the start. They had the blocks made for the guard's photo and that view of Carden Hall, and when they made up the page with these columns allotted to the story, it was short, stretch it how they would. So I'd say the chief sub called a youngster and told him to write to fill—write anything about it that came into his head, to bump the story out a bit. No agency'd send out a piece of garbage like that— and I know if I wrote such a huddle of rotten English I'd get fired one time. Done in the office, like the talk about record crowds at railway stations in holiday time."

"What's that got to do with this?" Wadden demanded.

"Nothing. Except it's done the same way. Some youngster is told to do a par on Victoria, or Euston, or any other terminus, and he just sits down and reels off what he saw as special representative on the spot, and the only spot he's seen is the full stop on his typewriter. This was done the same way—bet you anything you like. It hints at a sensation, the public gobble it down, and there you are. I'll bet you a new hat to a fag end that piece of tripe was never sent from here."

"Whoever concocted it, I'd like to wring his neck," Wadden said, as he took up the paper, folded it again, and tucked it under his arm.

"Why?" The pressman looked up interestedly. "Is there anything in it? Are you working along that line and want it kept quiet?"

"If you so much as hint at anything of the sort," the superintendent answered impressively, "your name in Westingborough won't be merely mud in future, but dirt, and devil a line of print will I ever give you."

"Not a word, supe. Leave it to me—not a word till the story breaks, and then for the love of Pete let me in on it early."

"You watch your step, then—that's all, young feller."

He returned to the charge room and put the paper on Harrison's desk.

"Finished with it, thanks, sergeant," he said. "Has Inspector Head looked in yet this morning, do you know?"

"He's in his room now, sir—been there an hour or more."

Wadden went along to Head's room and entered. The inspector turned from the window, where he had been standing, hands in pockets, gazing out into the flagged and brick-walled back yard of the premises.

"Come out of it, man!" Wadden adjured. "Make it a *dies non*, as it is. You'll come to it all the fresher tomorrow."

"One or two things to get out of the way to-day, chief," Head answered deliberately. "I'm going over to Crandon this morning."

"Umm-m! I'd rather see you take the day off. Head, I've just put in a spot of good work on young Butters. Remember that J 35 that you wouldn't believe in, and the old man scoffed at as well?"

Head nodded. "What about it?" he asked, with little apparent interest. "There is nothing in it, I feel certain."

"No, but there's a hint of something of the sort in Harrison's Sunday rag. Wherefore I buzzed over to Percy Butters, accused him of sending it in, and managed to get him nicely het up as to whether the case is going to develop into a secret service mystery. He'll go trailing around trying to uncover a secret service bump-off, which lets us out."

"Or, if it happens to be that, lets us in," Head observed grimly.

"Leads us straight to our man, you mean," Wadden dissented, with rather too obvious cheerfulness. "That young feller's got a nose for a case that would make a foxhound look like a splash of green paint. Head, we're not corpses yet, either of us. Stop looking like one."

"You're quite right, chief. I am not pleased with myself."

"You were just as unhappy, I remember, over the Gatton case—and the very next day it fell into your hand," Wadden remarked. "Well, *I'm* going to church this morning with the old lady, like a decent citizen, and then I want to go over a booklet I had sent me about a new fertiliser —some sort of radio-active compound, they say, that looks to me just the thing to make young tomato plants happy. And you're for Crandon, you say. Think you'll find anything there?"

"A talk with Marsden, to find out if any of his men saw anything early on Thursday morning that might give us a line of inquiry. He promised when I rang him that he'd go into it thoroughly for us. And then the ticket collector who comes on duty at the station an hour from now."

"Mr. X did not get off the train at Crandon," Wadden said.

"Rynewald," Head explained laconically.

"Rynewald?" The superintendent stared in utter incredulity. "But Thane gave him a clean bill, man! I'm sure of him, too."

"I'm sure of nobody till I find our man," Head retorted. "I'm not sure that I attach much to Thane's clean bills, either. He is not and owns he is not an observant man, and if that J 35 means anything Rynewald fits better than anyone else. Checking up on him does no harm."

"Have it your own way, since you won't take the day off as I'd like to see you do. And we'll get after Ashford's baggage first thing in the morning, and I'll ask the old man to give us another couple of days before dragging in the super-sleuths. You'll deliver the goods by then."

"A pessimist," Head observed sourly, "is a man who has to listen to optimists—in case you didn't know. I'm for Crandon, chief."

He took his hat and went out. Wadden followed, more slowly.

"The trunks'll give it," he told himself, and tried to believe it.

* * *

Taking the marsh road from Carden to Crandon added over five miles to Head's drive, but he was in no hurry, and a thought of Jevons induced him to turn off the main road so that he might pass within sight of the farmhouse. He expected—and gained—nothing by the diversion: the pleasantly-weathered frontage of the house, as he saw it from the road, gave no sign of life, nor was any smoke visible over the chimney tops. The deeply-set, rather small windows were all closed, or so nearly closed as to appear so at that distance: some hens were scratching and pecking in the straw of a cattle-yard at the side of the big barn, and for all that Head could see they had the farm to themselves. He had a momentary consciousness of the impossibility of seeing completely into other people's lives: one could never really know a man like Jevons, or a woman like his wife. And both, in some way, were connected with this case of Captain Ashford: their reactions went to show it.

Jevons was not the man of the train: the utter confidence with which he had offered evidence of a stone-wall alibi negatived the idea, but left him in some way connected with Ashford, angrily uneasy on being questioned about a possible connection. Through his wife? Who wrote to her from Jelalapur? She had changed her attitude utterly over something she had seen either in or near Head's car, and though he thought the initials on the trunk in the dickey had caused the change, he was not sure. Certainly Thomas, retired from service in India three years and more ago, had not been her correspondent. Nor, on the face of it, could there be anything to connect her with Thomas, unless his annual visits to the Carden Arms had been made because of her. But then, had that been so, there would have been talk in the district that would have come to the ears of men like Plender, no matter how careful the pair might have been. And, though a five-year-old rumour of something between her and Ashford was still current, there appeared to be nothing concerning her and Thomas. Had there been,

Plender would have known it, and passed it on when he mentioned her, Head felt sure.

Again, what was there about her that made Head himself feel that he ought to recognise her? He went over his mental picture of the woman carefully, but in vain. It was one of the half-memories that are irritating because they will not grow to completeness, a resemblance to something or somebody—picture, person, or even dream—that stayed just out of reach. She was like—like whom? Like what?

Ashford could not have seen her during the last five years. Would those trunks of his reveal any knowledge of her—intimacy with her?

Hope of a solution to the puzzle, Head realised, had narrowed down to the contents of those trunks. There seemed no other line of inquiry.

Inspector Marsden was not at Crandon police station. Like Wadden, he took Sunday off, and Head found him in his garden, prepared to lament the prolonged spell of dry weather and the early appearance of green fly, while he snipped at shrubs with a pair of secateurs.

"And I've no news for you, old man," he said. "I've had every blessed man jack on the mat and put 'em through it. Not only the ones on duty over the time that matters, but the whole lot, in case any one at all might have heard something I could pass on to you. Frankly, though, I didn't think I would get anything. The man who was daring and clever enough to plan and carry out that little lot in the train is not the sort to let a silly mistake trip him up. It's—it's quite unique."

Head let the solecism pass without so much as a smile. "Very good of you to take all that trouble," he said. "If you do hear anything——"

"Certainly, old man, cer-tainly! Only too glad to help if I can. But you're not in a hurry to-day, surely. Stop and help to commit an assault on the Sunday joint and veg., won't you? You're not *working* to-day, surely?"

"It's very good of you, but I want to clear up a few points in readiness for to-morrow," Head answered. "Look me up when you're in Westingborough, and we'll have a talk—I can't stop for one to-day."

He went on to the railway station, arriving in the yard just as a down train went on its way after depositing a dozen or so of Sunday travellers on the town. Just leaving the barrier as Head went through the booking-office was "Hoots" Aird, the grizzled and very Scottish collector who had been on duty over the period that Head wanted cleared up. A telephone talk to the station master had revealed Aird as the one concerned, and had revealed, too, that he was on duty to-day.

"I were expectin' ye," said Hoots. "Station master tell't me. Whit wey will I know anything, d'ye think? Thurrsday morrn, he said."

"You came on duty at what time on Thursday

morning?" Head asked.

"Time f'r the seven-ten. She's local, up."

"That is, from Westingborough. Who got off here on Thursday?"

Hoots pulled at his short, bristly whiskers. "Twa drovers an' Mrs. Kent, the porrk-butcher's wumman. Her sister at Westingborough's by way o' givin' birrth to a child. An' the drovers wanted the road to the farrm wheer was a sale o' live stock, Thurrsday."

"I want to find a tall, strongly-built man, with a sunburnt face and rather red nose, quite possibly not a stranger in this part of the world," Head said. "I think he would be wearing a soft felt hat, and either wearing or carrying a raincoat or some sort of overcoat. Arrived here, if at all, before midday on Thursday." He judged it best to describe his man, and find out if Hoots could remember him, before going through all the trains—both up and down—stopping here on Thursday morning and inquiring about arrivals and departures.

"One o' that sorrt—aye, 'twas Thurrsday morrn, too— an' theer were a furriner met him, off the eleven-fifty down," Hoots said slowly. "Firrst-class, from London. Taller'n yerself, he were, an' gey broad acrost the shoulders. An' a big red nose. Aye, I mind him. An' the furriner were nigh as tall but not so broad, wi' darrk eyes like a wumman's, a fine-lookin' man. Stannin' aboot an' lookin' at the clock ten meenits or mair till the train come in. An' he said—'I thocht maybe ye'd miss it,' an' the ither says—'got up earrly f'r once,' an' laughed. Aye, I mind 'em weel. An' the big one had a big case in his han', an' it were lettered wi' a E an' anither letter an' a R, but I dinna remember the ither letter. A bonnie lad in a fecht, he'd be, that one."

Rynewald, past question. Eleven-fifty Crandon reached Westingborough at twelve noon, having travelled express from London with no other stops. Since Rynewald had been on it, he could hardly have dropped off the last train of the preceding night to make that track through the woods. With a fast car waiting, he might have got back to London in time to board this express just before nine o'clock, but it was in the last degree unlikely. Having stopped to make the fire in the gully, he could not have got out of the woods much before four o'clock in the morning, which would give less than five hours before the eleven-fifty at Crandon left London. An almost perfect alibi, though not quite.

"Do you remember anyone else that morning who fits the description by which you remember this man, Aird. Off either up or down trains?"

Caressing his whiskers again, Hoots reflected deeply, and at last shook his head. "Nane," he said. "I mind anither nigh his size, but he were waitin' to meet a wumman off the eleven-fifty, not travellin' by train at all. He knew the furriner, an' they talkit a wee bit whiles they waitit. But ye'd no accuse him o' a red neb, I'm thinkin'."

"Did you hear what they said to each other?" Head asked.

Hoots shook his head. "I didna listen," he answered. "The eleven thirrty-three up were late, I mind, an' I were takkin' tickets off the passengers comin' up fra the subway till nigh on when the express come in. Then I mind the furriner said tae the ither—'Yon's my man, corrnel,' an' then they baith waitit an' said nae mair."

"And this colonel was meeting a woman?" Head suggested.

"Aye, a darrk an' han'some one, too. Bates hisself—he's the foreman porrter—fetched her luggage oot past me, an' I mind the corrnel tellin' him he'd see a Rolls in the yaird, an' the driver'd tak' the wumman's suit cases. I took a firrst-class London ticket off her."

Disposing of Colonel Thomas, who had driven over from the Carden Arms to meet his wife, Head reflected. He, too, could be ruled out, now.

"These are arrivals, Aird. Can you remember anyone corresponding to my description—big and red-nosed, say—getting on any train here on Thursday, at any time while you were on duty?"

"I dinna mind one," Hoots said thoughtfully. "Earrlier i' the week, Monday or Tuesday, I mind one o' that sorrt I clipped for Birrmingham, an' he come off a train from the norrth yesterday, the three-thirrteen up, it'd be. Great big men wi' red nebs are no so plentiful."

"I think them far too plentiful," Head dissented acidly. "Well, thank you very much, Aird, and congratulations on a good memory."

The interview had served little purpose, he reflected as he drove away, except that he could now dismiss both Thomas and Rynewald from his mind altogether as far as identity of either with the man in the train went. Jevons too. Major Fitton was not worth troubling about. Nothing more could be done until Ashford's baggage off the *Pathankot* arrived, and then, if it yielded nothing which would open up a line of inquiry, the chief constable would take the case out of Head's hands.

Between them, Ashford and his murderer had completely covered all tracks between Ashford's arrival in England by air, and the discovery of his body in the train. He had disappeared for some purpose of his own, letting his father and sister remain ignorant of his arrival, and, except for a snapshot of him mounted and in polo kit, the latest photograph they had of him was over five years old, and in that he was in uniform. Which meant that, if both photographs were circulated, there was practically no chance of their being recognised as his. Further to that, the murderer's theatrical and apparently purposeless trick of dressing Ashford's body in Thane's clothing, and taking away any baggage which the dead man may have had with him, revealed itself now as having been done with a very definite purpose. No description of the clothes Ashford had been wearing or of anything connected with him after his arrival was available for circulation, and, added to that, there was no telling whether he had been alone for the period of his disappearance, or accompanied by either man or woman. His heavy baggage might yield letters, photographs, or some other evidence of his associations of the past five years, but assuredly it would not reveal what he had done or where he had been during the last week of his life.

With the car back in its garage at the police station, Head walked to his home in time for the midday meal. The maid his wife kept had laid the table—for one, he noted—when he entered the dining room, and beside the plate was an unaddressed envelope which he opened, to read, pencilled on a half sheet of notepaper—

DEAR JEREMY,

Since you are much too busy to find time for me, even on Sunday, I am going over to Crandon for the afternoon. Susan is off for the afternoon, but I shall be back in time to get my own supper —and yours, if you condescend to come home for it.

CLARE.

"Justifiable, I suppose," he said to himself as he tore the missive to pieces and dropped it on the laid fire. Since the east wind was harsh and the sky had clouded over during the past hour, he lighted the fire. Clare would go to put flowers on her sister's grave in Crandon cemetery, and return in the evening to treat him with cool aloofness till bedtime. And he had done no real good—he might just as well have followed Wadden's advice, taken the day off and gone for a drive with Clare.

Everything was going wrong!

CHAPTER XV

The Warlingham

BACK in the charge room on Monday morning as usual, Sergeant Wells answered the inquiring look Head cast at him from the doorway.

"Nothing, sir, except a message from Mr. Thane that Sergeant Harrison took yesterday morning at ten thirty-five. Mr. Thane said you expected him to ring you, but since you weren't in he'd ring again about the same time this morning."

It being then only nine o'clock, Head went along to his own room and dealt with such routine correspondence as awaited him. He had just finished when Wadden entered, and seated himself beside the desk.

"Anything to tell the old man out of yesterday's inquiries?" the superintendent asked, as he carefully filled his pipe.

"Nothing whatever," Head answered curtly,

and taking off his telephone receiver, asked Wells to get through to Carden Hall and ask for Mr. Thane. Replacing the receiver, he sat back with tightly closed lips.

"Might get something from there," Wadden prophesied, gloomily.

Head did not answer, but sat still until the buzzer sounded, when he took off the receiver and listened. Then with—"Thank you, sergeant," he replaced it and leaned back again.

"Not there," he explained. "Left in the car, with Miss Ashford driving, nearly half an hour ago. I wonder——"

"Coming here—a pound to a penny on it," Wadden declared. "Nearly due, too, if they've been gone all that time. But there's one thing I've been thinking, Head. That likeness of Thane to the Ashford family gave me the idea while I was considering things last night."

"Well?" The monosyllable was hardly encouraging.

"Thane's only a distant relation, and yet there's that likeness. When you come to brothers, there's much more chance of a strong likeness. I was thinking about Jevons offering you a Midland Grand receipt, and offering to go to Birmingham with you to clinch the alibi. But supposing the brother who went to Canada stayed at the Midland Grand last Tuesday and Wednesday nights, and was so like this one that he felt safe in offering you that alibi? With the brother gone you can't check up on it."

"I think, chief, you've got Jevons on the brain," Head retorted coldly. "In addition to which, Thane said he was not the man."

"And you yourself said you don't altogether believe in Thane's verdicts, because he's naturally unobservant," Wadden pointed out.

On that, Head started up suddenly. "You've reminded me—if there's still time for it before Thane gets here." He took his soft felt hat and raincoat off their pegs as he spoke. "If I can get out to a chemist's and back in time, chief, you meet Thane when he gets here. Look mysterious, tell him you've got someone else for him to identify, and take him along to the cells to do it. Wells can tell you which cell—I'll get him to lock me in—if there's time."

"What the——?" Wadden began, rising to his feet. But he did not finish it, for by the time he had got the two words out, Head had gone.

The superintendent went back to his own room and sat there puzzling over this sudden move until Wells ushered Thane in to him. Then, mindful of what Head had asked, he rose impressively.

"Good morning, Mr. Thane. About that heavy baggage, I suppose?"

"Yes. A letter from the forwarding agents about it. Miss Ashford got hold of the letter and kept it from Sir Bernard. So far, the thought of the heavy baggage doesn't seem to have occurred to him——"

"I see," Wadden interrupted. "But before we go into that, another little matter of identification is bothering us, and Inspector Head said you might be able to help. Do you mind coming along with me?"

"Not in the least, if I can be any use," Thane agreed. "You don't mean to say you've got the man you're look for?"

"You'll see," Wadden answered. He led along the corridor to the charge room. "The key of that cell Inspector Head told you to give me, sergeant," he demanded, and Wells handed it over.

"Number five, sir," he explained.

With Thane following him, Wadden went along to the range of cells, unlocked and opened the door, and beckoned Thane forward. He had an idea of what Head intended to do, now, and his glance inside confirmed it. For there, with his back to the little light that came through the high window, his hat pulled down to hide more than half his forehead, and his overcoat buttoned to the throat, stood one whom even Wadden had difficulty in recognising as Head, at first.

"See what you make of him, Mr. Thane."

"Yes." Thane backed from the open door after one look at the forbidding, still figure. "That's the man. You've got him."

"Take just one more look, Mr. Thane."

It was Head's voice, and as Thane, staring incredulously, started forward into the doorway, Head took off his hat and unbuttoned the overcoat. He came out from the cell, and Wadden grinned at sight of his reddened nose and cheeks, while Thane almost whispered—

"It occurred to me last night, to test you if I got the chance, Mr. Thane," Head said. "I had just time to slip in at the chemist's along the street and buy some rouge and a pocket mirror. Nothing else."

"Then—it makes your nose look half as big again," Thane said. "And—you mean to say—but then, from what the superintendent said, I was expecting to see the man who drugged me, don't you see?"

"Exactly. And when you dined with me at the Carden Arms, and when you went to Jevons' place with me, you were not expecting to see him."

"Yes, but—I'm absolutely sure of myself, over them. Besides, I only took one look at you in this make-up—I had plenty of time to look at Jevons and at all the others you pointed out over that dinner——"

"Just one moment, Mr. Thane. All those others were in evening clothes—no, Major Fitton was not, I remember. But the others were. Now take any one of those three—Major Fitton, Rynewald, and Colonel Thomas. Pull a hat down over his face as I pulled mine, button him into an overcoat like this, and will you still be certain about them?"

"Not—not about Rynewald, perhaps. The other two—yes."

"Thomas, I think, we can ignore," Head said. "He met his wife at Crandon with the Rolls-Royce the next morning, which puts him at the Carden Arms the night before, probably. I can make certain of that from Cortazzi. But I calculated out that Rynewald, if he planned carefully, could just have got off the train when you pulled the cord and got back to London in time to come down again by the train Mirza Khan met. Of Fitton's movements I know nothing, and it will be worth while to look into them, I think, since you've proved so unreliable——"

"It wasn't a fair test!" Thane protested, interrupting. "The superintendent led me to expect—and as I say, your nose looks half as big again, while you had your back to the light and your face shaded——"

"Let's go along and hear about this baggage, Mr. Thane," Wadden interrupted in turn. "I'd say this was what errand boys call a fair cop, and when we do get our man you'll have to be careful what you say in the witness box." He led the way to his own room, and Head paused on the way to ask Sergeant Wells for methylated spirit with which to get rid of the rouge he had used on himself.

Still looking thoroughly disconcerted, Thane

took the chair at the end of Wadden's desk and handed over a letter which the superintendent unfolded and read in silence. Then Head entered, dabbing at his nose with the handkerchief he had soaked in methylated spirit.

"Listen to this, Head," Wadden bade crisply. "Addressed to Sir Bernard Ashford at Carden Hall, sent by Currie and Moss, continental and general carriers and forwarding agents, of Lower Regent Street."

"Miss Ashford told me Captain Ashford got them to handle his baggage the last time he was on leave, but she had forgotten their name until she saw it on their envelope—which came by this morning's post and she opened to prevent Sir Bernard from seeing it," Thane put in.

"It might be a gold mine, for us," Wadden said. "Listen, Head—

DEAR SIR,

We received instructions from Captain Ashford on the 27th instant, to clear through customs and deliver to your address four trunks, of which Captain Ashford forwarded us the keys at the same time, comprising his baggage on S.S. *Pathankot*, arriving to-day at Tilbury. Having seen the reports of Captain Ashford's death, we feel we ought to advise you that the baggage in question will be cleared through customs on Monday morning, and immediately despatched for delivery at Carden Hall, all charges to be paid by you as consignee on arrival of the baggage. Should you, however, wish to alter the instructions, you can do so either by telegram or telephone to us not later than noon on Monday. We shall be pleased to act on any instructions you may transmit to us by these means, and, failing receipt of such, shall despatch the baggage as desired by Captain Ashford, in which event it will be delivered at Carden Hall not later than 4 p.m. on Tuesday, April 3rd.

Assuring you of our best attention at all times,

We are,

Yours faithfully,

CURRIE & Moss. *p.p.* F. L. Richardson.

"Hand it over, chief." Head reached out for the letter. "I think it may prove a gold mine, as you say, if——" Glancing at the heading, he took off Wadden's telephone receiver and listened. "Oh, Wells—get me Currie and Moss, forwarding agents, and ask for F. L. Richardson"—he gave the telephone number on the letter heading—"put him through to me in the superintendent's room. Police priority, tell the operator."

He replaced the receiver, and Wadden nodded approval at him.

"Better scrub that nose of yours a bit more, laddie—it's a shade on the pink side, yet. Are you telling them to divert the baggage?"

"I'll hear what this Richardson has to tell me,

first," Head answered. "We may get something more important than the baggage."

"Miss Ashford asked me to tell you," Thane put in, "if you want to examine it, she'll tell whoever brings it to deliver it here, and repay you any charges they make on it if you let her know the amount."

"That will do admirably," Head agreed. "Whatever I get out of this man, I think we shall need to go through it. There may be letters or something that will bear on the case. But before that—Ah!"

For the buzzer sounded, and he took off the receiver again.

"I want to speak to Mr. Richardson, please —Oh, that is Mr. Richardson. A letter of yours addressed to Sir Bernard Ashford, about Captain Ashford's baggage off the *Pathankot*. You remember it?"

The other two heard a murmur from the transmitter.

"Yes. This is a police inquiry, in connection with Captain Ashford's death—in connection with the murder of Captain Ashford. We do not wish to divert the baggage—you are to deliver it in accordance with Captain Ashford's instructions. But I want you to tell me—can you lay hands on those instructions? They were written, of course, since you say in your letter that he sent his keys with them. Have you got them?"

Another, lengthier reply could be heard in the transmitter.

"Yes," Head said, look them up. "I'll hold on while you get them."

He waited, and Thane and Wadden sat silent. Then—"No, wait a minute! I don't want the text of what he says—not yet, at least. What I do want to know—from where are those instructions sent? What address, if any, is at the head of them?"

Another reply, at which Head frowned and made an impatient gesture.

"Never mind about it being crossed out! I want you to read me the heading, all you can decipher of it. Quite plain, is it? Well —Warlingham Hotel, Brendonbury Way, North. Right! Hold that letter. I am Inspector Head of the Westingborough police, and I will call for it to-day. Follow Captain Ashford's instructions about delivering the baggage. I shall call at your office for that letter this afternoon. Good-bye."

He replaced the receiver. Wadden drew a very deep breath, and exhaled it gently. Then he nodded in a satisfied way.

"I'll call the old man in a few minutes," he said. "Super-sleuths is orf, laddie. This uncovers the right end of the trail."

"Perhaps—and even if it does we have all the way to go," Head observed doubtfully. "But—yes. Mr. Thane, how did you get here?"

"Miss Ashford drove me," Thane answered.

"We decided you ought to see this letter at once—and it looks as if we were right."

"More right about that than some other things," Wadden remarked.

"It wasn't a fair test," Thane insisted, with a shade of irritation.

"Suppose we forget it, for the present," Head suggested. "What I wanted to ask—I understand there are two photographs of Captain Ashford available, and the one on horseback in polo kit shows his face clearly. I'd like those two to take with me. Will you ask Miss Ashford for me?"

"More than that—I'll fetch them for you," Thane offered. "I'm quite sure she'll do anything she can to clear up this mystery."

"The clearing up may prove a painful business, both for her and Sir Bernard," Head remarked gravely, "but you needn't tell her I suggested that it might. Can you meet me at the station here with those two photographs in time for me to catch the twelve-eighteen for London?"

Thane looked at his watch. "I'll be there by twelve-ten," he said.

"And if I'm not back by to-morrow afternoon, tell Miss Ashford we leave it to her to be here or not, just as she sees fit, for when the superintendent makes his examination of Captain Ashford's baggage."

* * *

The clock on the wall behind the dark, smallish, hook-nosed man at the roll-top desk stated the time as half-past four. Outside the office, the afternoon traffic of Regent Street roared and hummed and honked. The dark man held out a letter and Head took it.

"Was that all the communication you had from him, Mr. Richardson?"

"I believe he telephoned, first, and the girl who took the message asked him to write in and send the keys. He didn't come here. I'll get the girl in for you to ask her, if you like."

"Thank you—no. I haven't too much time, and this covers what I wanted to know. And the trunks have gone on, you say?"

"We are arranging to have them delivered from Carden station by our local agent to-morrow—they get there by the three-thirty passenger."

"Very good. That's all I wanted to know, thank you."

"All I wanted to know from you," he amended, speaking to himself as he crooked a finger at a crawling taxi, out in the street. He leaned toward the driver as the vehicle stopped beside the kerb.

"The Warlingham Hotel, Brendonbury Way, North London," he directed. "I want you to take the quickest way to it, not the cheapest."

"The quickest'll be the cheapest, sir," the driver said with a smile.

Head got in, and studied the letter in his

hand as the cab moved off. The text of it, simple directions for the delivery of four trunks at Carden Hall and a statement that keys were enclosed, did not interest him overmuch. He noted that Ashford had scored out the address at the top of the half-sheet of good quality notepaper, and had gone to a good deal of trouble to render it undecipherable. He had inked it over very thoroughly, and, since the lettering was not embossed, probably had believed he had blacked it out, but there was an iridescence in the printing ink which caused it to show through all that the pen had deposited over it, quite probably with more clarity now than when the pen-ink had first dried. Even the telephone exchange and number, in quite small type, were readable if the paper were held at a certain angle.

And, naturally, Ashford had not thought that this order to a business firm would ever be produced as evidence against him—or against his murderer, indirectly. Had he been alive to receive his baggage, it would never have come to light, of course.

The taxi-driver, keeping to other than main ways, crossed Oxford Street, went along Gloucester Place, and came out to turn up by Lord's toward Swiss Cottage. Beyond it, he kept on toward Golder's Green, passing the inviting end of the bye-pass road to the North, and then, unfamiliar with the northern suburbs, Head eyed his surroundings and found that they consisted mainly of "estates" of which the houses were for sale on the instalment system, except for such as were already in occupation. Pretentious frontages, boards advertising "show" houses—the taxi turned off from a road in which much building was still in progress, and went along by older, more substantial dwellings, to come at last to a mansion set back a good fifty yards from the road, with which it was connected by a well-kept, shrub-bordered, gravelled drive. A flamboyant notice board beside the open gates announced that the Warlingham Hotel possessed ten acres of grounds, with swimming pool, tennis and squash courts, a magnificent dance floor, sundry other amenities, and was open to non-residents, while Stanley Atherton was the resident manager. With this information, Head got out from the taxi and prevented the green-uniformed giant who had opened the door from snatching his suit case, after which he paid off the driver, feeling sure he could get another taxi with little difficulty when he had finished here.

"Staying, sir, or just tea?" the green-uniformed one asked.

"I want to see the manager," Head answered. "You can take him that card, and I prefer to carry this suit case myself, thank you."

"Just as you like," green-coat answered, with a vast diminution of respect after the one glance he gave the card. "This way."

He led along the opulently-appointed entrance corridor to a small room at the back of the premises, and opened the door.

"Wait there, and I'll tell Mr. Atherton," he bade.

The room was quite plainly furnished as a sitting room, contrasting very definitely with the showy and expensive fitments of such other apartments as Head had been able to glimpse in passing their doorways. He put his suit case on the centre table, and had had time to light himself a cigarette when a stout man appeared and entered the room to stand and stare with a mixture of apprehension and hostility.

"Mr. Atherton?" Head asked.

"That is my name. Inspector Head?" He glanced at the card he held.

"That is my name. I want information, Mr. Atherton, about a man I have reason to believe stayed in this hotel last week, possibly alone, and possibly not." He opened his case, took from it an envelope, and extracted the two photographs Thane had handed him at the beginning of this journey. He laid them both face upward on the table, and Atherton came forward to gaze down at them silently.

"Neither of them is very recent," Head said. "Can you recognise either of them as a portrait of anyone staying here last week?"

Atherton looked up at him suddenly. "We do not want scandal in this hotel, inspector," he said. "There was the Barrowby divorce case, not long ago. It did us a lot of harm, I tell you."

"You think this might involve a divorce case, then?" Head asked.

"What else?" Atherton shrugged his shoulders as he asked it.

"Those two"—Head pointed at the photographs—"are portraits of Captain Ashford, the victim in the train murder case, and I don't need more than your manner to tell me you recognise them."

"Mein Gott!" Atherton stared aghast at the photographs.

"When did he arrive here?" Head demanded sharply.

"He arrive—I think we sit down, Inspector Head. Mein Gott, yes! This is different. I did not know. Yes. He arrive here—Tuesday week. Yes. Eight days he stay here, altogether. To last Wednesday."

"Alone?"

"Alone? No! They never stay here alone. We have but three single rooms in the hotel. And he was the man they murder in the train!"

"Did he stay under his own name?" Head asked.

"No. Barnard, was the name he sign. Mr. and Mrs. Barnard. You have a photograph of the lady too—yes? I tell you, if you show me——"

"I have no photograph of her," Head interrupted him. "Tell me all you can about her.

Did they arrive together?"

"No. He arrive on Tuesday afternoon, and book the room for himself and his wife, he tell me—Mr. and Mrs. Barnard. I myself was in the office while the reception clerk have her tea. About five o'clock. The lady arrive in time for dinner. I do not know if they attend the dance after dinner, or go out. They hired a car for drives. He asked me, and I told him where he could hire the car. Drives in the afternoon."

"Yes. What was the lady like? Describe her as fully as you can."

"She was about my height, the rather tall medium height for a lady. Tailor made—a good costume, well-cut, but I see her only in the one suit all the time, in the daytime. And I do not notice more than one evening frock, which is not very low cut, and is I think black lace over yellow silk. Very good clothes, I think. She is dark, with nice dark eyes and dark hair, not too much made up, but very charming. They are very much in love with each other, I think, and talk much and earnestly together when I see them in the lounge or at lunch and dinner. She do not come down to breakfast, but he do. He say, when he come, that they want the room till Saturday morning—that is last Saturday—but on Wednesday afternoon he go to the reception clerk and say their plans is altered, and will she give him the bill. And their baggage is brought down on Wednesday after tea, one suit case his and one hers——"

"Any names or initials on the suit cases?" Head asked, interrupting.

Atherton shook his head. "Not often is there names or initials on the suit cases that come here," he said, "and there was not on those two, because I myself look to see when they are brought down. The case which I think was his have many labels, and one is pasted on the lid where the letters might be under, but I do not know if they are. It is a label of a hotel in Bombay, but I do not remember the name. Her case I think is nearly new, and there is only a piece of cloak-room ticket on one end."

"Did you hear him call her by any name?" Head asked.

"No. He call her 'darling' or 'my dear,' not any name that I hear when he talk to her so near that I hear. Except once I hear him call her 'Angel.' And she calls him sometimes 'Pixie,' and once I think it was 'Oberon' she call him. But at other times 'Pixie' always."

"Did you see either of them on Wednesday before they left?"

"Yes, I see him, when he ask for the bill, and her when she come down to go. I bid them good-bye and hope they come again."

"How did they appear to you that day? Happy, or troubled?"

"I think she do not look so happy when I bid them good-bye, though she smiled at me. He did not say anything, only 'Good-bye' to answer me. She say they have been very happy here, and goodbye, and no promise to come again like some give when they go—because the catering and the accommodation of this hotel is of the very best, I assure you."

One costume, one evening frock, dark eyes and hair. Head remembered Mrs. Jevons standing in the farmhouse doorway, almost too well-dressed for a farmer's wife caught at her daily avocations, and unprepared for any callers. He laid his hand on the two photographs of Ashford.

"You will swear, if asked, this is the man who stayed here with her under the name of Barnard?" he asked.

"There is no doubt," Atherton answered simply. "Yes, I will swear it, if asked. For this is different, not like a divorce case."

"Thank you for what you have told me." Head stood up and put the photographs back in their envelope, which he replaced in his case. "I shall be here again to-morrow or the next day, with a photograph of the lady who stayed here as Mrs. Barnard for you to identify. In the meantime, no word of the object of my visit to-day—no word to anyone."

"I promise you complete silence," Atherton assured him gravely. "It is not like a divorce case, as I have said. This is very serious."

"Now, where can I get a taxi?"

"I will ring for one for you, from the nearest rank."

In the taxi, bound for the next train to Westingborough, Head realised that, as he had observed to Wadden, he still had all the way to go. He had jumped to the conclusion that "Angel" was Mrs. Jevons, but he had yet to ascertain whether she had been absent from home while "Mr. and Mrs. Barnard" had been staying at the Warlingham. It occurred suddenly to his mind that Mrs. Thomas had arrived at the Carden Arms on the Thursday morning, and that she fitted Atherton's description of the woman as well as did Mrs. Jevons, except that she would hardly appear with only one costume and one evening frock for more than a week's stay. Also, Thomas had been at Carden to meet her with the Rolls, and thus did not fit if the murder were the crime of a crazily-jealous husband, while Jevons had not been at his home or anywhere near it on Wednesday night.

And Mrs. Jevons had corresponded with somebody in Jelalapur, while as far as Head knew Mrs. Thomas had not—or, if she had, there might be nothing in it, since she and her husband had been stationed there and would probably retain some associations with his regiment.

A photograph of Mrs. Jevons would settle the point.

CHAPTER XVI

"Angel"

SUPERINTENDENT WADDEN looked up as Head entered his room on Tuesday morning, bringing with him a rather bulky, paper-covered volume which he put down on the desk, opening it at the place he had kept by inserting his forefinger between two pages. Wadden looked at him, not at the page.

"This is so sudden," he said. "I didn't expect you till this afternoon or to-morrow. What's the bright idea of this?"

"The electoral register," Head told him. "Ashford stayed at the Warlingham till Wednesday afternoon, not alone. He called his companion 'darling' and 'my dear' in the manager's hearing, and once varied it by calling her 'Angel'. Now look at this."

Wadden gazed beneath the pointing finger, and read aloud—

"Jevons, Jeanette Angelina".

He looked up again, and sat thoughtful, while Head waited.

"And Thane swore he wasn't," he observed. "He's wall-eyed."

"This isn't proof," Head reminded him.

"Maybe. But it's enough to make you check up on that Birmingham fairy tale, enough to make you find out where she was for the period that matters—tell me the whole tale, though."

So Head told, all that he had learned from the hotel manager.

"And checks up for eyes and colouring, too," Wadden observed thoughtfully at the story's end. "Dress, too, by what you said of her. Well-dressed, as far as she could afford to be—good stuff, even if little of it. I dunno. It's a bit of a teaser, Head, even now."

"It looks too simple, to me," Head declared. "I feel sure there's a catch, somewhere. Either she was the woman and he was not the man——" He broke off, reflecting over it, and closed the book he had brought.

"The photograph will settle it," Wadden said, rather dubiously.

"And by getting it, I rouse her suspicions of what I'm after," Head pointed out. "Mind, even if she is the woman, there's nothing of which we can accuse her, as nearly as I can see. Once she suspects, I see her closing up like a Glasgow bar on a Sunday, and she'd be perfectly within her rights if she refused to tell me where she was during the days Ashford spent at the Warlingham. Staying there with him doesn't make her accessory either before or after. *She* didn't want him killed?"

"Jevons did, and he was away from home, too," Wadden pointed out.

"Did he?" Head demurred. "Chief, I'll go over there this morning, and be guided by their attitudes as to what I do—but it won't include an arrest. I daren't, on nothing more than surmise based on that manager's description. No. I'll go over, though, and then be on hand to overhaul Ashford's trunks when they arrive. I may get the photograph I want out of them. To put Jevons and his wife on their guard is the last thing I want to do—it may ruin my chance of getting evidence."

"Why won't you see him as I do?" Wadden asked abruptly.

"I can't tell you why. They are both connected with Ashford in some way—I feel certain of that. Feel it from the way both of them faced me, the way they took my inquiries—everything about them. And yet I've got a feeling that Jevons is not the man of the train, not the one who put Thane's clothes on Ashford's body. I can't account for the feeling, especially since I *know* they're both in this. There it is."

"'Angel—Angelina'—she's in it all right," Wadden averred.

"'Angel' may be just a pet name—not the woman's real name at all," Head dissented. "Didn't you ever call Mrs. Wadden 'Angel'?"

"A most indelicate question," Wadden said brusquely. "Stick to the case, man, and never mind what I might call my old lady. Yes, I did."

"Which goes to prove——" Head began, and did not end it.

"But that was a long while ago," Wadden said, "and proves nothing."

"There are Thane's other possible mistakes," Head remarked doubtfully. "Fitton, Thomas, Rynewald. There may be others. I seem myself to have concentrated too much on Jevons and the Carden Arms——"

"Man, you've got a line!" Wadden interrupted testily. "I told the big noise to hold off the super-sleuths because you've got a line. The others won't run away, or if they do they won't run far. They're all too easily traceable—people of their stamp just don't get away, in these days. Follow your line, and turn on to them if it frazzles out. You own yourself that both the Jevonses are in it, somehow."

He brooded, while Head stood silent beside him.

"Even if he's not the man," he added, "since they're in it they may lead you to that man. Get your photograph of her—follow your line."

"I'll go there, and question her point-blank," Head decided. "It's dangerous, and may damage my chance of getting evidence, but——"

"Don't be desperate, laddie," Wadden warned him. "Take it easy—think all round it—you can't move her to where she'll be recognised as Mrs. Barnard, but there must be quite a lot of little Mahomets in that hotel, and the manager might lend you one if you asked him."

"I'll think over it, Chief," Head said, far less decidedly, and, tucking the electoral register under his arm, went out from the room.

He was still thinking about it, still undecided, as he drove slowly along Carden Street, and, reaching the front gate of Potts the poacher, stopped the car and got out. Potts, busy with a digging fork on his land, recognised his caller and, shouldering his fork, came toward the front gate as Head entered by it. He smiled broadly.

"Brought them stamps f'r me to see, mister?" he inquired.

"I'm afraid I haven't, this time," Head answered. "I called because you will be able to tell me something I want to know, and I think will be able to hold your tongue over having been asked it."

"Able, both ways, mister," Potts agreed, "but if it's somethin' what might make it easy f'r your flatfoots to drop on me—well!"

"It won't," Head assured him, "because it does not concern your movements at all, but those of Mrs. Potts, during the last fortnight."

"The missus, huh?" Potts looked considerably

surprised. "Well, she don't go where the keepers don't want her. So why, mister?"

"She goes out for a day's work, occasionally, you told me," Head said. "Can you tell me—when did she last work at Jevons' farm?"

"Jevons', huh? More'n a month ago, till to-day. About a month, anyhow, it'd be. Call it three weeks for sure. Why, mister?"

"You're quite sure it wasn't last week, or the week before?"

"Dead sure, mister. Three full weeks, I'll take my oath. But why?"

"You said—'till to-day'," Head evaded the query. "Do you mean she has gone to work there to-day?"

"She have, mister. They're startin' spring-cleanin', an' Mrs. Jevons wrote a letter to my missus to ask her to go to-day. An' to-morrer, too. Arter that, I reckon, she'll say whether she want her next day."

"Yes. Well, that's all I wanted to ask you, Potts, thank you."

"What's it all about, mister?" Potts inquired curiously.

"Quite possibly about nothing. Can I trust you to keep quiet?"

"I got nobody to tell. If I had, I wouldn't, since you ask me."

"That's good enough. If you do come before the bench again, I'll put in a word for you, Potts. Any use telling you not to risk it?"

"Not a bit, mister!" and Potts laughed long at the idea. "I got it in my bones, I reckon—couldn't stop it if I tried."

"Mrs. Potts is not going to do all the spring cleaning there, I hope?" Head suggested. "It's too much for one, surely."

"Oh, they keep a gal," Potts told him. "Sly bit o' goods she is, too. Been wi' Mrs. Jevons ever since they married, she told my missus. Don't git on too well wi' him, but her an' Mrs. Jevons are thick as thieves together. A good-looker—maybe he tried tricks, an' she stood him off. I dunno. Queer lot, they are, wi' her actin' the lady like she do. Though my missus say she reckon she is a lady— or was, till she married him. These here wimmin will talk, y'know, mister."

"How long have they been married, do you know?"

"No, I dunno. Six or seven year, must be, though. All o' that."

"Well, don't forget, Potts. A still tongue saves trouble. I'll remember to bring my stamps for you to see, as soon as I have time."

"Thankye, mister, an' as for sayin' anything, you c'n trust me."

It would be useless to question the sly bit of goods, Head realised as he drove on, for Mrs. Jevons would have warned her both with regard to what might be said in Jevons' hearing, and, since Head himself had already been making inquiries there, as to what she should say in response to any questions he might put. Seeking for a pretext for calling, Head decided that he would ask Jevons for a sight of that Midland Grand receipt so freely offered on the last occasion. The man's reaction would be worth noting, and might lead to further revelations: he was, Head remembered, an inefficient liar.

It was the sly bit of goods, he felt sure, who answered his knock at the front door of the farmhouse. Decidedly a good-looker, in spite of her soiled apron and untidy blonde hair, but with shifty blue eyes which told why Potts had described her as he had. She stood silent, holding the door, and waiting for Head to declare his errand.

"Could I see Mr. Jevons, please?" he asked.

"Unless it's important," she answered pertly, but with no trace of dialect in her way of speaking. "They're drilling barley in one of the fields at the back, and he wouldn't want to be called away."

"I see. Is Mrs. Jevons in?"

"No." As, when he had first called here, Mrs. Jevons had looked past him at his car, so this girl looked now. There was no trunk in the dickey, nothing to distinguish the vehicle from any other well-kept old car, but it seemed to him that it had a significance for her. Potts had said that she and Mrs. Jevons were as thick as thieves together: had Mrs. Jevons warned the girl that he might call and question her?

"I will come in and wait while you tell Mr. Jevons I wish to see him," he announced, and her gaze came back to him from the car.

"All right," she said ungraciously. "I'll send the woman. We're spring cleaning—you'll have to wait in the passage. What name, please?"

"Head, of the Westingborough police. He will remember it."

She stood back to let him enter, and then closed the door. He was in a wide passageway running from front to back of the house, with doors giving access to the rooms on either side, and at the back a staircase to the first floor. The furniture was old: he noted a pair of coffin stools, a fine old oak box-settee, and a grandfather clock with the maker's name and date "1752" on its face. Over its ticking, as he stood, he could hear the girl giving sharp, irritable orders beyond a doorway at the back. His gaze rested on an enlarged photograph on the wall, just beyond the grandfather clock and shadowed by it. It showed a wedding group: Jevons stood awkwardly in a morning coat and with a silk hat in his left hand, while the right lay on the shoulder of Mrs. Jevons. It was an excellent likeness of her, and the man who had identified Ashford in his polo kit could not make any mistake about this—if she had been Ashford's companion at the hotel—in spite of her veil and wedding dress. Three bridesmaids and some elderly people completed the group, and after scant regard of them Head looked for the photographer's name and address. He read —"Roade, Art Photos," in the left-hand corner of the mount, and "Pagenham Newton" on the right, and moved toward the open door at the back, beyond which he could still hear the girl's voice.

"Don't trouble, please," he called. "Don't send for Mr. Jevons."

She reappeared. "Don't you want him?" she asked, with evident relief, standing in the doorway.

"I won't trouble him now," he answered. "I can call again."

"All right, then," she said. "I'll tell him you called."

As she made no move, he retreated to the front door and let himself out, closing it behind him. Jevons could think what he liked: he would not realise that Head had learned anything by his call here.

It was now mid-morning, and Pagenham Newton was a small town or large village a little more than thirty miles beyond Crandon. The petrol tank dip-stick showed Head that he had plenty of fuel for the run, and he got into the car and drove off, to accelerate to forty miles an hour where the road admitted it—the car would travel no faster on the level, while downhill, exceeding forty, it rattled like a crate of hardware badly packed. By twelve o'clock it was stationary in Pagenham Newton, and Head entered the small establishment of Roade, whose specimens of art photos looked a trifle faded and fly-blown in his window.

He appeared, a big, broad-shouldered man with a weathered complexion and a red nose, and took Head's card to gaze at it and then at its owner in a puzzled way. Then he smiled, engagingly.

"Police, eh?" he observed. "Well, what is it, Inspector Head?"

"Old photographs," Head answered. "I suppose you keep your negatives, as a rule?"

"Well, that depends. Some I do and some I don't. How far back would you be thinking of going, now?"

"Six or seven years. A wedding group, and the bridegroom's name was Jevons. The copy I saw was an enlargement, evidently. Can you turn it up—the negative, I mean—and print me a copy quickly?"

"Jevons. Jevons, now." The photographer thumbed his chin thoughtfully. "Can't say I remember the name, off-hand. Six or seven years is a very long while, mister—Inspector Head, I should say. Jevons. Can you tell me anything about him that might help?"

"A man about your size," Head told him, "a farmer, living now at a farm on the Castel Garde estate, the other side of Crandon——"

"I've got it!" Roade interrupted him. "Miss Cottenham that was—the younger of the two

Miss Cottenhams. Yes, I remember. His name was Jevons. Yes, of course! Bit of an excitement, that was, too."

"Why—how do you mean an excitement?" Head asked.

"Well, you see, inspector, old Mr. Cottenham —he was a widower, and lived over at Monk's Pagenham with his two daughters. Lovely girls, they were. Poor and proud, the old chap was —they had the Priory, and the old man left everything—what there was of it—to the other Miss Cottenham when he died. He wouldn't forgive this one for marrying beneath her, as he thought it. Let her be married from the Priory, but they say he washed his hands of her from that day—wouldn't have anything more to do with her. Lovely bride, she made. I took the photos, went along to the Priory to take 'em, and they ordered a dozen enlargements. I'm pretty sure I kept that negative, too, just in case."

"Of more orders," Head completed for him. "Could you look it out?"

"Well, I *could*." By his tone, he did not relish the idea.

"Then I should be glad if you would," Head told him unsympathetically.

"You don't mean now?" he asked, with a mixture of incredulity and dismay.

"Now," Head echoed, in solemn affirmation.

"Well, I s'pose I'd better see what I can do," he said heavily, and sighed his distaste for the task.

"What would you be wanting off it?"

"Two good, clear prints. I want the faces quite recognisable."

"Well, inspector, if you'll wait a bit, I'll see if I've still got the negative, first. I'm not dead sure about that, though I think I have. If you'll take a seat, I'll go and have a look for it."

Lifting a curtain at the back of the small front room, in which he displayed cameras, packages of films, and specimens of his art photos, he disappeared in what was apparently his studio, since a couple of big stand cameras were revealed in it until the curtain fell again. Instead of seating himself, Head inspected the wall cases, and gained the impression that the people in this part of the country would stand small chances in beauty competitions: alternatively, Mr. Roade was not good at posing his subjects. Twenty minutes passed, and then the photographer reappeared with very dusty hands and coat sleeves, and held up a half-plate glass negative between Head and the light from the window.

"That'll be the one, I expect," he suggested.

Head took the plate from him and, by holding it at various angles, managed eventually to get a positive effect. He handed it back.

"It is the one," he assented. "As I said, I want two very clear prints—for identification of one or more of the sitters, you understand, and there must be no mistake about them. For that, do you think this plate is good enough for contact prints, or will it be necessary to make enlargements. I must be quite sure of the faces."

"Well," Roade said doubtfully, "people take a good deal of identifying after seven years—that photo was taken just seven years ago, you see. I'll tell you what I'll do. I'll take a couple of bromide prints direct off the plate, and you can decide when they're finished off whether they'll do, or whether you want enlargements instead."

"Very good. How soon can you have the prints ready?"

Roade made some apparent mental calculations. "If I were to post them off to you to-night, you'd have 'em in the morning," he said.

"And if I were to go and get some lunch, and come back here at, say, about three, it would save you the trouble of posting," Head suggested.

"Three? Why, they'd hardly be dry by then!" Roade protested.

"Oh, yes! We do a little photography ourselves, at times, Mr. Roade. Just get a move on for once, please. I'll look back at three."

"Well, if you must have 'em by then——" Roade said dubiously.

"I assure you I must. Two good prints. And if it comes to enlargements, I shall have to take the negative and get them made at Westingborough to-night. I can't afford to wait over this."

"All right, Mr. Head—Inspector, I should say. You come back at three, and I'll have a pair of as good prints as the negative'll give."

Leaving him to his task, Head went out in quest of lunch. The sign of the Jolly Prior, picturing a mediæval cleric who, by the look of him, had a dispensation from fast days, was attractive, and Head entered the hostelry to find that the modern representatives of the prior catered in a way that would have won his approval. Mine host himself, yet another big man with a red nose, presided in the saloon bar, and after lunch, having still nearly an hour to spare, Head called for a drink from him and congratulated him on the quality of his food, as an opening.

"We try to do our best, sir, thank you," the landlord said modestly.

"I shall remember you next time I come this way," Head told him. "Not that I'm likely to forget your sign. It's the only one of its kind that I've ever seen—or heard of, for that matter."

"Well, you see, sir, I reckon it goes back to the old times—the good old times, some people call 'em, and they might have been, for all I know. In them old times, this place—Pagenham Newton—it was no more than a sort of back door to Monk's Pagenham. And after the old priory was broken up—a mighty big establishment it must have been, too, as the ruins go to show —when it was broken up, and people begun to travel about more, this place was on the main road and so it begun to get bigger. The names'll tell you theirselves. Monk's Pagenham, the one that belonged to the monks, and Pagenham New Town, d'ye see, sir? It's old enough now, but that's how it got the name, when the monks were turned out by old Henry the Eighth and the priory pulled down."

"Nothing but ruins left, eh?" Head inquired.

"All but what they say was the prior's own rooms, which have been built on to later to make what they call the Priory now, sir. The house named the Priory, I mean. The rest is all ruin, mostly at ground level."

"And that house is still inhabited?" Head persisted.

"Part o' the time, sir—not all. Old Mr. Cottenham used to live there, him and his daughters, but after the youngest one got married against his wish he soon died, and left the Priory to the eldest. She still come to live there sometimes, she and her husband, but I'd say eight months in the year there's nobody there but old Jim Furze and his missus. Caretaking the place. A regular waste, I call it, a fine old house like that. A bit gloomy, but a fine place. And the old chap—old Mr. Cottenham—one of the real old school, he was. They say when they had no more'n pea soup for dinner, he'd have all the silver out just the same, and old Jim Furse had to wait on 'em just as if it was a banquet. And the old man didn't last long after his youngest daughter got married and never come near him again. She was his favourite, though he did leave what little he had to the other one. Married a man from Crandon way, she did. Small farmer, they say—not their style at all. But you can never tell where a woman's fancy'll light."

He moved away, then, to attend to two men who had just entered, and a brisk conversation about the prolonged spell of dry weather, its effect on crops, and the high cost of feeding stuffs for cattle, began. The landlord spared a friendly nod for Head, who went out, since he wanted to get back to Westingborough as soon as possible. It was not yet time to go back to Roade for the prints, but Pagenham Newton might have other places of interest than its *Jolly Prior*. A stationer's with a big range of picture postcards, for instance, looked worth examination.

"Monk's Pagenham. The Priory Ruins," showed a range of crumbling walls little more than knee-high at any point, on a tree-dotted sward. Taking the card from its rack, Head entered the shop, and faced a spectacled, elderly woman who looked at the card, said "Tuppence, please," and handed over an envelope as she took the coins. "To keep it clean," she explained. "Thank you, mister. Will that be all to-day?"

"Have you one of the Priory—the house, I mean?" he asked.

She shook her head. "No-o, mister. That's private property, that is. Jim Furze'd scat anyone he caught takin' pictures there."

"Jim Furze? Is he the owner, then?" Head

inquired innocently.

"Oh, lawk, no!" she ejaculated. "Belong to Miss Isabel Cottenham, the Priory do. Miss Isabel that was, till she married. Jim, he look after the place —him and his wife. Miss Isabel don't often live there."

"Does her sister often come there?" Head risked the query.

"Miss Jeanette? Never been near the place since she married, mister. Why—did you know her?" She peered at him with sudden interest.

"I met her, once," he admitted. "I can't say that I know her."

"*I* knew her, when her hair was in pigtails. Lovely, she was when she grew up—so was Miss Isabel. Pity Miss Jeanette had to throw herself away like—but you say that'll be all for to-day, mister?"

"All, thank you," Head answered. Then, as the elderly dame evidently repented of her garrulity, he left her, and went to Roade's shop.

"Yes, Mr. Head, they'll be dry by now," the photographer assured him. "I was going to give 'em another ten minutes, but since you appear in a hurry I'll go and get 'em. And you won't need any enlargements to show the bride and bridegroom enough for identification, I assure you."

"I didn't say they were the ones I wanted to identify," Head told him. "There are more than a dozen people in that group."

"Well, all of 'em, then," Roade amended cheerfully. "Five shillings, sir, that'll be. Unmounted, of course. Did you want 'em mounted?"

"No. I'll take them as they are, if you'll let me see them."

Again he waited while Roade went through his studio and returned with the two prints. One glance at them was enough. Jeanette Angelina Jevons was almost stereoscopically lifelike, Jevons not less well portrayed, and with no regard at all for the other members of the group Head handed over two half-crowns and took the envelope in which Roade placed the prints. He had got what he wanted, and Jevons and his wife did not even know that he wanted it, let alone that he had it.

He made good time on the return journey until he came abreast the Carden Arms, and then at a shout and sight of somebody waving an arm at him from the hotel doorway he braked and turned into the forecourt, where another car that he recognised as belonging to the Ashfords was already drawn up. Thane came toward him, and put a foot on his running-board.

"I hope you don't mind my stopping you like that, inspector," he said. "About those trunks you and the superintendent wish to examine."

"Why—they haven't gone wrong, have they?" Head asked sharply.

"Oh, no! To report safe arrival—at least, I hope

it is that, or will be very soon. You see, Miss Ashford and I talked it over and decided that they mustn't come to the hall, because if they did Sir Bernard might see them, and though he wouldn't refuse to let you look at what is in them —we thought best to keep from him that you are doing it. So I went and waited at Carden station while Miss Ashford and he went to the funeral, and after she'd taken him home she came and joined me there. A van had been sent over from Westingborough to meet the train and deliver them at the hall, but we waited till the trunks came off the train and then ordered the man to deliver them to you at the police station."

"Very good of you to take the trouble," Head told him. "And of Miss Ashford, too. We shall deliver the trunks back as soon as possible."

"I'll tell her——" Thane broke off as Loretta emerged from the hotel, and Head got out from his car to face her.

"Good afternoon, inspector. Mr. Thane has been telling you——?"

"I can only thank you for thinking of it, Miss Ashford," he said, as she left her question incomplete.

"In case—my father might have seen the trunks and wondered, asked us about them," she explained. "So, you see"—she smiled slightly —"it was for his sake and our own, rather than for yours. And now I can thank you for the lovely wreath you and the superintendent sent.

I do, and so does my father. Such unexpected sympathy, he said."

"The very least we could do." Inwardly, he blessed Wadden for the thought, which in his own preoccupation over the case had not occurred to him. "I hope he is—hope the strain of the day has not been too much for him."

"Not—I don't think you'll see him back on the bench again, Mr. Head," she said rather uncertainly. "He's turned his face to the wall. And since he wouldn't let me stay with him after we got back, Mr. Thane suggested tea here instead of at home, after we'd seen about the trunks at the station——"

"Knowing that an hour away from the house will do you all the good in the world," Thane broke in. "But we're delaying you, inspector. No news yet, I suppose?"

"Nothing whatever. Miss Ashford shall know, as soon as I have anything to report."

"I am not sure that I wish to know, Mr. Head," she said. "You were a good friend to me—once before—and then not so much by what you told me, I think, as by what you kept back. You see, nothing you may do can make any difference. To us, I mean. You can avenge, but that will not bring him back to my father, or lessen the tragedy for him."

"I am not trying to avenge, Miss Ashford," he told her gravely. "My work consists of protecting those who keep the law by bringing to justice those who break it, a far different thing from vengeance. But now I think of it—if I may trouble you for a minute." He took out the envelope Roade had given him, extracted one of the two prints, and handed it to her. "Do you recognise any of these people?"

She scrutinised the portraits, and pointed to Jevons as she held the print so that he could see where her finger rested.

"That man—the one who stopped the hunt from going over his land," she said. "Jevons—the one you asked me about. None of the others."

He took the print back. "Thank you. I won't keep you any longer. And you shall have those trunks delivered at the hall as soon as possible. To-morrow, probably. If we need to keep anything out of them, it shall be returned to you with the least possible delay."

As he drove away, Thane took Loretta by the arm and turned with her toward the hotel entrance.

"I wanted to ask him what he found in London yesterday, with those other two photographs," he said, "but it didn't seem possible."

"Nor would it have made any difference if you had," she averred. "We must be quick over tea. I ought not to have agreed to come here for it, really."

"You're not sorry you did, are you—cousin Loretta?"

"Not sorry—no. Why did you insist on it, really?"

"Well"—he hesitated over it—"for one thing, I wanted to get you out of that drawing-room and all it means, for to-day. The associations it must have—you've been through enough, for one day. And there was another reason. Head made me look rather a fool, yesterday morning, and I wanted to have a good look at other people who may be taking tea here to-day, to make sure I was right in what I told him about them."

"So I was not the only reason?" she asked coldly.

"You were the first—the only one that really counts. I may have more to tell you about that, some other day. For to-day, I'd like you to realise me just as a prop for you and your father to lean on, just as long as you need such a prop. Both of you."

She did not answer until they had seated themselves and the waiter had left them after taking the order for tea. Then she looked Thane straight in the eyes.

"Thank you, cousin Leo," she said.

CHAPTER XVII

Love is Not Everything

A SLIGHT twinkle of amusement appeared for a second or two in Sergeant Wells' eyes when Head asked him if any trunks had been delivered at the police station that afternoon.

"Yes, Mr. Head. Two big ones and two little ones. The superintendent paid the charges and signed for 'em, and they're in your room."

"In my room? Who said they were to go in there?"

"Mr. Wadden, sir. He said he wasn't going to have his office messed up unpacking 'em, and if there was any glory in it you'd claim it."

"As, undoubtedly, you will," Wadden said from the charge-room doorway. Then he blew gustily at Wells. "Sergeant, I'll get a toasting fork and rake your liver for giving that full report of all I said—when I've got time to attend to you. All Mr. Head wanted to know was the present whereabouts of the trunks, not the whyabouts. Brought anything back with you out of your little tour round the country, Head?"

"Only the photograph I went to get," Head answered, and went out from the charge-room to go to his own. "Now we can see——"

"Not so fast, laddie—not quite so fast!" Wadden adjured him. "I want six half-crowns off you. One wreath for the funeral to-day, thirty shillings, and I won't charge you anything for putting your name on the card that went with it, nor will I take one penny for saving your face by remembering to send it—from us both. Remember it—fifteen bob. And now—how did you get the photograph? Hold him down till he choked?"

"I got it from the photographer, and details can wait," Head answered as he opened the door of his room and entered, with Wadden following. "You haven't opened any of these yet, I suppose?"

"No. I didn't know if Miss Ashford would want to be here while we overhaul her dead brother's belongings. I feel squeamish about it, somehow. The idea of prying into those things, if you understand."

"I do, chief, but I'd feel a lot worse if the man who strangled him and slashed his face about got away with it. Keys—ah, yes!" He took them off his desk, with their big linen label on the cord that held them together. Two small trunks stood

on two large ones, and he fitted a key to the
lock of the topmost, turned it, and slipped back
the hasps. Opening the lid, he revealed books,
loose papers neatly banded, and a small pigskin
attaché case, which he lifted out and put on his
desk.

"By the look of it, chief, this is the one we want
most," he observed, and lifted out a pile of books.
"Drill manuals, veterinary handbook, musketry
training——" he put the books on his desk backs
upward, merely glanced at their labels, and took
out a bundle of papers. Examination notes, by
the look of them," he remarked, and took out
another bundle which he placed on top of the
first without comment. Within three minutes he
had emptied the trunk, and then he took up the
pigskin case.

"The key to that would have been on him,
I expect," he remarked after trying the hasps,
while Wadden closed the trunk lid and lifted it
down to place it under the window. "Wait a bit,
chief—don't open any more yet. We must get
these things back in their proper order for Sir
Bernard to see, and we mustn't risk mixing the
contents of one trunk with any other lot. He was
a very neat packer, by the look of it."

"Are you going through all those papers?"
Wadden asked.

"Not till we must. It depends on what we get
without them. I imagine this case might yield
something—he kept it locked, you see. What do

we——" He produced a bunch of keys from his own pocket, and tried one of the smallest. The pair of locks clicked one after the other, and he slid the hasps back. "Just as I thought. Unless you go to Bramah or Chubb, all attaché cases yield to one out of three keys, and I tried the right one of the three first. Now I wonder? Diaries— yes, regimental stuff, by the look of it. Oh, damn! Urdu writing! That's beyond us, chief, and we'll have to find a translator. Either Urdu or Arabic, and I can't tell the difference. Nominal roll—his troop or squadron, or whatever it was. Chief, you're right. This feels like taking hold of his dead hand, almost, and I *don't* like it! And yet... wait a bit!" He took out a small book bound in black leather, and as he opened it two sheets of blue notepaper, covered with close writing and folded together, fluttered to the floor. He picked them up and compared them with the writing in the book from which they had fallen, and then sat down at his desk to read.

"What have you found?" Wadden asked.

"What we wanted, I think," he answered. "Wait a bit, though. I make it to be a woman's writing, and this is a continuation. Also"—he turned over first one sheet and then the other —"the end of it's missing. Unless she gives her name in the script, or it's in the book——"

He did not end the sentence, but scanned the closely-written sheets and put them down to take up the black leather-covered book. "Not there, on either of them, and this is very nearly cypher," he said complainingly. "Concerns two people beside himself, apparently, and he represents one by a circle and the other by a square, by the look of it. Instance—'circle seems afraid for square, postmaster resenting arrt.' Which means arrangement, I take it. It's a diary of sorts, chief, and I'll have to study it carefully. To-night, I think. Meanwhile"—he put the book in his pocket, and took up the blue papers —"listen to this. I've no compunction in reading it out to you, and quite possibly, as I begin to see things, it may have to be read in court, yet."

He found the beginning of the fine, neat script, and read: "—consent to such a step, I do not know, and, Pixie, I dare not ask." Head broke off to explain—"I take it that the first words there would be 'whether he——' 'Whether he would consent,' you see, chief. And 'Pixie' was what the woman at the Warlingham called him. We're on the right track, in a way. Now I'll read on."

"The 'he' of the sentence being the man of the train," Wadden suggested. "And—but would any woman's husband kill like that?"

Head waved the query aside with an impatient movement, and read on—

"—Pixie, I dare not ask. For you are still more than two years away from me, and I could not come back there to you, while I know well that the man who gives up everything for the sake of a woman always regrets it in the end. There is no exception to that rule, as so many women who have let their men take the risk know in bitterness.

"More than two years away—more than two years before I can hear your voice and realise your love again. Will it last so long with you, fed on memory and no more? As for me—'each hour a pearl, each pearl a prayer——' for one sight of you, one moment's sound of your voice. So it will go on, I know, because—oh, Pixie! I hate myself for it, but I just cannot do what you ask, come to you completely. For your sake as well as mine. Say that I'm selfish, say that I will not give up what I have for all you could give—and I *know* all you could give is more than everything. But you wouldn't go on giving it, if I did that. Your father's son couldn't face all that would come of it and remain the same. Pixie, the worst of it is that love isn't everything—and yet I love you, love you, love you—unforgettably, achingly, and truly enough to know what would happen to us if I did that, came finally to you."

"The woman's got sense," Wadden remarked. "But doesn't she give one solitary hint of whether she's Mrs. Jevons, anywhere in it?"

"Wait a moment, chief. Here's something that may link up with the diary in my pocket. I'll finish this and then we'll look at the other trunks. There might be a photograph of her in one of them."

"Small hope," Wadden said. "He'd pack all his

papers together."

"Probably. Listen to the rest"—and Head read on——

"Pixie, remember always when you write to me. There must never be anything to show that what you write is to *me*—'me underlined, chief'—though I want you to tell all as I tell you. Because when I saw, in this last letter of yours, your name for me—I don't know if he ever heard that name spoken as mine, but you remember what we told each other. That if any letter of yours or mine should come to light, there should be nothing in it to tell who had written or to whom it was written. Only that way can we go on writing, for I wouldn't feel safe about it in any other way. And you remember I told you I'd assure the postmaster of that, because he *does not like*—'underlined again, chief'—the arrangement. Never forget, darling, for safety's sake."

Breaking off there, Head looked up from the letter. "That's where it links on to the diary, as I see it," he commented. "That sentence I read out —'postmaster resenting arrangement.' And he's kept names out of the diary, too. Who are square and circle and postmaster?"

"Jevons and his wife and——" Wadden broke off dubiously.

Head took the black-covered diary from his pocket, put the two sheets of paper inside, and replaced the book. "I'll save all that up for the midnight oil," he said, "and we'll go through the other three trunks, if you don't mind, and then see if there's anything bearing on it among these papers on the desk. I think he'd keep a photograph."

"I dunno," Wadden demurred. "Remember, when he started back off leave last time, you have Sir Bernard's statement that Mrs. Foster was the most favoured nation in his treaty. The one who wrote that letter may not have meant nearly as much to him as he did to her. She may not be the one who stayed with him at the Warlingham, even. Sir Bernard's remark about his women costing too much goes to show that he wasn't what you'd call exclusive in his amours. But let's put his drill books back, make sure none of those bundles of papers are interesting, and then get on with the other trunks. It looks like a long session, to me."

They kept at it for the best part of three hours, unfolding every article of clothing to make certain that nothing was concealed in either pockets or folds, scrutinising every paper—even measuring each trunk before repacking it, inside and out, to assure themselves that there were no false bottoms, compartments in the lids, or other secret hiding places. And, when the last trunk had been repacked and locked, Head had nothing to show for their work beyond the black-covered diary, and the two sheets of paper covered by a woman's handwriting.

"And," he said, scrutinising them again, "it's not worth while to read you the rest of it, chief, for it gives no more enlightenment. A woman of the world—Mrs. Jevons struck me as being that, too—who is determined to eat her cake and have it. Not going to sacrifice her position, whatever that may be, but holding on to Ashford, all the same."

"Jeanette Angelina Cottenham's father left her nothing—left everything to her sister," Wadden pointed out, "and as Jevons' wife she's got a position of sorts. If she'd thrown it up and gone to Ashford, he'd have had to resign his commission, and Sir Bernard would have cut him out—wouldn't have stood for it. She could see them being reduced to the conventional garret if she tried it, which is why I said she's a sensible woman. And she'd reason, in a few years at most, Sir Bernard has got to die, which means her man would have the hall and the title and pretty much everything else. If she could hold on to him till that happened, divorce would be a horse of a different colour, and she could go to him from Jevons without breaking up everything, as she would if she'd done it in Sir Bernard's lifetime. So there you are."

"And still I don't see Jevons as the man we want," Head remarked thoughtfully. "I propose we look in at the Black Lion on our way, since we've worked overtime and earned one apiece, and then I'll go home and settle to studying this diary. The trunks can go to Carden to-morrow."

"And you can get your photograph identified at the Warlingham," Wadden suggested. "Then get Birmingham to prove Jevons a liar, and you're on the way to the finish. I told you to stick to that line."

"When it breaks, I'll remind you of that remark," Head promised.

* * *

"Well, what did you make of the diary?" Wadden inquired, when Head looked in on him as usual the next morning.

"I think it's time to remind you that you told me to stick to the Jevons line, chief," Head answered. "I don't think she's the woman of the Warlingham, and in that case he's not the man of the train."

"Amplify that—as the old man would say," Wadden bade sourly.

"The diary is concerned with four people in addition to Ashford himself," Head explained. "They are defined by a square, a circle, a left-handed angle of ninety degrees or less, like the letter L turned the wrong way, and the title 'postmaster.' It's all very obscure, and what I did get out of it I got by degrees—by finding his way of thinking and expressing himself, to some extent. Many abbreviations like that 'arrt' for 'arrangement'. I think, but am not sure, the square represents someone in sympathy with him and the circle, the angle stands for the circle's husband, and postmaster is somebody who knows about the affair but is not in sympathy with them over it. Why he should have that title I can't see, unless he is a postmaster. And that seems rather absurd, to me, though he may be. The idea of making the husband an angle is clear enough—he's part of the inevitable triangle. I gather Ashford's idea was that if anything happened to him, and the diary fell into wrong hands, it should give nothing away—and he's very nearly succeeded in making it that, too."

"Remember Mrs. Jevons' letters from Jelalapur," Wadden urged reflectively. "Supposing Mrs. Jevons were the circle and Jevons the angle, the square would be somebody who persuaded Jevons there was nothing in it, and even claimed the letters as hers, since there's no name in them, by what she said in that one you read out, to say whose they are. And then postmaster would be—who would postmaster be?"

"It doesn't fit together very well, does it?" Head suggested rather ironically. "Unless he were square's husband, and the murderer—which again is absurd, because square is not the one who wrote the letter."

"Doesn't make it absurd," Wadden objected. "She was in it, Ashford might have preferred her to the letter-writer, and got her to go and stay at the Warlingham—told her when he'd arrive in England——"

"The diary is explicit enough for us to rule that out," Head interrupted. "If either of them is the woman of the Warlingham, it's the one he records in the diary as a circle. Further to that, I'm as certain as I can be that the angle is not square's husband. Postmaster may or may not be. He appears to be an antagonistic onlooker."

"I used to play a game years ago—what was it called, now?" Wadden reflected aloud. "You took little black and white things and jumped 'em over each other—halma, that was it! This is like that game. Squares and circles and angles and postmasters, and you jump 'em about, juggle 'em into what you think are their places, but are they?"

"The manager of the Warlingham can bring us a step nearer the answer to that," Head observed. "I can get back to-night, too."

"M'yes. And whether Jevons is our man or no, if Mrs. Jevons is the woman you won't have much difficulty in making her talk. Oh, now I think of it! There's an inquiry through this morning for the trunk that fell off the back of that car, the one you took back to Cortazzi."

"For return of the trunk to Colonel Thomas, you mean?"

"No—people who call themselves the Crompton Hire Service want it, apparently, and offer a five-pound reward. They're not in any hurry—you took it to Cortazzi last Friday, and the inquiry only came in this morning. We'd have had it last Saturday if they'd put it in at once."

"At the latest," Head agreed reflectively. "Don't do anything about it, chief. If you instruct Cortazzi to send it, he'll get that five pounds, and it ought to be divided between Potts' boy and Hawker, your man of weight. I shall be over that way to-morrow, almost certainly, and I can pick up the trunk from Cortazzi and get it sent back from here. Then we can make sure the reward goes where it ought."

"If it's the right trunk," Wadden said.

"It is, I know. Thomas jobbed the Rolls from the Crompton Hire Service, and they are his initials on the trunk. You'd think, since it's worth a five-pound reward, the inquiry would have been through sooner."

"The Crompton people might have forgotten about it till he jabbed 'em in the memory-tank," Wadden suggested. "Anyhow, it's not important, though Hawker and that boy will think it is when they get their doubloons. I suppose you aim at catching the ten-three up, don't you?"

"And since it does not run a restaurant car," Head answered assentingly, "I can have a late lunch at the Warlingham while Atherton makes up his mind about that photograph, and then come straight back here."

"Do you mind if I have a look at said photograph?"

Wadden asked. "You've got plenty of time for the ten-three, even if I do look at it."

Head took the photographer's envelope from his breast pocket, and handed over one of the prints, leaving the other in the envelope.

"Which one—of course, though. Jevons is the bridegroom, isn't he?"

"Obviously," Head answered. "The group was hanging on his wall, an enlargement with the photographer's name on it. I went and got him to make me two prints—neither Jevons nor his wife know I've got it."

"Ah! And thundering good portraits of 'em, too—clear, I mean, and since you're content with it I suppose it's like what they are now. Good-looking bridesmaids, too, but those hats rather disfigure 'em. Not the sort of patty-pans they wear on their heads nowadays. But the bride ain't got no hat, of course, which is all to the good for you. Head, she's a bit out of the ordinary, that woman, if this is anything like her. It was her day out, of course, but she's exceptionally good-looking, all the same, and buried in a place like that, with a man like Ashford coming along—not but what Jevons is a fine figure of a man."

He handed the print back, and Head replaced it in the envelope and put it away. "Jevons doesn't look as good-tempered as that, now," he remarked. "At least, he didn't when he came out to talk to me."

"Naturally, knowing what you were after. Well, catch that ten-three, check up on her and make sure she's the one, and then even if he's not our man you can probably get enough out of her about who is to carry the case through. Frighten her into telling all she knows, at least."

"'If' once cost a man his life, chief, I remember."

"The worst it can cost you is a super-sleuth from the Yard making faces at us provincial rozzers, my lad, and Providence put this pretty picture into your hands to stop that from happening. Here, it's sessions to-day! I'd very nearly forgotten all about it."

"Expect me back about half-past seven, chief. I'll just go along to my room and collect a few things, and then make for the station."

"Good luck, laddie. If the old 'un rings through, I'll tell him you're hot on it, and there's nothing for him to worry about."

But, as Head went to his own room, he felt dubious as to whether he were so very hot on it, for instinct still told him authoritatively that Jevons was not his man. He had Ashford's diary in his pocket for further study during his three-hour journey, and now, unlocking the cupboard in his desk, he took out the package containing the partly burned shoe soles, the cord with which Ashford had been strangled, and a wisp of paper containing the buttons from Jelalapur, all of which articles he placed in a small attaché case. It would be well, he felt, to have these things with him, in case need should arise for investigation of any of them. A minute's reflection decided him that there was nothing else he need take: he had all those names the expert in footwear had given him, together with all other addresses and notes on the case that he had recorded, in the pocket-book he usually carried.

Thus he set out. At about half-past two that afternoon Wadden, just returned from lunch, took off his telephone receiver as the buzzer sounded, and heard Sergeant Wells at the switchboard say—"Here you are, sir—Mr. Head, superintendent." Then Head's voice—

"Just to say I shall not be back to-night, chief."

"Uh-huh! Did that hotel manager identify Angelina?"

"No. It wasn't Angelina."

"Oh, hell! Who was it, then?"

"I'll report everything when I get back to-morrow, chief. Can't stop, now. Oh, while I think of it——"

"If it wasn't Angelina, who the hell was it?" Wadden roared into the instrument, interrupting whatever thought had occurred to Head.

"No, it doesn't matter, though," the quiet voice in the transmitter said, and Wadden blew fiercely as he detected a note of amusement in it.

"I'll be back to-morrow, chief. Good-bye."

"Here——"

The click of the receiver-rest at the other end spoiled his protest, and he replaced his own receiver and sat back in his chair.

"I'll scarify his liver with a meat-chopper, when he does get back," he promised himself.

But he knew quite well he would do nothing of the sort.

CHAPTER XVIII

The Shadowed Face

THE green-uniformed lord of the Warlingham doorway appeared inclined to accord Head a greater measure of respect on this second visit. The manager, probably, had corrected the man's attitude.

"Mr. Atherton said you was to wait in the lounge, sir, if you did call again before he got back. 'E's hout—I mean, he's out, had to go into London, but he won't be later'n three o'clock."

"I see. Would it be possible to get some lunch while I wait?"

"Yes, sir, of course. If you'll just come this way."

It was already two o'clock, and, after a wash and brush-up, Head found that he had the dining-room of the hotel to himself. Good food and good service brought him to the end of his meal just as the manager entered the room and came over to him.

"Good morning, Mr. Head. I trust you have been well served?"

"Very well indeed, thank you," Head assured him, quite sincerely. "And you arrive at the right moment for my purpose."

"Ah! The photograph of the lady, I believe you said. Well, I expect it will be quite easy to settle the point, if you let me see it."

Head took out one of the prints and handed it over. As a beginning, Atherton gave it an almost casual glance, but this lengthened into a stare. He narrowed his eyes to regard it as an artist might in passing judgment on a picture: he held it close to his eyes and peered at it, and tried it at arm's length. Then he shook his head.

"One moment," he said. "I will get——"

He went off and disappeared through the doorway of the room without saying what he would get. In a minute or so he reappeared, carrying a handled reading glass, with which he went to the dining-room window to continue his examination in the best available light, varying the distance between print and lens until he got the correct focus. Eventually he came back to where Head was seated and put the print down beside him.

"I realise it is important, Mr. Head, most important that there shall be no doubt," he said. "I realise perhaps it will be for me to go into the witness box and testify to what I say now, that it is correct on my oath. I must make no mistake. The lady standing nearest to the seated one—that is the one who stayed here as Mrs. Barnard. Yes. The face is in shadow, and without the magnifying glass I was not quite sure. There is the hat, too, the hat which looks so strange against the fashions of to-day. That and the shadow make it difficult. But with the magnifying glass it is quite certain—there is no mistake at all. That one."

He put his finger momentarily on the bridesmaid standing nearest to the bride, and offered Head the reading glass.

But, for the moment, Head did not take it. He recalled how the enlargement he had seen had hung in shadow from the grandfather clock, and saw, too, that the upper parts of all the bridesmaid's faces were shadowed by the hats they wore. But he ought to have seen! He ought to have given other faces than that of Mrs. Jevons closer scrutiny—he ought to have seen! As he saw now, even without the reading glass.

He took it from Atherton's hand. "Sure you've never seen the bride before—the seated woman in that photograph?" he asked.

"Never." The reply was quite positive. "There is—well, a little resemblance, I think. Not much. About the chin and lips, perhaps. Between her and the woman who stayed here as Mrs. Barnard, I mean. But I know I have never seen her before, and the other is Mrs. Barnard."

The resemblance that had puzzled Head with a consciousness that he ought to have been able to place Mrs. Jevons when he saw her, that she had reminded him of somebody, some portrait or even dream....

He knew of whom she ought to have reminded him, as he took the reading glass for which he had no real need, and got the shadowed face in focus. Sisters, of course—the wedding had taken place from the Priory, and who but the sister of the bride should be chief bridesmaid? There she stood, the resemblance between them more marked at that time than in this present. Jeanette Angelina Cottenham's sister, the "Miss Isabel" of the old lady in the stationer's shop.

Isabel Thomas!

Then Isabel Thomas was "circle" of the diary, Mrs. Jevons was "square," and Jevons was "postmaster." It fitted better than when Head and Wadden had discussed it, and allotted parts to the people represented by those symbols. The angle was Thomas—yes. Mrs. Jevons had received letters from Jelalapur, and when they reached her sister Thomas would have no suspicion, since the address would be in his wife's sister's handwriting. And "postmaster" Jevons had objected to his wife being party to the subterfuge. Yes, but that did not prove Thomas the murderer: he had met his wife at Crandon with the Rolls Royce from the Carden Arms, the morning after the murder.

"I am very much obliged to you, Mr. Atherton." He put down the reading glass and took up his print. "Your help has opened up a line of inquiry on which I must get busy at once, so if I could have my bill——"

"Mr. Head, there is no bill. I am happy that you should be my guest for the lunch, and happy that I have been of any service."

"It's very nice indeed of you," and Head smiled at him, "but you must realise that the lunch will go among my expenses."

"Still I say you shall be my guest, and we will take no money," Atherton insisted. "There is time for a coffee and liqueur with me."

"I am afraid not. But—yes, though. You told me when I was here before that you have three single rooms. Can I have one of them tonight? Not as your guest, but to go on the expense sheet?"

"I shall be delighted to reserve one, Mr. Head."

"Many thanks—and for this excellent lunch. Now, if I might have a telephone call, I'll begin my afternoon's work, and hope to get back here in time for dinner. If not, in time to sleep."

He rang Wadden, and then green-uniform got him a taxi.

"Runton Mews, somewhere off Queen's Gate," he directed the driver. "The people I want call themselves the Crompton Hire Service."

The drive would give him time to think, to make readjustments.

* * *

If Wadden had not so persistently thrown Jevons and his wife at him, so to speak, as principal actors in the tragedy....

Monk's Pagenham was little more than thirty miles from Carden. Mrs. Thomas would have suggested staying at Carden to her husband, so that she could be near her sister, go over in the Rolls to see her....

She could drive over, too, during the brief intervals they spent at the Priory....

She had travelled out on the same boat as Ashford when she went to her marriage with Thomas. Had that been the beginning of the tangle, or had she and Ashford met on one of those occasions when she went to see her sister?

Ashford and Mrs. Jevons had been seen together in Crandon during his period of leave five years before. Had Isabel Cottenham and he been lovers then, and had he, knowing that Isabel meant to marry Thomas and was still in love with himself, arranged the circuitous correspondence?

No, though, for Thomas had been with the regiment, then. Much more probably, Isabel had made the arrangement after Thomas had resigned and got back to England with her. The pair might have begun their illicit traffic only a little while before Thomas' resignation took effect.

The pair of them had intended staying at the Warlingham until Saturday: on the Wednesday, something had happened to make them change their plans. Was Thomas that something?

Even if he had been, how could he arrange to travel on the same train to Westingborough as Ashford, and how would he know what train his wife would take for Crandon the next day?

On the face of it, Thomas could not be the murderer. He could not have arranged both to commit the murder and to meet his wife as he had done. If he had tracked Ashford to the train, he would have lost track of her: if he had been at the Carden Arms to learn by what train she would arrive, could he have been on Ashford's train? Could he have slipped unseen into the hotel in the early hours? It was scarcely possible.

He *could* have been in both places, but without the confederates of whom there was no sign, and whom he would hardly employ if he intended murder, how could he have obtained the information on which to base his plans both to kill Ashford and to meet his wife?

They had left the Carden Arms before the identity of the victim was generally known, but not before it was known in the hotel, thanks to Potts and his trout-selling errand there. Had she feigned illness to cover her agitation over her lover's death, or——?

What excuse had she made to Thomas for

her absence during the time she spent at the Warlingham? Had that excuse aroused his suspicions? Yet, apparently, he had not followed her to London—

Cortazzi must give a full account of Thomas' movements, tell whether he had been in the hotel on Wednesday night—

If not Thomas, who had murdered Ashford? Did that J 35 mean anything? If so, the Ashford—Thomas liaison must be disregarded.

Those notes in Urdu that Ashford had made would not refer to secret service work. Men in that service did not trust to writing, in any language.

Ashford may have had some idea that, by going to Carden on the Wednesday night instead of waiting till Saturday, he might claim if accused of having been with Mrs. Thomas that he had come straight overland, or from Paris, while for her part she had stayed the night in London to establish that she had not been with him. They had both left the Warlingham in some haste just after tea on Wednesday—

"'Ere you are, sir. Crompton 'Ire, you said."

Head came back to realities and found himself in a cobble-paved mews, in which stood a dozen or more cars, two of them in process of being washed by men in long boots. He got out, paid his driver, and entered a little office in which a small man, seated with his back to the door, turned his head to reveal a pair of horn-rimmed spectacles on a nose many sizes too large for his face.

"And what can I do for you, sir?" he inquired without rising.

Without speaking, Head put down a card on the table at which the small man sat. It evoked a rather perturbed "Oh!" and no more.

"You hired out a Rolls Royce to a Colonel Thomas," Head accused.

"It's due back in any minute," the small man said. "Why? Has Albert had a smash with it?"

"Not to my knowledge," Head told him. "Albert being the chauffeur, I suppose. Albert James Smith. Are you Edward John Smith?"

"I am." He got on his feet as he said it. "You seem to know a lot about us, Inspector Head. Not much we can tell you, is there?"

"You say Albert will soon be back. Where is he now?"

"Why, out with the Rolls on hire to Colonel Thomas! Why ask me, when you've just owned you knew we'd hired it out to the colonel?"

"Ah, but I was referring to a previous hire period," Head explained. "I understand it came back from hire to the colonel last week."

"Oh. It's about the trunk, then, is it? Because he kicked up a rare old fuss about that, and I'm instructed to pay the reward——"

"When were you instructed?" Head interrupted him to ask.

"It'd be—let me see! Yes, Monday. I put over a

description to the police at once, and offered the reward. Have you got the trunk?"

"Not here. You mean Colonel Thomas kicked up this fuss on Monday?"

"No, that was when he knew he'd lost it—said he'd knock Albert's block off. I believe Albert told him to try. It wasn't till Monday he rung through and said he wanted the reward offered, and we got busy."

"You mean he ignored it, between Friday and Monday?"

"Looks like it, don't it? But if you haven't got it——" he broke off and scratched the back of his head to express disappointment.

"Do you know where Colonel and Mrs. Thomas are now?" Head asked.

"A place called Monk's Pagenham, I believe. Albert was to drive them there. She keeps a car of her own there, and——"

He broke off again, this time in blank surprise. For Head reached past him to the telephone on the table, took off the receiver, and dialled "999," while Edward John Smith stared open-mouthed.

"Police, Westingborough," Head said to the transmitter. "Westingborough, a police trunk call. Yes, this is——" and he gave the number.

A silence, and the voice of Sergeant Wells sounded to him.

"Head speaking, Wells," he said. "Get through to Plender at Carden, and tell him to go to Cortazzi—at once, mind!—and take away the trunk lettered P.W.T—the one I took back to Cortazzi. Plender is to say it is by my instructions, and he is to go at once, get the trunk, and hold it for me. He must get it at once, before others can."

"Very good, Mr. Head. The trunk lettered P.W.T. I'll instruct him."

"Thank you, Wells—that's all. Good-bye."

He replaced the receiver. Thomas would not have got to the Carden Arms yet. That trunk, in view of the new aspect of the case, might prove far from unimportant, though Thomas had not troubled about it till Monday. In that very delay Head saw something that called for thought.

"Now I wonder what that's all about," Smith remarked pensively. "Whatever it is, you'll have to pay for that call."

"I expected no less," Head said, and put down a half-crown on the table. "That covers, I think. You say Albert is due back any time?"

"He's back," Smith told him. "The Rolls went past the window while you made that call. It's got a theatre job for the evening—I s'pose they'll want to do about fifty miles for their twenty-five bob, as usual, and give him sixpence tip when he drops 'em at their door——"

"Will you tell him I want to talk to him?" Head interrupted.

"What—in here?" The query sounded rather incredulous.

"I didn't see any armchairs out in the mews,"

Head retorted drily.

"Well, if you must, I s'pose you must," Smith observed with obvious reluctance, and went out. He returned after a brief interval with an alert-looking man of about his own size, attired in dark blue, box-cloth chauffeur's outfit, and with a nose that proclaimed some relationship to Edward John Smith, who introduced him as "My brother Albert, inspector," and then scratched the back of his head and waited.

"Howdedo, inspector," said Albert, cheerfully. "I've heard a bit about you, the times I been shoverin' the colonel and his missus, and now Teddy tells me you want to hear a bit about me, or maybe about him. It'll be about that trunk of his that dropped off, I reckon."

"You can tell me all you know about that, for a beginning." Head pulled Edward John's chair round and seated himself on it. "Also you'd better sit down and have a cigarette, if you care for one. I want to know about other things beside the trunk. That first, though."

"Well—thankye, sir." Albert took the cigarette and a light, and seated himself on the edge of his brother's table. Edward John shook his head at the offered case, stuck his hands in his pockets, and went to stand in the office doorway, looking out into the mews. "The trunk—yes. We stopped for lunch at the Grand at Leicester—he'd told me to take it easy on the run, and when I opened the door for them to get out I heard him tell her he'd get a private room. She looked like death warmed up, I thought. I got my lunch and then looked round the car and found one trunk was gone, strap and all. He'd been going to have it inside, at first, so they were strapped separately—it'd have been a nuisance inside, as I told him when it was brought out at Carden. When they come out to go on, I told him about it, and he flew into a fury, and when he talked about pushing my face in I told him he'd better start in on it. Then he calmed down and thought a bit till a policeman come along and told him the car couldn't stand there all day. I said what about having inquiries made along the road, but he said he'd make his own arrangements, and mind my own business. Then he went to the back and tried the strap on the other trunk, while the policeman hung around to see we didn't stop too long there, and he—the colonel, I mean—he said if we used rotten old straps like that what could we expect, and I'd got to get a rope or something to make sure the other one didn't get lost. I'd got about sixteen foot of cord that'd hang a bullock up, in the tool box, and I got that out. He took it and corded the trunk himself, slip-knotted it, and when we got to the end of the run beggar me if I could untie that knot. I had to cut it—they don't like you if you stand too long in the Savoy yard, even with a Rolls——"

"Where is that cord?" Head interrupted the recital.

"Why, back in the tool box. I was careful to cut it near his knot, so as not to shorten it more'n a foot or——"

"Fetch it here for me, will you? I want it."

"But it was on the other trunk, not the one that fell off," Albert protested. "And it wasn't put on till after I'd found out——"

"Never mind," Head interrupted again. "Fetch it here for me."

Albert got off the table and went out, and Edward John turned to face into the room and observe— "I don't see what all this is about."

"Afraid I don't feel like enlightening you," Head told him.

He resumed his survey of the mews, and Albert returned. Head took the cord, a length of stout, braided white cotton threads, immensely strong, and cleanly cut beside a knot that still remained in it near one end. He opened his attaché case and dropped the cord inside.

"I'd like that back, some time, sir," Albert said in an injured tone. "I keep it in case of a tow, and might want it."

"You shall have it back," Head promised, "but it might be wanted elsewhere for awhile. You left Colonel Thomas and his wife at the Savoy, I understand, when you cut this rope off the trunk?"

"And come straight back here for a wash down," Albert resumed his story. "Teddy wished another job on me that same day."

"When did you next see Colonel Thomas after that?"

"This mornin', sir. He put in an order to Teddy last night to take him and Mrs. Thomas down to the Priory at Monk's Pagenham, and I went to the Savoy for 'em. Made it slippy, because of this theatre job I'm going on to-night. She looked better, I thought, but not as lively as she does as a rule. Bit quiet and peaky. Generally, she's got a word or two for me, but nothing of that sort to-day. Oh, no!"

"Haven't they a car of their own?" Head asked.

"Some sort of old bone-box down at the Priory, sir—I believe it's for her to drive when they're there. They don't take it away from there, though. They're abroad more'n half their time, and when they're in London they job here. Seem to live in hotels most of their time when they are in England—like when I took 'em to the Carden Arms. This is the third year I've been down there with 'em—and that's how I come to have heard about you, sir. That business at the Angle, I think the house was called, and the Forrest case the other side of Westingborough——"

"We'll take them as read, Albert," Head interrupted him. "This last trip to Carden, now. You took both Colonel and Mrs. Thomas, or did he go alone and she joined him there?"

"No, sir. I took 'em both there from the Savoy. Something she said—I got an idea they'd just come over from Paris and only stopped a night at the Savoy that time, but I'm not sure about that. Three weeks ago last Saturday it'd be I took 'em down. And an easy time—it always is that, when I take 'em to Carden. He's dead set on flyfishing, puts in nearly all his time at it, and I run her to see her sister at a farm out Crandon way. This time, she went to stay with the sister."

"Does he ever go there with her?" Head inquired.

"Him? Lord, no! No fish, there. Besides, I got the idea he's much too high and mighty to go to a place like that—I heard him say once—it'd be the first time they went to Carden—something he said to her about not marrying her family, but her. It was a little bit of a row they had about just that, I made it. No, he never went near there."

"And she went to stay there this time, you say. When would that be—how long after the Saturday of three weeks ago?"

"It was on the Monday, week before last," Albert said after a pause for thought. "I always stop at a cottage in the village, because they can't put me up at the hotel, and when I went along in the morning for orders as usual, he told me Mrs. Thomas was going to stay with her sister for a few days, and I was to come for her at eleven. Which I did, and out she comes as happy as a sandboy, with only a little hand case which she chucked in the car when I opened the door, and said something about no use taking fine clothes, or nice clothes, to stay on a farm——"

"Spinning it out, ain't you, Albert?" Edward John inquired, turning about in the doorway. "They're good clients of ours, remember."

"And I'm saying nothing against 'em, either!" Albert snapped back. "I'm telling Mr. Head what he asked sir?"

"You'd got to where you took her to the farm," Head said, "and I want all the details you can give me of what happened after that, until you drove away with two trunks on the back of the car on Friday last."

"Yes, I reckoned that was what you wanted, sir, which is why I'm spinning it out—plenty time to hose down and get away on that theatre job, Teddy. What about some tea, too? About time, ain't it?"

"It'll be along in a quarter of an hour or so," his brother answered, "but I can't make out what all this is about."

"You never can," Albert told him, with scant sympathy. "Now, Mr. Head, where was I? Oh, yes! I took her to the farm, and she said the colonel'd let me know when I was to come there for her, but she reckoned it'd be about Friday or Saturday week—that'd be last Friday or Saturday. Then I went back and amused myself—he didn't want the car that day. I turned up the next morning for orders, and the next, and still he didn't want the car. Fishing all the time, like he always does down there. It's what he goes for, and so she can go and see her sister when she feels like it. So I keep on turning up morning after morning and no orders for me till—let me see! Yes, either the Monday or the Tuesday, it'd be, and I'm pretty nearly sure it was the Monday. I goes for orders in the morning as usual, and the colonel says to me—'Nothing for you to do to-day, Smith, and telling you that is getting a bit monotonous, don't you think?' Something like that it was he said to me. And then he said Mrs. Thomas had the use of a car where she was—they've got one there, I know—and he wasn't likely to want me. He'd send word to the cottage if he did. Mrs. Thomas would want to be fetched back on the Friday, or else Saturday morning perhaps——"

"Wait a minute," Head interrupted, and did not explain his request. Edward John in the doorway faced about to look at him, and Albert waited as bidden, while Head thought out the implications of Mrs. Thomas' return.

Yes, of course, Ashford, apparently arriving by the *Pathankot*, could not reach Carden Hall until fairly late on the Saturday night, for the boat would not dock much before noon, and, had he been alive, he would have been there to meet it and clear his four trunks through the customs, to give verisimilitude to his pretence of having come all the way by sea. Meanwhile Mrs. Thomas, back at the Carden Arms before he appeared, ostensibly from a visit to her sister, would have been in no way traceable to the Warlingham. Something had happened to frighten them into parting on the Wednesday afternoon, though: was it Thomas?

"Go on with the story," Head bade, "and miss nothing out."

"That's what he told me," Albert said. "She'd want to be fetched back then, so I was to turn up on the Friday morning for orders as usual unless I heard from him at the cottage before. He'd send if he wanted me in the meantime, but he didn't think he would, because all the use he had for a car was to get somewhere, and driving for driving's sake was no use to him— didn't appeal to him, was the words he used. So back I goes, quite happy. If he liked to pay for me and the car to hang about idle, that's his look out, and the hire money's mounting up all the time to put smiles on Teddy's face there. And nothing more happens till the Thursday. I turns up every morning to give the car the once-over in the garage, and on Thursday I goes back to the cottage, reckoning to make the rest of the day out with a nice bit I know down there, since he's not sent for the car, and when I gets back there's a telegram. From her, not from him. It says to meet her and Mrs. Jevons at Crandon station eleven-fifty that morning. 'Oho!' says I to myself. 'They've been up to town on a blind together, and want to be taken back to the farm, and he's to know nothing about it.' For she'd reckon he'd be busy at his fishing, you see, and wouldn't want the car, and when I met 'em she'd ask me to say nothing to him about their little jaunt together, most likely. No reason why he should know, of course. So off goes me with the car to be there in time, and when I gets there, it's not her and Mrs. Jevons—her sister, that is—coming out of the station together, but her and him. They comes to the car, and she's what you might call chatful, but he don't look too pleased. Along comes a porter with the case she'd taken to the farm and another one, but she stops him when he starts to put 'em both in the back of the car. 'That one isn't mine,' she says, 'it belongs to the lady there'— and I looks and sees Mrs. Jevons standing back all haughty, and I reckoned he'd told her off which was why she wasn't any nearer. So the porter took that case back and didn't get any tip from us, because I drove straight back to the hotel with 'em and I reckon Mrs. Jevons had to take a cab to the farm, or else walk. What puzzled me was when he went to London to come back by that train, because I'd——"

"How do you know he did go to London?" Head interposed.

"Well, I don't, of course, because I hadn't seen anything of him since the Monday, when he told me he'd let me know if he wanted the car. But he came off that train with 'em—if he'd been meeting it from the hotel, he'd have got me to drive him. He wouldn't have walked all that way, I know. It's seven or eight miles, at the least."

But, remembering what Hoots Aird had told

him, Head knew Thomas had met the train, and had not travelled by it. Had his wife wired him at the hotel to say that she would arrive by the eleven-fifty? And, if he had been there to receive the wire, he could not be Ashford's murderer. Or could he? Surely it would be impossible to steal into the hotel in the small hours of the morning, unperceived? Yet—the knot that slipped only one way, in the cord from Ashford's throat, and the knot in the heavier cord Albert had brought in —abruptly Head reached for his case, opened it, took out Albert's cord, and held it out to him.

"Tie me a running noose in the unknotted end of that, as if you had it round a trunk on the back of the car, and wanted to pull it tight," he bade. "I want to see how you'd tie it."

Edward John, in the doorway, looked round again. "I'm beginning to have an idea what all this is about," he observed. "Go on, Albert."

And Albert made a running noose that would run only one way, with a knot exactly like that in the cord from Ashford's throat.

"Like that, you mean, sir?" he asked.

"Just like that," Head assented, and, taking the cord, put it back in the case and closed the lid, knowing that Albert had nearly—not quite, but nearly—spoiled the value of that piece of evidence.

"Well, I reckon that's about the whole story, sir," Albert remarked. "They didn't want me again that day—Thursday—and when I went round for orders Friday morning he told me what time we'd start, and we did. I've told you what happened about the trunk, and how I left 'em at the Savoy. I don't think there's anything else."

Again Edward John turned, and this time came forward from the doorway. "Tea," he said, and was much more amiable than he had appeared till then. "Shall I ask 'em to fetch another cup for you, inspector?"

"That's very good of you," Head assented.

"Yes, ain't it?" Edward John agreed ironically, "but you see, I'm beginning to see what all this is about, now."

"I wish I could," Head remarked thoughtfully.

"Why—you don't mean to say——" Edward John stared at him incredulously, and left the sentence incomplete.

"I might have an idea that you run this business," Head told him, "but I couldn't prove it to other people. For that, I need evidence."

"I do own it!" Edward John exclaimed. "That is, me and Albert do. Why, I could show you our cheque signatures, and there's the car licences, and the lease in our names——" He broke off, looking indignant.

"Exactly—evidence," Head said quietly. "Not merely an idea."

"Take your brain out and dust it, Teddy," Albert advised. "I see what Mr. Head's getting at. Yes, miss, the tray can go here, and we want you to bring another cup and saucer and a third ration of solids—buns and things. That'll be yours, Mr. Head—help yourself to milk and sugar, and I'll have a bun till she fetches the other cup."

* * *

"You are Mr. Peto?"

"That is my name, sir. What can I do for you?"

Head offered his card, and the grave, elderly man looked at it, and then, without taking it, gave the inspector a look of silent inquiry.

"To ask you if, among your customers, you have a Colonel Philip Woodford Thomas, retired from the Indian Army about three years ago."

"No, sir," Peto answered without hesitation. "A Mr. George Thomas, a stockbroker, has been on our books for the past twenty years, but we have no other client of that name. Of that I am certain."

"Do you do any cash sales—to customers whose names you would not know?"

The other man smiled pityingly as he shook his head.

"I am afraid, sir"—momentarily, he glanced down at Head's feet—"you do not realise the quality of the footwear that we supply, or you would not have asked that question. I can assure you that, without exception, we do not."

"Thank you very much," Head said. "That's all."

Outside the shop, he paused to reflect. Yes, there would be just time, before establishments of this kind closed, for one more call. And Winter's of Maddox Street was nearest. If he drew blank there, he must begin on the others in the morning.

CHAPTER XIX

Belief is Not Proof

THE superintendent ordered Jeffries, police clerk, chauffeur, and general handy man, to bring Mr. Head's tea into his—the superintendent's—room, and to bring him another hot buttered bun at the same time.

"My old lady says things about my figure sometimes, but I *like* hot buttered buns," he said defiantly as he observed Head's smile. "Besides, I don't go on trips to London and get lushed up and petted by managers who want to keep on the right side of the police. Carry on with the tale, though, till your tea comes along."

"I turned out from the hotel this morning," Head resumed his recital, "and went on with the shoemakers. If that manager, Atherton, had made me feel I was somebody, I very soon forgot it. The way they all looked at my shoes made me feel like a tramp with his toes showing, and I wanted to put my feet in my pockets, or anywhere out of sight. Those chaps don't make the sort of shoes you and I wear, chief. They put diamonds in the heels instead of nails to take the wear, and the uppers are made of angels' skins lined with cloth of gold—twenty-four carat gold. I worked through my list of names without result, and by that time I was thoroughly footsore—because I don't wear their shoes, I expect. And a worm would look jaunty, compared with what I felt like. Every one I interviewed was old and crusted, but not a bit mellow after looking at my feet. The last one I visited was a shop in Sloane Street—Calman was the name—and when I came out and knew I had to give it up I saw across the street, nearly opposite, another shop of the sort that was not on my list, but as mouldy and respectable as any of them. Waterfield was the name over the front, and I went in. Waterfield makes shoes for colonel Thomas. They all know their customers as they do their own children."

"If they're the modern sort of parent, a lot better," Wadden declared. "Here's your tea. Give Mr. Head the other bun, Jeffries—I want that big one. Carry on, Head—the less you eat, the more you can talk."

"But Waterfield—I saw him himself—couldn't definitely identify those soles as belonging to a pair of shoes he had made for Colonel Thomas," Head pursued. "He had one of his workmen into the shop, and with my permission they dissected the second sole and heel—even went so far as to take scraps of waxed thread and soak away the wax in some sort of liquid to unravel the threads. The workman matched up the threads with some unwaxed stuff he brought in, and declared he'd done that stitching, but I doubt whether that statement would hold under cross-examination. Waterfield, too, was prepared to swear the shoes were his make, and I think he could make good on it in the witness box. But there wasn't enough left from the fire for him to be absolutely certain those shoes were made on the special lasts he keeps for Colonel Thomas, because Thomas has perfectly normal feet for a man of his size. In fact, Waterfield said, it might be possible for a man like that to wear ready-made shoes without discomfort, but by the way he said it I knew he'd sooner forgive a man for paraffining his mother and setting fire to her than for a crime like that. I kept my feet well under his counter while he explained it all to me. And I had an idea, chief."

"You needed it, by that time," Wadden observed. "What was it?"

"Whoever crossed the Idleburn and made that trail through the woods burned his own shoes in the fire and put on Ashford's—and I'm not saying yet that it was Thomas," Head said. "He didn't do it because his own shoes were wet and the others were dry, either. He'd had a torch or something to prevent him from stepping on earth that might take a footprint, but he knew all the same that he might have made a print and not known it. He didn't, but he couldn't be absolutely sure of that. But, when he made that fire, it wasn't far short of dawn, and there'd be light to show him where to step for the rest of the way. So he burned the shoes that might have left prints, and put on Ashford's as an extra precaution against being traced. If a print should be found, you see, no shoe could be found to fit it. Colonel Morrison pointed out the difficulty of getting rid of such evidence as a pair of shoes, and our man got rid of them—or thought he did —at the first opportunity."

"Thomas did, you mean," Wadden said, and finished his second bun.

"I thought it was Jevons," Head observed with gentle irony.

"You're not sure yet that it wasn't," Wadden retorted with considerable energy. "That Smith feller's story merely tells you Thomas was at Crandon station when his wife got there, and he didn't go by car. No more than that. He must have been at the Carden Arms to get some message that told him when she'd arrive, and in that case I don't see him on the train the night before with Ashford. Further to that, from what you say he didn't turn pale and stagger as he ought to have done when he saw Thane with you at the Carden Arms that night. Seeing Thane there, and being afraid of being recognised, ought to have blown his lid off and started him shouting for burnt feathers. And it didn't."

"As I recollect that," Head said slowly, "Mrs. Thomas came down the stairs and through the lounge with him following. She didn't know what had happened to Ashford then, remember, didn't suspect anything at all had happened to him, only that there had been a peculiar sort of murder in a train somewhere near, with a naked man concerned in it. She didn't hurry down, knowing as she did that she was the best-dressed and best-looking woman in the hotel. No, she gave everybody time to realise it, and that gave Thomas behind her plenty of time to see Thane and make up his mind what to do about it— that is, if he were the man of the train and feared Thane might recognise him. Thane's man had a red nose, he says, and Colonel Thomas has not a red nose. Therefore, if he were the man of the train, he must have trusted to his normal appearance in dinner kit as opposed to his disguised appearance in pulled-down hat and buttoned-up overcoat to carry him through. And it did."

"Sound. Oh, sound!" Wadden reflected pensively. "And it leaves us exactly where we were before, don't it? What next?"

"I'm going over to see Cortazzi," Head answered, and stood up. "To find out whether Thomas slept in the hotel last Wednesday night."

"I'd go on from there and have a word with the Jevonses if I were you," Wadden advised. "Watch their reactions when you point out that they were party to Mrs. Thomas staying at the Warlingham with Ashford, which was the cause of his being murdered—whether that's true or no. Frighten 'em—hint at what must come out under cross-examination in the witness-box, and watch how they stand up to it. Or don't, maybe."

"If it's not too late when I've finished with Cortazzi," Head assented. "Meanwhile, will you get through to whoever is in charge over the Pagenhams, find out if the Thomases are still there, and ask for us to be informed at once if they move away?"

"It shall be done—leave it to me," Wadden promised. "If he is our man, the fact of his going there proves that he's far too wily a bird to rouse suspicion by running away or altering his normal habits."

"Believing, of course, that we don't suspect him," Head observed. "And on the face of it, since she appears to be still with him and we haven't made a move a week after the murder, there's no reason why we should. He'd reason that if we'd found out about her being at the Warlingham, we should have been after her, if not him, before now."

"Assuming——" Wadden said, and left it at that.

"Quite so, chief. When he saw Thane, he didn't blench, as far as my recollection goes—and he hasn't got a red nose. And if she knew he'd killed Ashford, she'd leave him—I don't think she could live with him and not learn it from his manner toward her."

"Postulating what a woman will do—you might as well try to count the green fly on a tomato plant," Wadden said "Hie along and pump the local Mussolini, and then you'll have time to go on to the Jevonses."

* * *

As usual, Cortazzi was most anxious to afford Head every assistance, and, outwardly, not in the least curious—unlike Edward John Smith—as to what it was all about. He assented readily to the suggestion that they should talk in his own office, a mere cubby-hole of a place back of the desk on which lay the register of visitors, and pulled down the sliding pane covering the opening through which their conversation might have been overheard in the lounge. Then he seated himself facing Head, and waited placidly.

"Colonel Thomas has not come back," Head asserted, by way of opening.

"'E do not come back, Mr. 'Ead. I 'ave let ze room. I am fool."

"I want to take your mind back to last week,"

Head said slowly. "Before the Thursday, when Mrs. Thomas returned here in time for lunch. Was Colonel Thomas here all the time, till he brought her back?"

"Larst week," Cortazzi reflected. "I theenk—when I am fool, Mr. 'Ead, I 'ave to theenk if you arsk me about larst week. So—yaas. Mrs. Thomas go to stay with 'er sister, not larst week, but ze week behind it. Yaas. Ze man which drive ze car, 'e tell 'Arry 'e take 'er to stop with 'er sister. It ees a farm where 'er sister live with 'er 'usband, an' 'e take 'er there. Yaas. Not far, that farm. An' she come back with 'im—you say it was Thursday. You see, Mr. 'Ead, 'e pay all ze taime for them both, because when I am quaite fool I do not let a man single ave ze room double unless 'e pay ze double. Noh. I move im in ze single room unless 'e pay ze double to keep ze double room. An' ze colonel pay ze double all ze taime, because Mrs. Thomas is to come back after she stop at her sister. I 'ave much to theenk. Ze buying for ze meals, ze staff, ze rooms, ze laundry, flowers on ze tables—all of it I do. An' you arsk me where is one man which pay ze double an' all day go after ze feesh. Per'aps 'Arry tell you more, an' Lena, for she make ze beds. Me, I theenk ze colonel was 'ere all ze taime."

"We will have Harry in, please," Head asked.

Cortazzi jumped up and went out, to return with his head waiter, who inclined his head respectfully as he stood just inside the door of the tiny office. Cortazzi closed it behind him.

"You tell Mr. 'Ead all 'e arsk, 'Arry," Cortazzi bade, "an' if you tell anyone what 'e arsk, it is ze fineesh of you 'ere."

"An inquiry about the movements of Colonel Thomas, before his wife came back here last week, Harry," Head told the man. "You would be able to tell me if he were in for meals, I expect?"

"As far as I can remember, sir, he wasn't in for any meals either on the Tuesday or the Wednesday," Harry answered. "Very often when he's here he doesn't come in to lunch, but asks me for sandwiches. He took sandwiches Monday and Tuesday, but not after that. Both he and Mrs. Thomas were in for lunch on the Thursday—you lunched here that day, sir."

"And dined too," Head agreed. "Colonel Thomas asked you for sandwiches on the Tuesday. Yes. Was that the last you saw of him?"

"No, sir—I remember, now. Four—five of 'em wanted sandwiches that day, and I took 'em into the lounge. The colonel was in the telephone box at the time. The others took their packets, and he came out and took his packet off me and stood looking at it in what I thought was an odd sort of way, and didn't thank me for 'em as he generally does. Turned round and went up the stairs with the packet and his fishing bag and tackle, and as nearly as I can tell that's the last I saw of him."

"This was on the Tuesday?" Head asked.

"Tuesday morning, sir. He wasn't in to dinner,

and he wasn't down to breakfast next morning, either, so I asked Lena—that's the maid who does the rooms, sir—whether he was up in his room. She said no, and his bed hadn't been slept in, but I didn't pay much notice to that——"

"You be careful, 'Arry!" Cortazzi interjected with visible anxiety.

"Let him go on, Cortazzi," Head bade. "Why didn't you pay attention to the bed not being slept in, Harry? Because Mrs. Thomas was away?"

"That's it, sir." The faintest semblance of a smile appeared on the man's face. "With the cat away—well, you never can tell, even with the best of 'em. And Mr. Cortazzi can't be everywhere ——"

"I am most careful of ze morals, Mr. 'Ead. Most careful!" Cortazzi protested indignantly. "I sack one girl which was ze best girl I ever 'ave 'ere, in every uzzer way. I sack 'er in one minute, when I know."

"But what happened once might happen again, you thought, Harry," Head suggested. "Quite naturally—don't blame him, Cortazzi, or yourself either. And that little incident, Harry, would make you notice when the colonel next turned up for a meal in the dining room, I expect?"

"It did, sir. Of course, if it had made any difference on the meal slips, I'd have noticed at once, but with him it didn't. He was paying full rate for the two of 'em all the time, whether they were in or no, so as far as he was concerned there wasn't any slips to be turned in. But as you say, sir, I did notice, and the next I saw of him in the dining room was on the Thursday for lunch, when you lunched here and Mrs. Thomas had got back. They were both in to lunch."

"He didn't sleep in his own bed on Wednesday night?"

"I couldn't say, sir. I didn't ask Lena, but she'd know."

"I will go an' fetch Lena," Cortazzi said, and opened the door.

"Don't," Head bade, and stopped him. "If I need her, I know where to find her. Remember, Harry, and you too, Cortazzi, absolute silence over what I have asked and what you have both told me is essential."

"Ze man which keep 'otel, 'e never talk," Cortazzi said. "'Arry, if ze 'ead waiter of ze 'otel talk, 'e is not 'ead waiter any more. If I am fool or empty, it is all ze same. One word, an' 'e go."

"You needn't worry about me, Mr. Cortazzi," Harry said serenely. "I'm too well off here to take any risks of that sort."

"I am going to use your telephone, Cortazzi," Head said, rising to his feet. He went out to the lounge and, entering the glass-walled box there, shut himself in and dialled "O."

"Police, operator," he said in reply to the inevitable query. "Is that Miss Willis on duty now?" Carden exchange, he knew, was operated by two girls working in turns, and he thought he recognised this voice.

"It is—and that's Mr. Head," she asserted rather than asked.

"Quite correct, and I want you to do something for me, Miss Willis. Can you look up the record of any trunk calls to or from the Carden Arms on Tuesday morning of last week, and give me the telephone numbers of any persons who made incoming calls?"

"Certainly, Mr. Head." It was not the first time she had been of service to him in this way. "It may take some time to get incoming numbers, though. Shall I look up outgoing trunk calls first?"

"If you'd be so good. Shall I hold on while you do it?"

"Oh, yes! It won't take more than a minute or two."

By his wrist watch, it took just three minutes, and then she reported that no outgoing trunk calls were booked from the Carden Arms during the morning in question. Local calls, Head knew, were untraceable on the dial system since only the fact of a call having been made was automatically recorded for accounting purposes.

"And if you want the callers' numbers for incoming calls," she said, "I'm afraid it's no use holding on. Can you ring again in half an hour?"

"Yes. I'll wait and ring you then," he promised.

He seated himself in the lounge to wait, and reflected that there would still be time to interview Mr. and Mrs. Jevons before returning to Westingborough. It began to appear that Thomas was the man of the train by which Ashford and Thane had travelled, but, so far, nothing that had come to light would carry weight with a jury after even a mediocre defending counsel had cross-examined on it. And Thomas was evidently a man of considerable wealth, one who could afford the best counsel money might buy.

Cortazzi came out from his office and looked at Head inquiringly, but, since he won no response, did not approach. Ze Miss Tomsongs came in, and as they went toward the stairs one twittered to the other that it was the most delightful walk they had found yet, and how dear Mary would have enjoyed it. Still twittering, they vanished beyond the turn of the stairway, and Rynewald entered with Major Fitton.

"Pints, in tankards—you order them," he bade, and left Fitton to advance and stand over Head. "How are you, inspector? Seeing you reminded me of an appointment I failed to keep with that large superintendent. Wadden, I believe is his name. An appointment with a bottle. Do you mind telling him I fully intend to look in next time I'm his way?"

"Not in the least," Head answered. "Is that all the message?"

"I think so—yes. No, though—you might remind him at the same time that betting is a vice of which I'm never guilty—never have been. I don't know if you've met Major Fitton, but I'm quite sure he would agree that a famous man like yourself might have a tankard with us. Can I ask you to join us in one—we are just about to lay the dust."

"Thank you very much, but"—Head got out of his chair—"I was waiting for a telephone call— to make one, I mean—and the time has come to do it, I see. So you must forgive me for declining, this time."

"Next time, then," Rynewald suggested with a smile, "and the honour will be mine. I'll rely on you to give the superintendent my message."

A little too friendly, Head reflected as he entered the telephone box and carefully closed its door. Was Rynewald's cordiality intended to prevent suspicion of him? Head took off the receiver and dialled.

"Miss Willis? Yes. Now what news of incoming calls, if any?"

"One only, Mr. Head—nine minutes, it was. Originating from Regent exchange"—she gave the number—"at ten-two a.m."

"You don't know who is represented by that number?"

"No, Mr. Head. You didn't ask me to find that out for you."

"Quite right, Miss Willis. Careless of me to

forget it, but I expect you're glad to be saved the trouble. Thank you very much. Now will you put me on to police, Westingborough, please?"

As he had expected, Sergeant Wells took the call.

"Inspector Head speaking, sergeant. Take down this number, please," and he repeated the Regent number he had just taken down. "Find out for me whom it represents, their address and business, if any, and have the information ready by the time I get back—seven-thirty at latest."

"Very good, Mr. Head."

"Tell the superintendent I'd like him to wait for me. That's all, sergeant. Except—if I'm not there by seven-thirty, he needn't wait."

Emerging from the box, he went straight out to his car, paying no heed at all to Rynewald, who put down his tankard and moved as if to intercept him and renew the offer of a drink. And, as Head drove away, he saw Rynewald standing and gazing through the glazed upper part of the entrance door, anxiously, it appeared.

Was the man anxious over anything? Had he some cause for anxiety, apart from his errand in connection with Nevile dyes? Over that, Head knew, nothing had resulted, so there was no reason for Rynewald to stay on in the district —Raymond Nevile would not alter his decision. It might yet be necessary to ascertain what Rynewald had been doing on that momentous Wednesday night.

Such evidence as had come to light pointed to Thomas as the mystery man in the train, and now, with Harry's statement, there was nearly enough to justify belief in his guilt. Nearly, but not quite.

And there was a vast difference between belief and proof.

CHAPTER XX

Proof

ALTHOUGH, as the landlord of the Jolly Prior had observed to Head, the "Newton" part of Pagenham Newton refers to the newness of the town, it is a village rather than a town, and for the most part the houses on either side of its one straggling street are greyly old, for the name was bestowed on it long ago. They are mostly of stone, too, and here and there in a wall can still be seen traces of carving, which declare the reason for the scant remains of the old priory in their original place. Pagenham Newton is built of the priory stones, for the greater part: there are not more than half a dozen brick houses in the village.

After the last prior had been hanged over the doorway that gave access to his apartments, as seems to have been a practice of those good old days, the priory and a good portion of its lands were granted to one Robert Hoddal, or Hoddle—both spellings are extant—who did some effective dirty work for the Lord Protector Seymour during the reign of the boy king, Edward VI. He built himself a mansion which no longer exists, using the priory stones for his purpose, while others also raided the fabric for building materials. But, either because the last prior had dangled over his doorway, or because the stone from other parts of the great range of buildings was of better quality or more easily raped away, the prior's dwelling remained intact while the Hoddle family pursued a more or less nefarious course—one of them was burned at the stake on account of a traffic with the evil one which involved the procuring of children, after the manner of Gilles de Retz, and another was executed in the last part of James I's reign, for being careless over poisoning his wife. Three other people were killed by the poison, in consequence of which that particular Hoddle died rather horribly.

There were good Hoddles as well as bad, or it may have been that some were more careful than others, for the priory estates remained in the family until, during the Civil War— they were all staunch Puritans by that time— the male line was extinguished. There remained Isabel Hoddle, who married Hugo Cottenham, a poor gentleman whose family was ruined by adherence to the Royalist cause. After the Restoration, the second Charles graciously permitted Hugo to take possession of his wife's lands in return for services rendered. The family mansion had been almost destroyed by Royalist cannon in the course of the war, and Hugo, rather than attempt rebuilding there, restored the prior's dwelling and added a wing on each side of it. He made, by any architectural standards, an ugly, patchwork frontage of it: the three original floors that he restored, of one room width, revealed the best characteristics of renaissance work. The wings were hardly worth calling Jacobean, and did not match each other at that. They were given steep roofs, tiled, while the centre portion retained its flat leads, in the middle of which a roofed doorway stuck up like a monk's cowl, to give access to the leads from the top story. Viewed from the front, the whole gave a cock-eyed effect, owing to the lack of symmetry of the wings.

The Hoddles had been schemers, sly plotters, criminals, and swashbucklers, with here and there one who tried, by good works, to atone for the general badness of the family. Such a one, apparently, was Let-Not-Your-Heart-Be-Troubled Hoddle, who was one of Ireton's trusted men, and who came to a glorious and gory end at Marston Moor. The Cottenhams, on the other hand, claimed descent from the old nobility that became almost extinct when Tudor tricksters laid the foundations of modern plutocracy. They had held a barony, which was attainted before Bosworth field put an end to the Yorkists, and, though the Cottenhams had been staunch Lancastrians, was not restored to the family, for the Tudor rewards were granted only to followers who might be regarded as assets, and, poor and proud, even then, the Cottenhams ranked more nearly as liabilities.

The blend of the two families produced curious results. There were in it men like Richard Cottenham, the father of the two girls Isabel and Jeanette Angelina, honourable gentlemen who won the respect of all who knew them: again there were such as Hugo Cottenham, a younger son in the days of the first George, who swung in chains in Execution Dock after a career of piracy in which he rendered himself notorious for fiendish cruelty—and in those days it was no mean feat to attain notoriety in such a way. There were saints among the women of the family, and again there were outstanding sinners, of whom the less said the better. By the end of the nineteenth century the once-prolific family had fined down to Richard and his wife, who bore him his two daughters and no other children. He was the last male Cottenham.

Jeanette, the younger of the two girls, was first to marry, and in so doing displayed Cottenham spirit and Hoddle taste. Farmer Jevons was not the sort of man that old Richard Cottenham would admit to his house, even as an acquaintance, but the girl was determined to have him and have him she did. The letter Isabel wrote to Bernard Ashford defined her as nearly all Hoddle: selfish, deceitful, planning to hold both Thomas and Ashford, at least until the latter succeeded to his father's title and estate: arrestingly beautiful, as had been many Cottenham women before her, she must have possessed some siren quality of attraction, some holding power both greater and rarer than surface charm.

Perhaps old Jim Furze and his wife, who had served old Richard Cottenham at the Priory and acted as caretakers there after he had died and Isabel had married Colonel Thomas, could have told what passed between the pair after Albert Smith had left them there; but Furze was the old type of family servant, and he told no more than he must, while his wife was equally tight-lipped. Warned that the colonel and his wife would arrive, they summoned Maria, Jim's niece, to act as housemaid, and got in provisions, lighted fires and aired the beds, and had all in readiness when "Miss Isabel" and her husband entered by the doorway over which the last prior had once dangled.

It was a small retinue, but in spite of his age Furze was still an exceptionally good servant, while his wife managed the kitchen and Maria, in addition to other duties, found time to act as maid to Mrs. Thomas.

On the word of Maria, all was not well between the colonel and his wife. Usually, on their visits to the Priory, they went about together, called on neighbours in the district, had people to tea, and the like. This time, Maria heard the colonel haranguing his wife after she had left them in the dining room, the night of their arrival, and next day Mrs. Thomas took the car and drove off alone, while the colonel got out his tackle and went fishing. There was a trout stream of small merit near by that had been good enough in old time to serve the monks for their Fridays, though the fishing was not to be compared to that obtainable in the vicinity of the Carden Arms.

That day, the colonel did not return for lunch. Mrs. Thomas was late for the meal. In mid-afternoon she got Furze to unlock the door in the roof which gave access to the leads, and went up there with a book to sit on the knee-high parapet over the front entrance. Since the April afternoon was chilly in spite of brilliant sunlight, she wore her fur coat, and sat there in it with the book held down on her knee while she gazed across the crumbled ruins at the lands she knew. A dwarfed, lonely figure she made at that height—it was Maria who used the word "lonely" in describing how she had sat there. Maria had had to go to Pagenham Newton because the grocer's errand boy had one of his epileptic fits that day: she had looked back at the beginning of her journey and had seen Mrs. Thomas seated on the parapet with her head drooped, not reading, but just idly gazing: as nearly as she could tell, the lady had not altered her posture in any way when Maria returned, over an hour later.

What were Isabel Thomas' thoughts, that spring afternoon?

She had probably descended from the roof by the time Head drove away from the Carden Arms after instructing Sergeant Wells to identify the telephone number that Miss Willis had obtained, for sunset had brought a cold wind and promise of another fruit-destroying ground frost during the night.

Driving along Carden Street, Head pulled up level with Potts' front gate: dusk was so far advanced that it was nearly time to switch on sidelights—too late to go on to Jevons' to-night. Besides, if he did go, what of value could he learn? That Mrs. Thomas had sent a message to her sister, asking her to be at Crandon station with a suit case, on the platform with it, to make it appear that they had both gone to London and had returned together, when the chauffeur appeared to meet them with the Rolls. Thomas, appearing instead of the chauffeur, either had or had not detected the imposture: it was of little consequence, either way; Mrs. Jevons had not been with Mrs. Thomas in London.

"Hello, mister!" Potts, in shirt-sleeves, bobbed up from behind his thick privet hedge. "Brought them stamps along?"

"Not this time, I'm afraid," Head answered. "I stopped only to turn round and go back, having remembered something."

"Ar! I thought you was the sort that never forgot things. Perishin' hard for the garden, this here weather is. Looks like we ain't never goin' to get no rain, it do, an' these here night frosts is enough to drive a man to drink. Water gettin' scarce, too. The river's down to next to nothin', when you reckon what it ought to be this time o' year."

"Not so low, I understand, as to stop you from having trout for sale," Head observed. "I shall have to draft an extra man into Carden, if this goes on. You're breaking out in a new place, it seems."

"Lord love you, mister, that ain't fair, now! Two lots—well, call it three. And they was crowdin' each other in the water, they was—I ain't sayin' what water. It might be a hunderd mile from here."

"And might be twenty-eight days hard," Head pointed out.

"I reckon I'll leave them fish alone," Potts said dubiously. "I dunno, though. Anyhow, I'll keep an eye out for that there extra man o' yours. Which one'll it be, mister?"

With a laugh, Head put in reverse and backed the car across the road to turn about. He swung to face the other way, put in first gear, and depressed the accelerator. Potts' voice followed him—

"Don't forgit them stamps next time, mister!"

A hundred yards or so brought the car to Plender's neat cottage, and Head drew in again and went to the door. Mrs. Plender opened it.

"My husband's out, Mr. Head. Gone over Todlington way, I believe."

"That's all right, Mrs. Plender. He should have a trunk here—I sent instructions for him to get it from the Carden Arms."

"Yes, sir—it's here in the front room. Do you want it?"

"I'll take it, if you don't mind my coming in to get it."

"Well, I could fetch it out, sir. It isn't heavy."

But Head entered, and recollected how Mr. Hawk, the Carden stationmaster, had once brought vital evidence to that front room. There he saw the trunk, plastered with labels which told of much travelling in many places: Paris, Cologne, Baden, Montreux, Buda-Pesth, Copenhagen, the Eastern Exchange Hotel at Port Said, the Continental-Savoy at Cairo, the Queen's Park hotel in Port of Spain, and others half-hidden by later pastings. And, not obscured by labels, the initials—"P. W. T."

He took it out to his car—as Mrs. Plender had said, it was not heavy—and, having bidden her good-night, drove off, switching on his side lamps. Wadden would have gone home by the time he reached Westingborough, and the trunk and all else must wait till to-morrow.

And supposing all that he had learned proved futile, and Thomas was not the man? Rynewald? Somebody out to destroy J 35?

Well, Colonel Morrison would call in Scotland Yard, and he, Head, would resign. Inevitably. Of all the cases——

The two-seater chugged laboriously up Condor Hill.

* * *

"That was Inspector Head, surely?"

Thane, with Loretta beside him, had just reached Carden Hall gateway when the inspector passed in his car, they having walked down the drive before going in to dinner. They stood still while the tail light disappeared.

"I didn't notice the car in time to be sure," she remarked.

"And it's not my place to be sure— of him or anybody," Thane said, remembering his identification of Head in the cell at Westingborough.

"Let's go back—it's getting cold," she suggested. "You can tell me what you mean by that as we go."

"Merely that I thought a certain man had a red nose, so Head reddened his and I jumped to the conclusion he was that man," Thane explained.

"He fooled me over it, when you drove me there and waited for me outside the police station—when we took that letter about the baggage."

"He had a reason for what he did," she said with conviction.

"Possibly, but I don't feel any smaller ass for that," Thane rejoined rather acidly.

"Even a philosopher can be unphilosophical, it seems," she remarked after a silence in which they walked slowly along the drive.

"Are there any about here?" he inquired. "Where do you keep them?"

"You proved yourself one the other day, when you corrected my perspective," she explained. "Altered my outlook, say. And now——"

"Philosophy is the art of not being disturbed by other people's troubles," he asserted. "I maintain that if Plato had sat on a hornets' nest, he'd have used just as bad language as an ordinary man."

She laughed momentarily at the simile, and Thane took her arm.

"That's the first time you've laughed since we met," he told her.

"And even now I feel I ought not," she answered. "All this—the tragedy that has been, and the trouble to come. When they find the man who killed him, I mean. All that may have been behind it, things about him—about my brother—that may come to light then——"

"For which you are not responsible," he

reminded her. "Loretta"—it was the first time he had used her name in such a way—"when you come to the end of things, you'll have to answer for one life—your own. And what any other person has done can only darken your outlook for a little while—all things pass. I'm not being intentionally priggish, but so very glad to have heard you laugh I want to hear it again."

"Some day, cousin Leo," she said, as they came to the hall entrance.

"Don't you think we know each other well enough now to omit the 'cousin' part of it?" he asked, pausing on the step and still holding her arm. "It's a very distant relationship, you know."

"I'll think about it." She smiled at him as she answered. "You are—my father asked me to-day how long I thought you wished to stay, and said how glad he was to have you—somebody like you —with us just now. And he said, too—if they find the man, you'll be wanted at his trial. And so ——" She broke off, and drew back from his hold on her arm.

"And you?" he asked. "Do you wish me to stay —Loretta?"

"For his sake, yes," she answered. "For myself —don't ask me yet, please. I am—things are changing so much. Let's go in—Leo."

* * *

"Did you find out about that telephone

number, sergeant?"

"Yes, sir. I had some trouble, because it's what they call ex-directory—not listed. But I got it as a police inquiry. The name is Cossar, the address Planet House, Shaftesbury Avenue, and they describe themselves as a private detective agency."

"Ah! I'll take this trunk along to my room— has the superintendent gone home yet?"

"Yes, sir. Left about ten minutes ago."

"Well, see if Mr. Cossar or any of his sleuths are available at this time of night, and if you can get anyone, put him through to my room."

Taking up the trunk, Head went to his room and sat for awhile at his desk, reflecting. The trunk must be opened—if at all—in the presence of witnesses: Wadden and himself, Jeffries, and —he took off his telephone receiver in response to the buzzer's warning.

"Mr. Cossar himself on the line, sir. Here you are?"

A rather high-pitched voice said—"Hullo?" querulously.

"Mr. Cossar, I understand?" Head asked.

"That is my name. What do you want? I was just closing down."

"Spare me a minute, Mr. Cossar. Inspector Head of the Westingborough police talking. You have been conducting inquiries on behalf of a Colonel Thomas, I understand?"

"This is a Private detective agency, Inspector

Head," Cossar retorted, "and my clients' affairs are strictly confidential."

"Quite so, but when a charge of murder becomes mixed up in them, you may have to violate a confidence in the interests of justice. Do you know anything about police work?"

"Well!" Cossar barked a caustic little laugh. "Considering I retired as a detective-sergeant when I started this office——"

"You do," Head assented. "That being so, you will understand when I tell you that you will be wanted here to make a statement in connection with a murder charge, not later than"—he paused to think of the times of arrival of trains from London—"twelve noon to-morrow."

"Is that so?" The query was caustic to a degree. "And supposing I don't appear there at twelve noon tomorrow, Inspector Head?"

"In that case, Inspector Byrne of the C. I.D. will call on you—you may have heard his name at some time or other. He happens to be my cousin and very good friend, but you won't find him at all friendly if he has to call on you. You, I know, are in possession of information that we require in connection with the train murder case, and we want you here to give it. Your expenses will be paid."

A silence. Then Cossar spoke in an altered tone.

"I'll be there. I see what you're getting at. Yes, I'll be there."

Replacing the receiver, Head sat awhile in thought again. Then he took another call, late though it was.

"Get me that Crompton Hire Service, sergeant."

When the call came through, he recognised the voice, easily.

"Good evening, Mr. Smith. Inspector Head speaking, from Westingborough. I want to speak to Albert. Is he available?"

"Just a minute, Mr. Head. I think I can get him for you. Do you mind telling me what it's all about?"

"This being a long trunk call, I'll leave Albert to do that later," Head replied. "See if you can get him to come to the 'phone, will you?"

"Hold on. I think he's about somewhere."

A long silence, and then Albert's voice—

"Hullo, Mr. Head. What have I been doing now?"

"I don't know—fortunately for you, perhaps. It's about what you did when I had that talk with you. Do you remember my asking you to tie a slip-knot in the length of rope you found for me?"

"I remember it all right. When are you going to let me have that rope back? It's expensive stuff, that rope is."

"Quite so, and you'll get it back undamaged when we've finished with it. But just now, Albert, I want to ask you. Where did you learn to tie that particular kind of knot? It's rather unusual, I mean, except for people who have to make a practice of all sorts of knots."

"Well, it's rather odd you should ask me that, Mr. Head. As a matter of fact—you remember I told you the colonel tied that trunk on the back of the car himself outside the Grand at Leicester, when he was afraid the strap might break?"

"Yes," Head assented. "I remember it. Why?"

"Well, you see, I stood by and watched him do it, and I thought to myself that's a mighty useful sort of knot. Because, before he put a couple of half-hitches on the rope to make sure, he tried the trunk, and I could see the knot wouldn't slip down, though it had slipped up easy enough. And when I got a bit of time to myself I started practising the knot till I got it right. It ain't easy, and I know even now if I tried it I'd have to think before I could do it, and might not get it right first go. And when you asked me I thought I'd try it, remembering how he'd done it—and I got it right first time, you remember."

"Yes, I remember. Thank you very much, Albert. That's all I wanted to know. I'll see that you get your rope back as soon as possible."

"Hold on just a second, Mr. Head. Teddy here is asking me what it's all about."

"Tell him I hope to find out, shortly. Good-bye, Albert."

Again, after replacing the receiver, he mused awhile. Then he rose to his feet, and looked down at the trunk.

"Proof," he said. "But he won't run away to-night."

And, being very tired, he went home.

CHAPTER XXI

A Pair of Links

THE trunk stood on the desk in Head's room, which he had cleared to make space for it, and Head himself, together with Superintendent Wadden and Jeffries, the police clerk, stood watching while Sergeant Wells tried key after key on the locks, and, as each one proved unavailing, the superintendent blew softly. There were two keys untried when he spoke—

"I think I'd get away if I were you, Head. We're not likely to find anything in the thing that bears on the case. Remember, he let it go a long while before he offered any reward or tried to get it back."

"Which is why I think we shall come on something connected with the case," Head objected as Wells tried the last key but one, which appeared as if it might turn and save further trouble. "He left it alone until he felt certain it would not be opened by us, or by anyone likely to connect him with Ashford, and then put out that reward to get it back and get rid of any evidence it might contain. No use, sergeant?"

"The last is always the right one, sir," Wells answered, and tried the one remaining key on the ring. But it was only another wrong one.

"What now—break it open?" Wadden inquired. "Or do you go?"

"I'd like to see inside that thing first," Head said. "Any more keys of about that size anywhere, Wells?"

Jeffries drew a half-dozen or so on a ring from his pocket. "One of these might fit, sir," he suggested, and handed the keys to Wells.

The sergeant looked at them and shook his head. "Only one stands a chance," he said. "The others are much too big."

"That man Cossar—what about him?" Wadden asked. "You won't be back when he gets here. Do you want me to tackle him?"

"Leave him to me," Head answered. "He's essential for the completion of the case. Hold him here for me—— Ah, sergeant! It works, eh?"

"Luck at last, sir," Wells assented, as, after turning Jeffries' key in the second lock of the trunk, he clicked back the catches and raised the lid—to reveal, for a beginning, a pair of fishing waders.

"Possibly," Wadden grunted, "though it

doesn't look over lucky to me. Who's the searcher? You'd better empty it, I think, Head, and we're the witnesses. Take an inventory as he lifts 'em out, Jeffries."

"One pair of waders," Head announced and put the down on the floor.

Following these came two suits of soiled underwear, one tweed coat, one pair of trousers, two pairs of golfing shoes, a pair of rubber goloshes, another tweed suit, and a silk dressing gown. Then, looking into the almost empty trunk, Head drew a long breath, and took out yet another pair of shoes. He looked inside one, and handed it to Wadden.

"On the stiffened leather inside the heel, chief," he said.

Wadden read aloud—"Chotu Pershad, Jelalapur."

"Originally in gilt script," Head observed, gazing into the other shoe. "There's just a trace of the gilt left, and the stamping is plain enough. Just as well I stopped till this was opened."

"We'll try the pockets of these suits," Wadden suggested calmly.

He took up the coat of the second tweed suit that Head had lifted out from the trunk, while Head himself took the other coat. Presently Wadden dropped the coat and held out his hand.

"Look, man!" he almost shouted. "This is why you found no sleeve-links among the ashes."

Head took one of the links from Wadden's

palm. It was a flat-faced pair of ovals of plain nine-carat gold—plain, that is, except for a monogram engraved on one of the ovals. Head dictated to Jeffries—

"One pair of sleeve-links, monogrammed with intertwined B, G, and A. Which," he added, "are the initials of Bernard Gordon Ashford."

"And we three witness that they were found in the left-hand side pocket of this brown tweed coat," Wadden observed, "as we witness that a pair of shoes, marked inside as made by Chotu Pershad of Jelalapur, were also found inside the trunk initialled P. W. T. And why the fool kept the links—I can understand his not finding it easy to get rid of the shoes, but why didn't he sink those links down a well or somewhere?"

"Took them out of the cuffs in the train, and then forgot where he put them—thought he'd left them in the shirt and they were among the ashes of that fire—anything," Head suggested. "By the time he'd dressed Ashford's body in Thane's clothes, I'd say, he was worked up to a point that would admit of a mistake like this, even. And until that trunk fell off the back of the Rolls, these things were safe enough."

"You might call it the luck of accident," Wadden remarked, "but I'd say myself it's another proof that God don't love murderers. But——" he looked at Head, significantly, and pointed at the door.

"Yes. Turn out the saloon, Jeffries, and you'll

drive—to Monk's Pagenham, beyond Crandon. Turn off halfway through Pagenham Newton street—it's a narrow turning on the right. I'll take Sergeant Harrison, chief, and—Jeffries, tell Williams he is to go with us. Warrant for Philip Woodford Thomas, chief—you know the rest. It'll be sessions opening time in a quarter of an hour, and you can get whoever is on the bench this morning to sign the warrant, and then send it back to me by the time Jeffries has got the saloon out—or nearly. I expect Miss Ashford will be able to identify these links as her brother's."

* * *

"That's the place, Jeffries. A gable on each side of a flat roof, was the description. And this lane should take us to it."

As Head pointed through the windscreen of the saloon, the silhouette of the Priory roof was still fully a mile distant. The horizontal line of the original flat roof, between the two inverted V's of the wings, was broken by the little pent-house in which was set the door leading from the top floor to the leads, and also by a human figure, a little to the right of the pent-house, as Head gazed at it. The distance, together with the clouded, rather misty air, rendered him not quite sure as to whether the figure were that of a woman, but he believed it was. For a little while a high hedge masked the Priory roof-line, and, when it came into view again, the figure was no longer visible. She—or possibly he—had gone down. They were near enough, then, to see that the door on the roof had been left open by whoever had descended.

The saloon turned on to a drive, so badly-kept and potholed that both Harrison and Head took hold of the side-straps to steady themselves. The oval of gravel before the entrance on which Jeffries brought the car to a standstill was tufted with grass, and shrubs that bordered it were ragged-branched, untended. The heavy oaken door was half-opened; beyond it, the big ground-floor apartment to which the doorway gave direct access showed dimly as Head, first out from the car, waited for Harrison and Constable Williams before entering the place. But, before they ranged themselves with him, he started forward and stood over a patch of reddish-brown directly in front of the half-opened door. That which had caused the stain had not had time to soak into the hard gravel fully, or to dry from redness. He looked up, and against the wrack that drove across the sky it seemed that the frontage of the Priory travelled, as the moon will appear to move in the sky when clouds pass near it. Thirty—forty feet, perhaps—above his head the parapet towered.

With Harrison and Williams beside him in response to his beckoning, he stepped forward and—there was no bell-push or handle, that he could see—took hold of the heavy knocker and beat a half-dozen imperative blows with it. And, as he beat, an old man in a rusty black suit and starched cuffs and collar ran swiftly down the stairs at the side of the gloomy, dark-panelled room, and hurried toward the door.

When he reached it, not ten seconds had passed since the thunderous clatter of Head's knocking had ceased. He gazed at the three men who prevented his exit as he advanced toward them, and then stretched out his hands before him as might a swimmer beginning a breast stroke, as if he would thrust them all aside to pass.

"Hold on, whoever you are!" Head bade sharply. "Didn't you hear me knock, or are you quite deaf?"

"Deaf—no! Let me go—let me go!"

But, as his hands fell to his sides, Head saw that they were blood-stained. He reached out and, grasping the old man's arm, shook him.

"Oh, no!" he said. "Who are you—why do you want to get away?"

Accepting without resistance the fact of being held, the old man looked up at his questioner. The half-panic urgency of his manner gave place to reason, and the stare of horror died out from his eyes.

"I—I'm sorry, sir. Police, too! Yes, police'll be wanted—you come at the right time. And it's no use going for a doctor—I thought I'd go for a doctor, but of course it's no use now. She's dead."

"Who is dead?" Head demanded. "Mrs. Thomas?"

"Aye—Miss Isabel—she's dead. And now there's only Miss Jeanette, and she's—yes, only Miss Jeanette. Nothing to be done—she's dead. Police—yes, it'll be for the police. She jumped down."

"Threw herself from the roof?" Head thought of the stain on the gravel, just behind him. "Or was she thrown down, man?"

"Nay, who'd hurt Miss Isabel? I was out there"—he pointed past Head and the two men —"and the colonel waved to her on the roof as he came along the drive—you'll have to know everything, being police. I can't understand how you come to be here like this, though——"

"Where is Colonel Thomas?" Head interrupted the man.

"The colonel? He picked her up and carried her in. I heard her whisper—childish, it was, and I expect in that last moment she was back in her childhood. 'Pixie—sorry' was the words—it wasn't more than a whisper, but I was helping him to lift her poor broken body, and I heard her —look, the blood is still on my hands! Hers. She jumped, just after he'd waved to her as he came along the drive. I didn't see—I was turned his way, and only heard the fall. And there she was, all broken. The blood is there yet to show. He came running, and took her in.

"Your name?" Head asked. He wanted to delay action, though he knew the urgency of it. To arrest a man over the body of his dead wife!

"Furze—James Furze. I've served Cottenhams all my life."

"Yes. Now you must take me—us—to Colonel Thomas."

"Very good, sir."

He backed through the doorway and pointed toward the staircase by which he had descended. "If you'll follow me—he carried her up."

He led on, and Head and his two men followed. The staircase went all the way to the top of the building, but on the first floor old Furze turned aside from it to open the door and stand back from it—

"The police, sir," he announced.

They entered the room, and Colonel Thomas got up from his knees beside the bed. He had covered that which lay on it with the eiderdown quilt, all but the face, which was free of any marks of Isabel Thomas' fall. Her open eyes gazed up toward the ceiling, not staringly, but as they might have gazed in life at something in which she had little interest. Lovely, wonderful eyes. Thomas had so arranged the quilt that it held her lower jaw from falling, and her lips were only a little parted as she lay, the agony of death already passed from her face.

Her blood had stained the man's chest and arms and hands, and there was a smear on his forehead, too. He looked at the three.

"I think you have been very quick," he said. "But then, I had lost count of time. She died in my arms, as I carried her here."

"Philip Woodford Thomas, I am a police officer...

"...may be taken down and produced as evidence against you."

The time-worn formula effected no change in Thomas' attitude or expression. Nor did he resist when Head manacled him, nor when they searched him after leading him out from the room and down the stairs. And from the moment when Head began to speak the charge, until they led him out to the car, he did not speak. Before entering the car, he looked back at the Priory frontage towering against the sky.

"With Isabel gone, nothing is left," he said.

When they came to Pagenham Newton, Williams got out from the car to inform the local police of the tragedy they had left at the Priory. Between that point and the drawing-up of the saloon in the yard at the back of Westingborough police station, no word was spoken by any of the four men in the car. Nor did Thomas speak when Head asked him to get out. He complied, and stood waiting until they led him to the charge room.

"Did he say anything in answer to the charge?" Wadden asked, later.

"Nothing that affects it—nothing to produce

as evidence," Head answered. "It was a devilish murder, chief, and yet——"

"I know, laddie, but—what was it old Omar said? 'Not all thy piety nor wit'—something like that. And I'd forgotten—that chap Cossar. Went over to the Duke of York to get a bite—I let him go, and told him to come back here for you to talk to him when you got back."

"I'll go over there and talk to him," Head said. "The—yes, the mechanism of it. It's got to be clear, to complete the case."

They stood, then, in the corridor of the police station, outside Wadden's office. As Head went out to cross the street, the superintendent did not enter his doorway, but stood gazing through the front entrance of the police station. He saw that Head went draggingly, like one reluctant, disliking his errand.

"It'd been far better if Thomas had showed fight," Wadden said to himself as Head disappeared in the doorway of the hotel.

* * *

"Yes, I see that. I've been in the force, Inspector. Giving evidence won't do my agency any good, but you won't have to subpœna me."

"I am glad to hear it. By the way, have you been paid for the services you rendered to Colonel Thomas?"

"Oh, yes! I took care of that. Cash down is my

rule, in all cases of that sort—divorce evidence cases, I mean."

"He intended to divorce her, then?"

"I don't know about that. On the whole, I'd say not. His instructions were to be most careful as far as she was concerned. It seemed to me that he wanted me to find out whatever she was doing, and put a stop to it—from what you say about his being the man who killed Ashford, too, I should say that was all he wanted. To get her back fully —get rid of everything that might hold her away from him. Ashford."

"Yes. I reach that conclusion too. Now, the mechanics of it."

"I don't get that, Mr. Head." Cossar gazed inquiringly across the lunch table in the hotel dining room.

"What part, exactly, did you play? For completion of my case—you will have to state it in evidence, and might as well give me the gist of it now. I know Thomas employed you, you see."

"That is so," Cossar agreed, slowly, thoughtfully. It wouldn't pay me to try and get out of it. This is one hell of a mess, you know. I don't like it at all. Whatever I do, it'll damage me —the agency."

"Assisting justice straightforwardly will damage you least," Head pointed out.

"Quite. Oh, quite!" Cossar assented, half-ironically. "Well, he wired me to meet him at Crandon, he paying all expenses, and I came down after a telephone talk with him about it at that hotel—the Carden Arms—to arrange terms. We had our interview in the station waiting-room, and he told me he wanted his wife watched when she went to stay at a farm tenanted by some people named Jevons—do you know about that?"

"Yes. She was supposed, then, to be staying there till last Saturday, and then rejoining him. Go on, though."

"Yes. He fixed things with me the day before she went there. I put a man on to watch. The day after she got there, he traced her to London, and followed her into Southampton Street post office, just off the Strand. She'd left a taxi outside, and so had my man. He heard her ask for letters or telegrams for Mrs. Barnard, *poste restante*, and followed her out. Going up Constitution Hill his taxi had a puncture, and he lost her. I could have killed him. All I had was that name, Barnard— he'd heard her spell it. I took a chance on hotels, and found her late on Monday night at the Warlingham. You know about that, though."

"I know about it." Head assented again.

"I rang him at the Carden Arms on the Tuesday morning and told him I'd located her," Cossar went on. "Located Mr. Barnard with her too. Thomas came to me in London, and asked if I could give her the impression she was being watched, so that they'd separate. I told my man on watch to do just that, and Thomas told me he wanted to keep track of Mr. Barnard, not of her. He was so quiet and decent over it that I counted on no more than a horsewhipping for Barnard, common assault of some sort, and instructed my man. He traced them to the Russell on Wednesday afternoon—no, it was the evening by the time they got there—and I got Thomas where he was staying and told him. He went with me to where my man was keeping tag, and stayed with him to watch. When Barnard—as I knew him—came out alone, late that night, Thomas went after him. And that, of course, was for the murder, though I didn't associate the name Barnard with Ashford till you got on to me. I'd no idea what had become of Barnard and Thomas, you see, and the dead man's name wasn't out till after the inquest. Meanwhile, by Thomas' orders, my man kept tag on Mrs. Thomas at the Russell. She'd booked a double room for herself and Mrs. Jevons there for the one night. Mrs. Jevons never turned up."

"No. Mrs. Thomas told her to meet the eleven-fifty at Crandon, to make it appear that she had stayed with her sister in London," Head explained. "Your man, I suppose, saw her to the train next morning——"

"And rang through to my office to tell me," Cossar carried on the story. "Thomas had told me he'd get in touch with me during the morning, and he rang me at my Office, about ten o'clock, it'd be. I told him Mrs. Thomas was due to arrive at Crandon at eleven-fifty—my man had been on hand when she asked for her ticket—and he said that was all he wanted to know and he'd send me a cheque in settlement. I got the cheque next morning, and put the case out of my mind—till you rang me last night. I considered it closed, you see. To me, there was no connection between Thomas or Barnard and the murder of a man named Ashford."

"You suspected nothing?" Head eyed the man keenly as he asked it.

"As God is my witness—nothing, Mr. Head," Cossar answered sincerely.

* * *

The crowded assize court emptied slowly. When Jevons came out with his wife, his arm was round her and she leaned against him both for support and guidance, blinded as she was by the tears that coursed down her cheeks, all unchecked. Superintendent Wadden watched them enter their car, and stood waiting while Jevons drove away.

Then, as he still waited, Thane and Loretta came out together, and approached him. He lifted his hand to his uniform cap in salute. Loretta's eyes showed traces of tears, he noted, and Thane, holding her arm, looked sombrely grave as he returned the salute.

"Inspector Head, Mr. Wadden?" Loretta asked.

"You won't be able to see him for a good while, Miss Ashford, maybe quite an hour. He's got all sorts of formalities to settle."

"I'm sorry. I'd have liked to thank him. For all his consideration, I mean, the way he spared my brother's name all he could."

"I'll tell him for you, if you wish," Wadden promised. "It was a stonewall case, you see. Those links finished it, practically."

"I—that was why I had to appear, I know. But after—to have to stay through the rest of it. Why did they make me?"

"It's the rule," Wadden told her. "After a witness has once entered the court to give evidence—any one witness might be recalled to the stand, you see, and if they were let go—well, it's the rule."

"I see. Tell Mr. Head I do thank him, for my father as well as for myself. I'm afraid I don't feel like waiting—we have a long drive back to Carden, and it's late now. Good-bye, Mr. Wadden, and thank you too," and she shook hands with him, as did Thane.

He listened to scraps of discussion by others who passed him as, waiting for Head to appear, he filled and lighted his pipe.

"It's not a cap at all. Nothing but a little square of black stuff. It was the chaplain who put it on his head, I heard."

"Gruesome business, that sentencing. Terribly impressive."

"Yes, a fine-looking girl. Nice voice, too, and what little she had to say she said quite distinctly. I liked her eyes, especially."

"Well, all I've got to say is, if there's any hint of a reprieve, it ought to be squashed at once. I s'pose he'll appeal—they all do."

"Didn't look capable of it, I think. More in it than meets the eye, most likely. She was at the bottom of it, of course."

"What I want to know is, if that Inspector Head is all he's cracked up to be, why didn't he find out where Thomas was between the time he made that fire and when he got to Crandon station to meet her? The defence might have made more of that, I should think."

"What does it matter? It was that pair of Ashford's shoes, and his sleeve links, that decided the jury. And the judge too—didn't you listen to his summing-up?"

"I don't think he was fair. Dead against Thomas, I thought."

"And he put that man Thane's clothes on Ashford because he thought nobody could identify Ashford in them."

"Wasn't that railway guard funny about it?"

"I think the most unconcerned of anyone was the man in the dock. He didn't seem to care much, even when the judge was passing sentence."

"Well, that's the first time I've ever been to a murder trial, and it'll be the last. I don't believe in capital punishment, either."

"What would you do with them, then? You can't let murderers loose on the world, to murder again if they felt like it."

"Oh, don't be silly! You know what I mean."

"'Fraid I don't. Do you?"

"Got my exes all right, Teddy. That Head's a good sport."

"Tomfoolery, half of it, I say. I could tell as soon as I got in the court the man was guilty. When it come to all that fuss and forms over it, Albert, I can't see what it's all about."

"Carm on, man. Time for a livener before we catch our train."

"Think they'll hang him?"

"If I was in his place, I'd sooner that than penal servitude. If they don't, he'll be an old man when he gets out."

"Yes, but he's rich, and life's sweet."

"I think they ought to get up a petition. Provocation, and all that sort of thing. Thousands of people would sign it."

"Some people are fools enough to sign anything."

"Oh, so I'm a fool, am I?"

"I didn't say that! You're so hasty, picking things up like that."

"Well, you shouldn't——"

"A most fascinating case, I call it, what? Lucky to get in, were we not, what? The old judge —wasn't he a scream?" At that Wadden blew, violently, and, as he had a mouthful of smoke, the youth who had been delivering comment found himself enveloped in tobacco fumes—and it was not often that the superintendent cleaned his pipes. Fiercely the youth turned on him.

"What the devil do you mean by that, constable?" he demanded. "I—I'll report you, what? Filthy, disgusting brute, you!"

"Young feller," Wadden said, "if I were to hit you once, you wouldn't wake up to report me before August bank holiday, and if I were to take you in charge and hand you over to a constable for using abusive language—— Oh, well! Move along there—move along, please!"

The youth's companion clutched his arm.

"Don't be a silly ass, Fred," he urged, as Wadden's fierce eyes turned on him. "Come along—he's not a constable at all. Come along, man!"

"Man?" Wadden queried after they had passed, with savage irony.

* * *

At the top of Condor Hill, Thane swerved his new car on to the railed parking width beside the road, expertly. Since he had not yet attained to the dignity of a full licence, the car bore a red "L" front and back, but there was nothing amateurish about his driving.

"Think I'd pass my tests, now?" he asked.

"I think we must not stay here," Loretta

answered. "It's long past dinner time, and—it's been a terrible day."

"I know," he said, "and you're tired and hungry—yes. But now it is all finished—everything—and you can look for silver linings."

"Can l?" she asked wistfully—asked it of the future, not of him.

"There is a balance," he said. "It has swung away from you enough. If it were not for that memory you keep—it was just here you told me of it—remember? Else—but that's not all, I think."

"What else?" she asked.

"Oh, nothing—much," he answered.

"And—you remember? You told me he'd laugh down from his Valhalla and want to see me giving the memory its rightful place. I do, now."

"And that place?" he asked.

"A yesterday, not a to-day in which to live. Something I shall keep—impossible not to keep it. We're so late, Leo—time to go."

"Time to go—yes." But he sat still.

"You've been so good to us—my father and me."

"Loretta?"

She looked up at him, questioningly.

"I'd never try to spoil the memory you keep. But——"

"Yes?" Still she gazed up at him.

"Could you—some time, when this worse memory is a little less keen—could you give me second place? In—in your thoughts?"

She leaned toward him and pressed her head against his shoulder.

"You are the most wonderful man in all the world, for me," she said, rather indistinctly. "Don't you know it yet? I do. Leo, it's so late. Shall we go home, please?"

THE END